DADDY and the Beanstalk

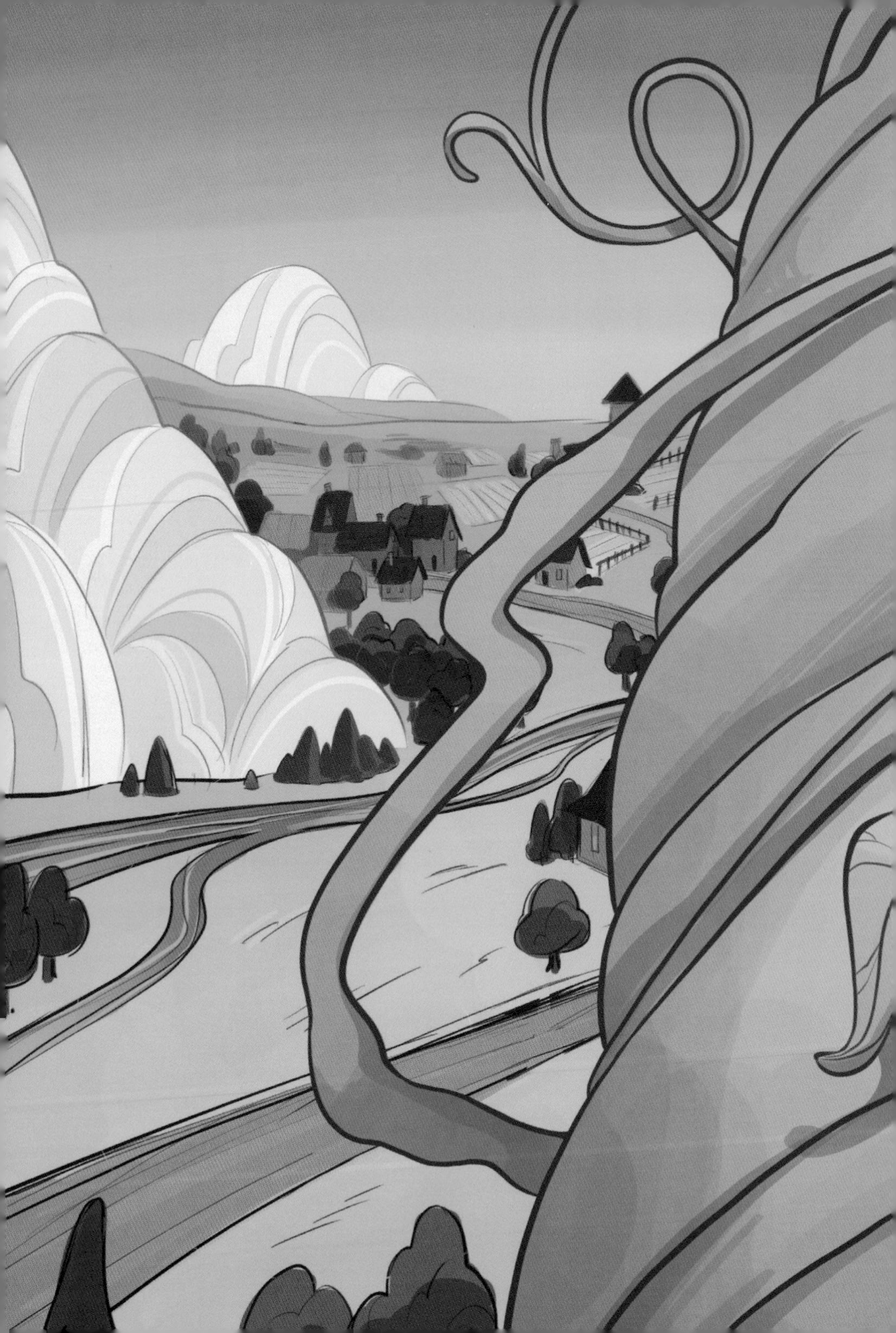

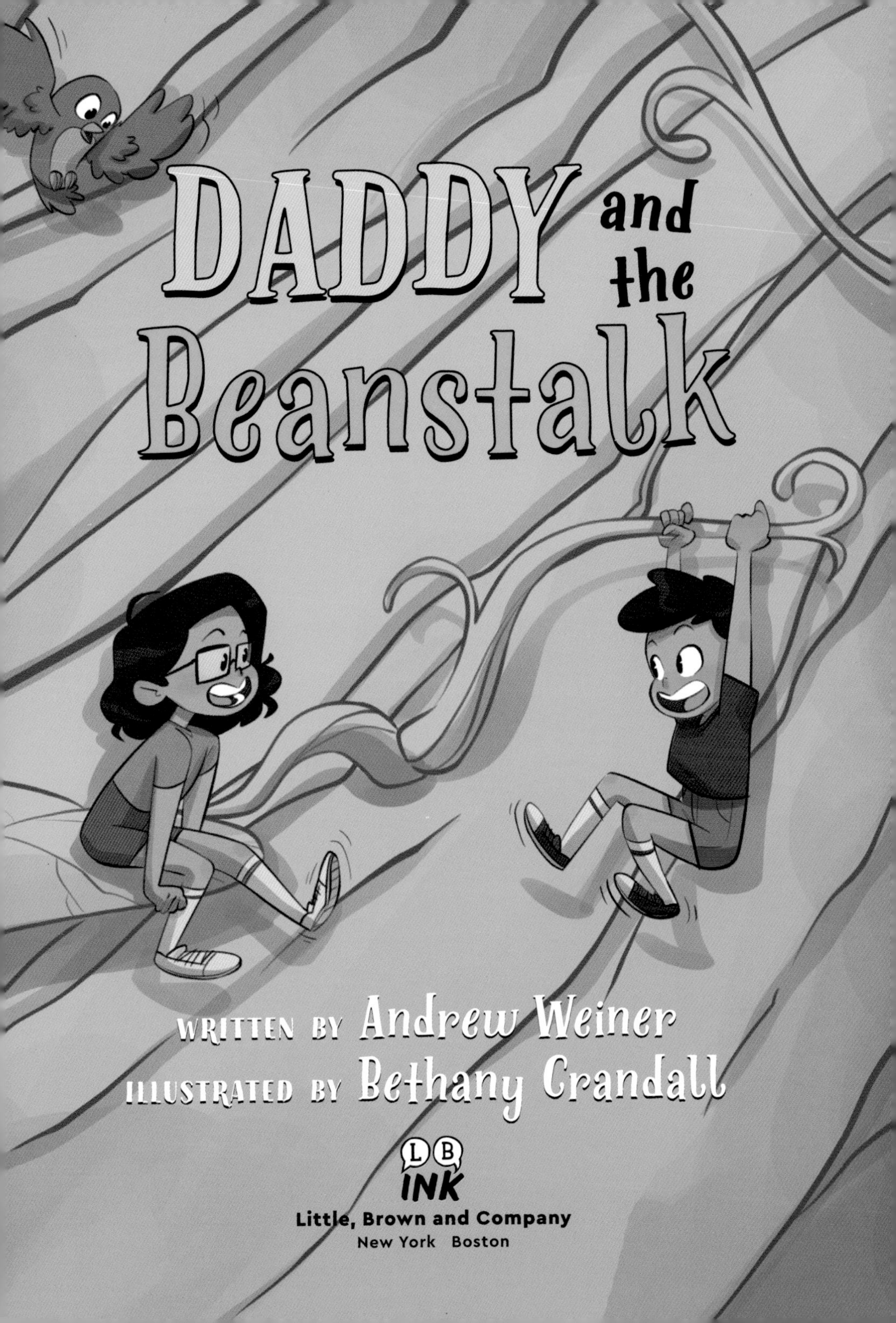

DADDY and the Beanstalk

WRITTEN BY Andrew Weiner

ILLUSTRATED BY Bethany Crandall

LB INK

Little, Brown and Company

New York Boston

ABOUT THIS BOOK

This book was edited by Andrea Colvin and designed by Megan McLaughlin. The production was supervised by Bernadette Flinn, and the production editor was Marisa Finkelstein. The text was set in Sequentialist BB, and the display type is Tarot Regular.

Little, Brown Ink
Hachette Book Group
1290 Avenue of the Americas, New York, NY 10104
Visit us at LBYR.com

First Edition: November 2023

Little, Brown Ink is an imprint of Little, Brown and Company. The Little, Brown Ink name and logo are trademarks of Hachette Book Group, Inc.

The publisher is not responsible for websites (or their content) that are not owned by the publisher.

Little, Brown and Company books may be purchased in bulk for business, educational, or promotional use. For information, please contact your local bookseller or the Hachette Book Group Special Markets Department at special.markets@hbgusa.com.

Library of Congress Cataloging-in-Publication Data
Names: Weiner, Andrew, author. | Crandall, Bethany, illustrator.
Title: Daddy and the beanstalk / written by Andrew Weiner; art by Bethany Crandall.
Description: First edition. | New York : Little, Brown and Company, 2023. | Summary: To help her fall asleep, the author tells his daughter a bedtime story from his mischievous childhood when he bought magic beans with his mother's grocery money.
Identifiers: LCCN 2020050707 | ISBN 9780316592918 | ISBN 9780316592901 (ebook)
Subjects: LCSH: Graphic novels. | CYAC: Graphic novels. | Bedtime—Fiction. | Fathers and daughters—Fiction. | Storytelling—Fiction.
Classification: LCC PZ7.7.W397 Dad 2023 | DDC 741.5/973—dc23
LC record available at https://lccn.loc.gov/2020050707

ISBNs: 978-0-316-59291-8 (hardcover), 978-0-316-15248-8 (ebook), 978-0-316-59290-1 (ebook), 978-0-316-66973-3 (ebook)

PRINTED IN CHINA

APS

10 9 8 7 6 5 4 3 2 1

There are two heroes in this story:
my daughter, Estella, and my sister, Karen.
This book is for them. –AW

To my parents, who always supported my
passion for art, and only got a little anxious when I
said I wanted to make a living doing it. –BC

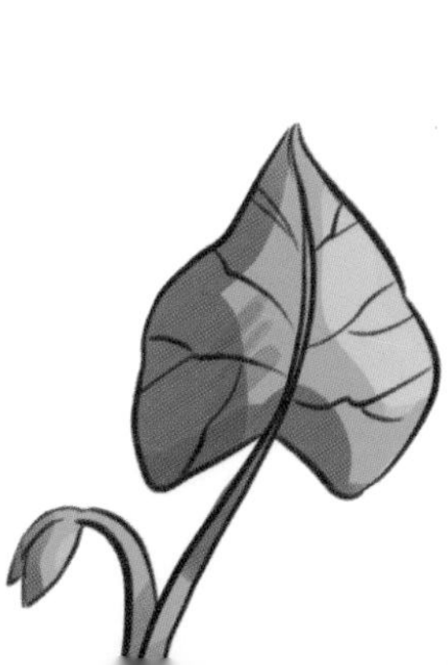

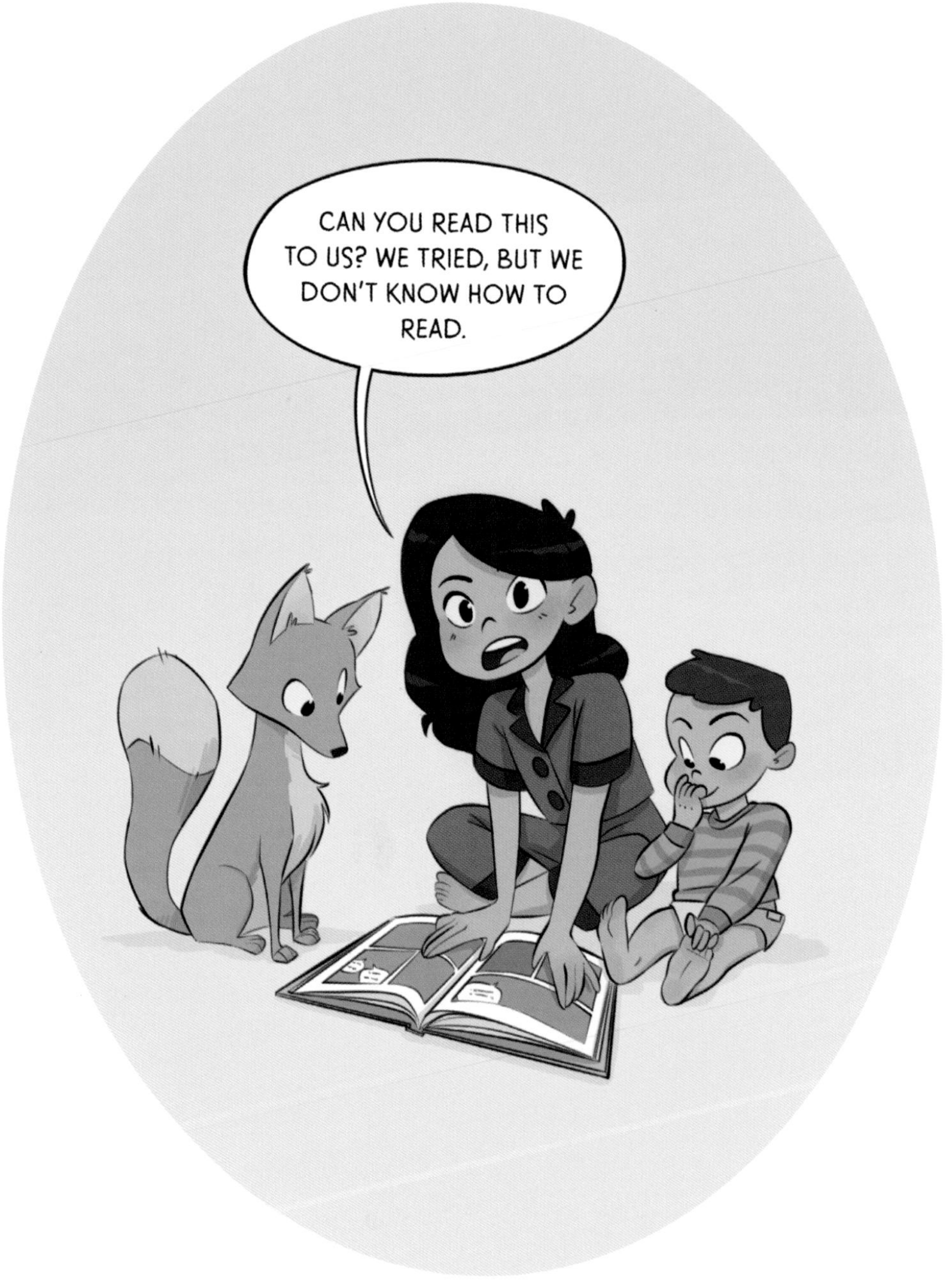
CAN YOU READ THIS TO US? WE TRIED, BUT WE DON'T KNOW HOW TO READ.

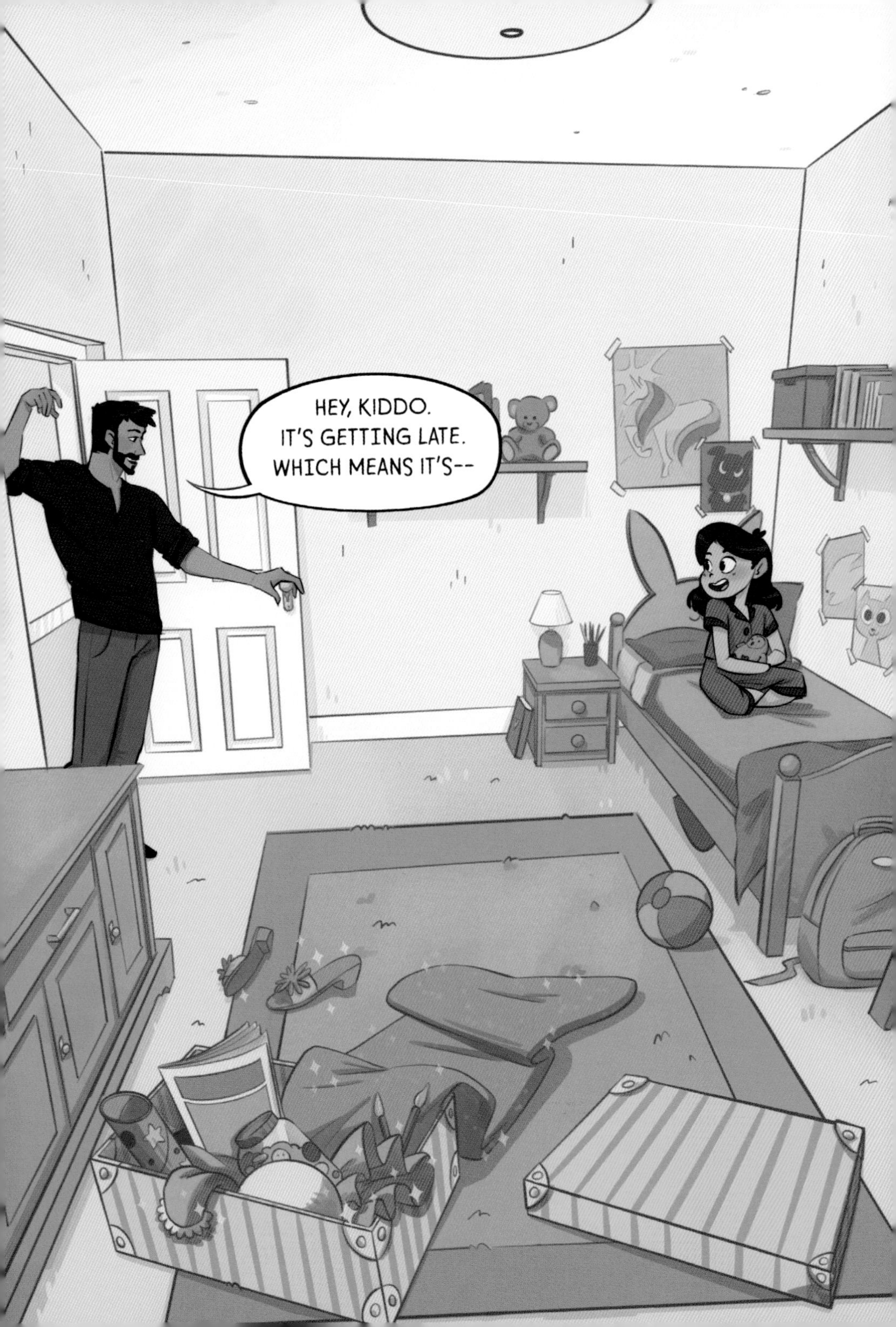
HEY, KIDDO. IT'S GETTING LATE. WHICH MEANS IT'S--

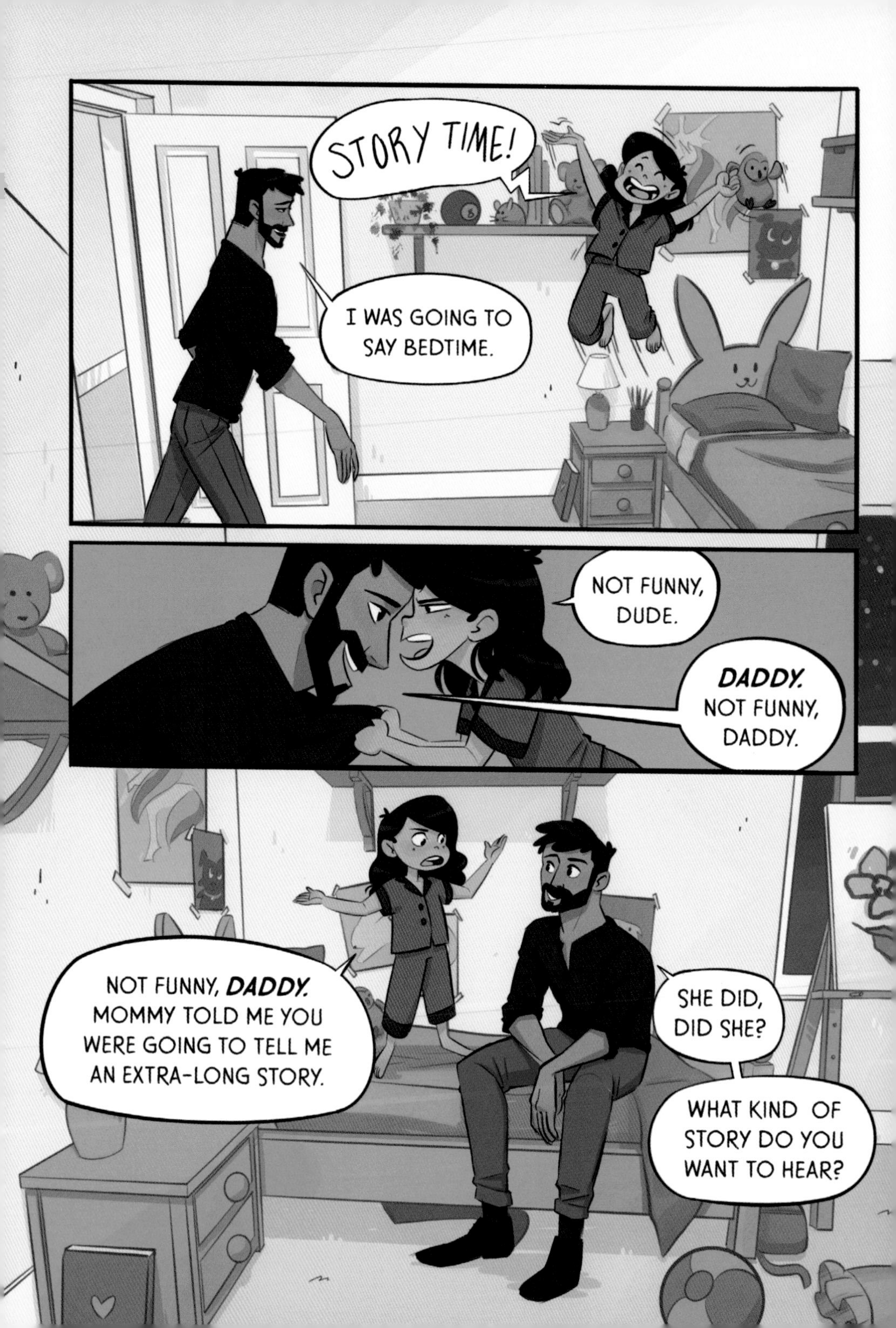
STORY TIME!
I WAS GOING TO SAY BEDTIME.
NOT FUNNY, DUDE.
DADDY. NOT FUNNY, DADDY.
NOT FUNNY, DADDY. MOMMY TOLD ME YOU WERE GOING TO TELL ME AN EXTRA-LONG STORY.
SHE DID, DID SHE?
WHAT KIND OF STORY DO YOU WANT TO HEAR?

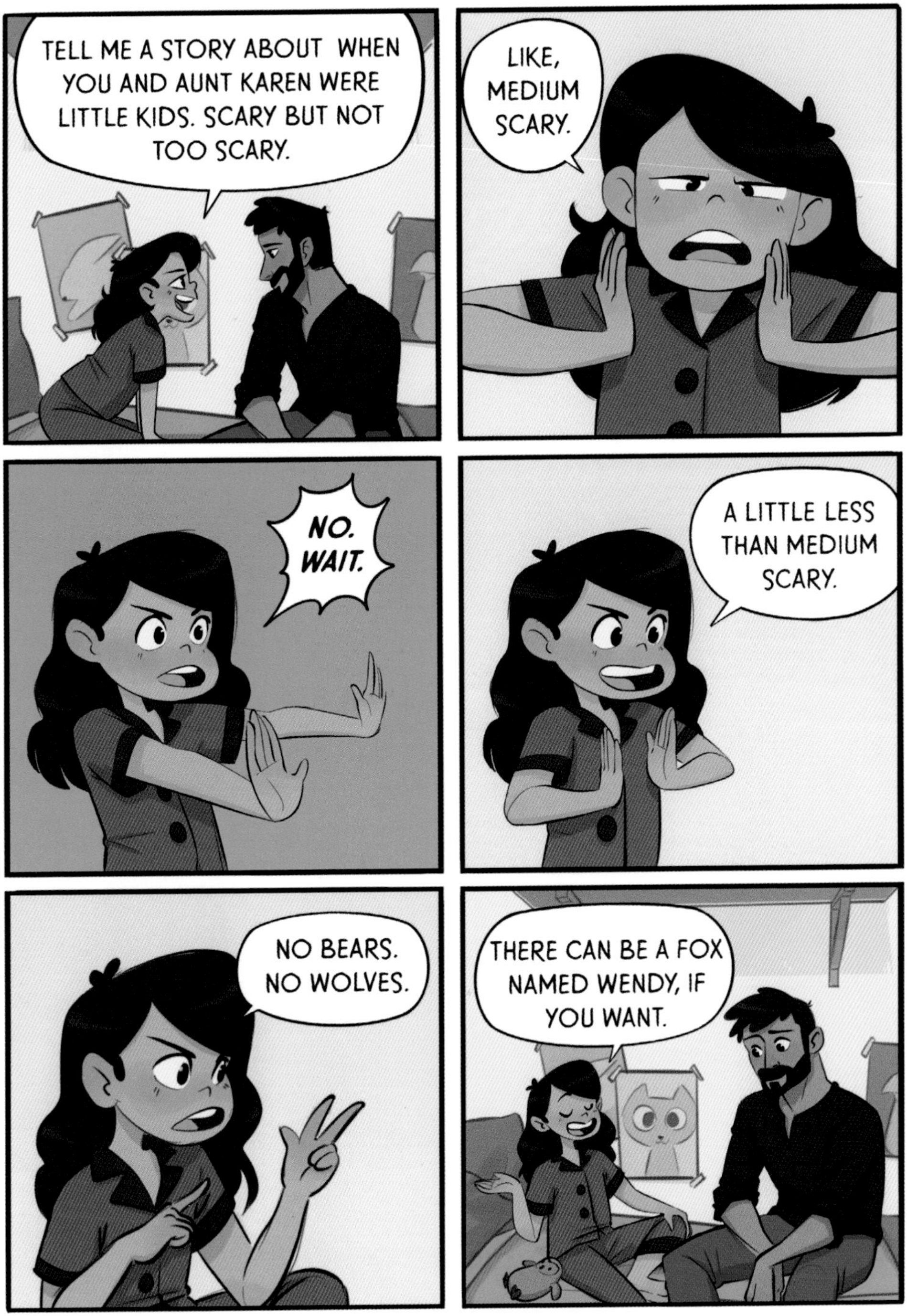
TELL ME A STORY ABOUT WHEN YOU AND AUNT KAREN WERE LITTLE KIDS. SCARY BUT NOT TOO SCARY.
LIKE, MEDIUM SCARY.
NO. WAIT.
A LITTLE LESS THAN MEDIUM SCARY.
NO BEARS. NO WOLVES.
THERE CAN BE A FOX NAMED WENDY, IF YOU WANT.

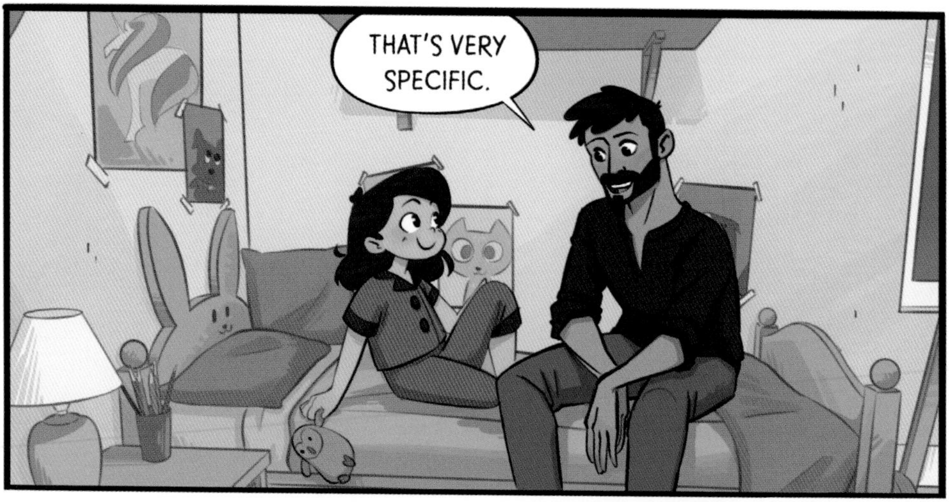
THAT'S VERY SPECIFIC.

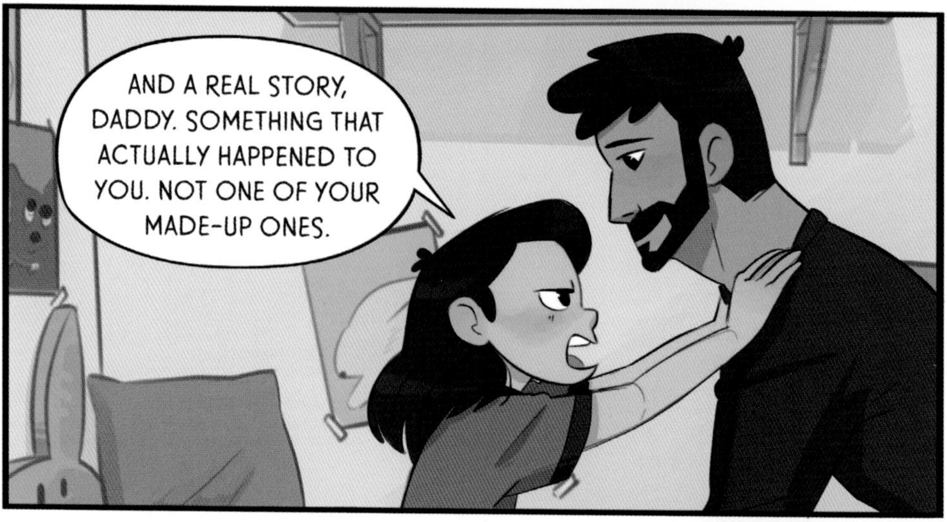
AND A REAL STORY, DADDY. SOMETHING THAT ACTUALLY HAPPENED TO YOU. NOT ONE OF YOUR MADE-UP ONES.

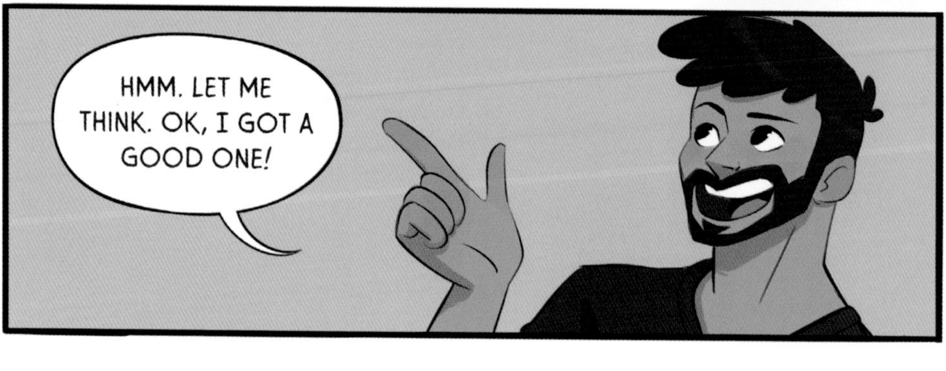
HMM. LET ME THINK. OK, I GOT A GOOD ONE!

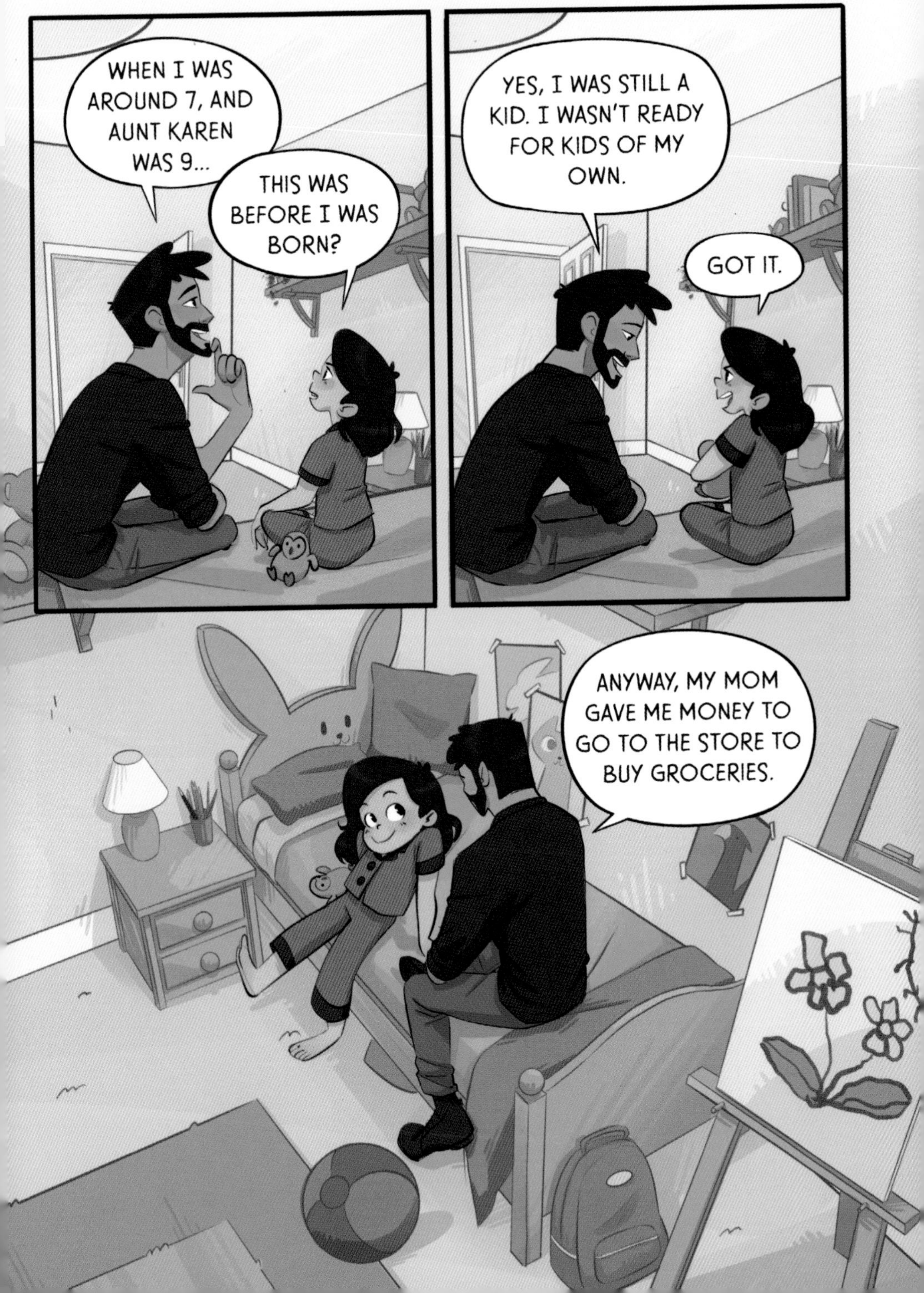
WHEN I WAS AROUND 7, AND AUNT KAREN WAS 9...
THIS WAS BEFORE I WAS BORN?
YES, I WAS STILL A KID. I WASN'T READY FOR KIDS OF MY OWN.
GOT IT.
ANYWAY, MY MOM GAVE ME MONEY TO GO TO THE STORE TO BUY GROCERIES.

HERE'S $3.52. WE NEED EGGS, BREAD, PEANUT BUTTER, AND KETCHUP.

HOW COME YOU GOT TO HOLD THE MONEY? KAREN'S OLDER THAN YOU. I WOULD NEVER LET LEVI HOLD THE MONEY.

WELL, YOUR BROTHER'S NOT EVEN 3 AND DOESN'T KNOW WHAT MONEY IS. ANYWAY, I GOT TO HOLD THE MONEY BECAUSE I ASKED--POLITELY.

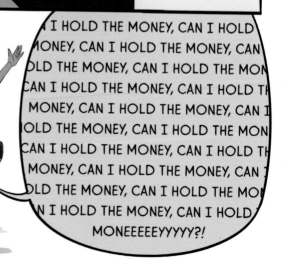

...N I HOLD THE MONEY, CAN I HOLD ...MONEY, CAN I HOLD THE MONEY, CAN ...OLD THE MONEY, CAN I HOLD THE MON... ...CAN I HOLD THE MONEY, CAN I HOLD T... ...MONEY, CAN I HOLD THE MONEY, CAN I... ...OLD THE MONEY, CAN I HOLD THE MON... ...CAN I HOLD THE MONEY, CAN I HOLD T... ...MONEY, CAN I HOLD THE MONEY, CAN ... ...OLD THE MONEY, CAN I HOLD THE MO... ...N I HOLD THE MONEY, CAN I HOLD ... MONEEEEEYYYYY?!

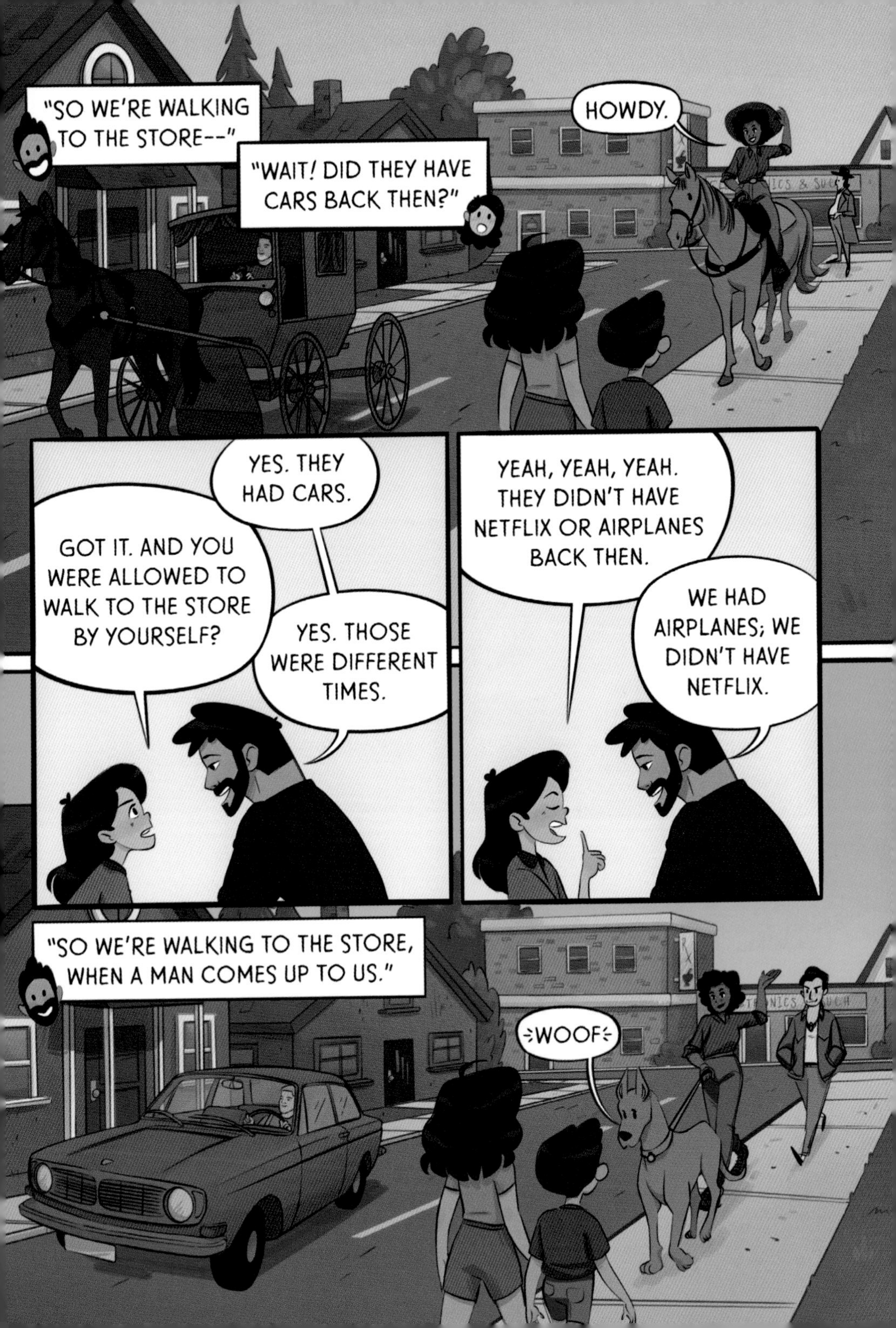
"SO WE'RE WALKING TO THE STORE--"
"WAIT! DID THEY HAVE CARS BACK THEN?"
HOWDY.
YES. THEY HAD CARS.
GOT IT. AND YOU WERE ALLOWED TO WALK TO THE STORE BY YOURSELF?
YES. THOSE WERE DIFFERENT TIMES.
YEAH, YEAH, YEAH. THEY DIDN'T HAVE NETFLIX OR AIRPLANES BACK THEN.
WE HAD AIRPLANES; WE DIDN'T HAVE NETFLIX.
"SO WE'RE WALKING TO THE STORE, WHEN A MAN COMES UP TO US."
WOOF

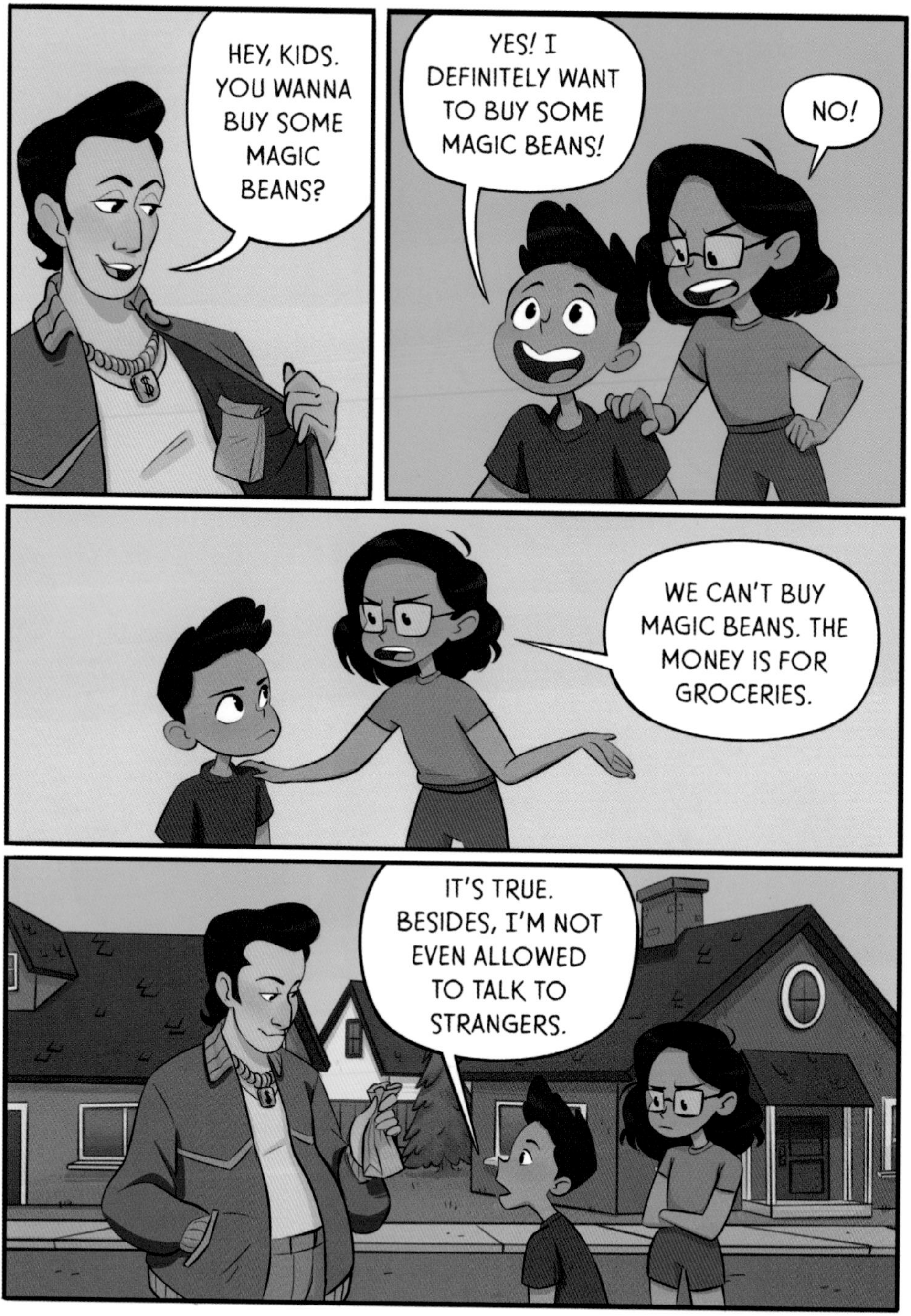
HEY, KIDS. YOU WANNA BUY SOME MAGIC BEANS?
YES! I DEFINITELY WANT TO BUY SOME MAGIC BEANS!
NO!
WE CAN'T BUY MAGIC BEANS. THE MONEY IS FOR GROCERIES.
IT'S TRUE. BESIDES, I'M NOT EVEN ALLOWED TO TALK TO STRANGERS.

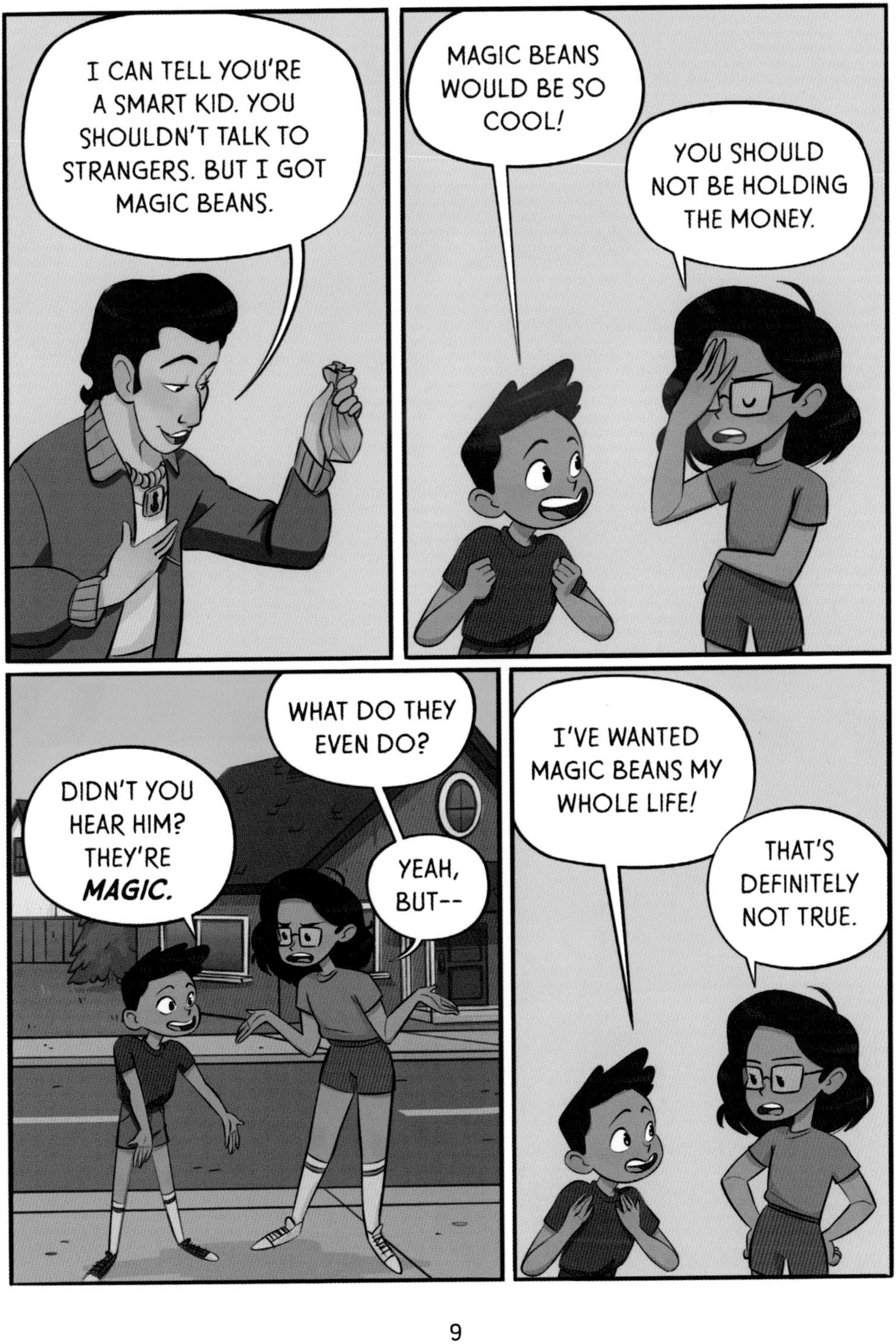
I CAN TELL YOU'RE A SMART KID. YOU SHOULDN'T TALK TO STRANGERS. BUT I GOT MAGIC BEANS.
MAGIC BEANS WOULD BE SO COOL!
YOU SHOULD NOT BE HOLDING THE MONEY.
DIDN'T YOU HEAR HIM? THEY'RE ***MAGIC.***
WHAT DO THEY EVEN DO?
YEAH, BUT--
I'VE WANTED MAGIC BEANS MY WHOLE LIFE!
THAT'S DEFINITELY NOT TRUE.

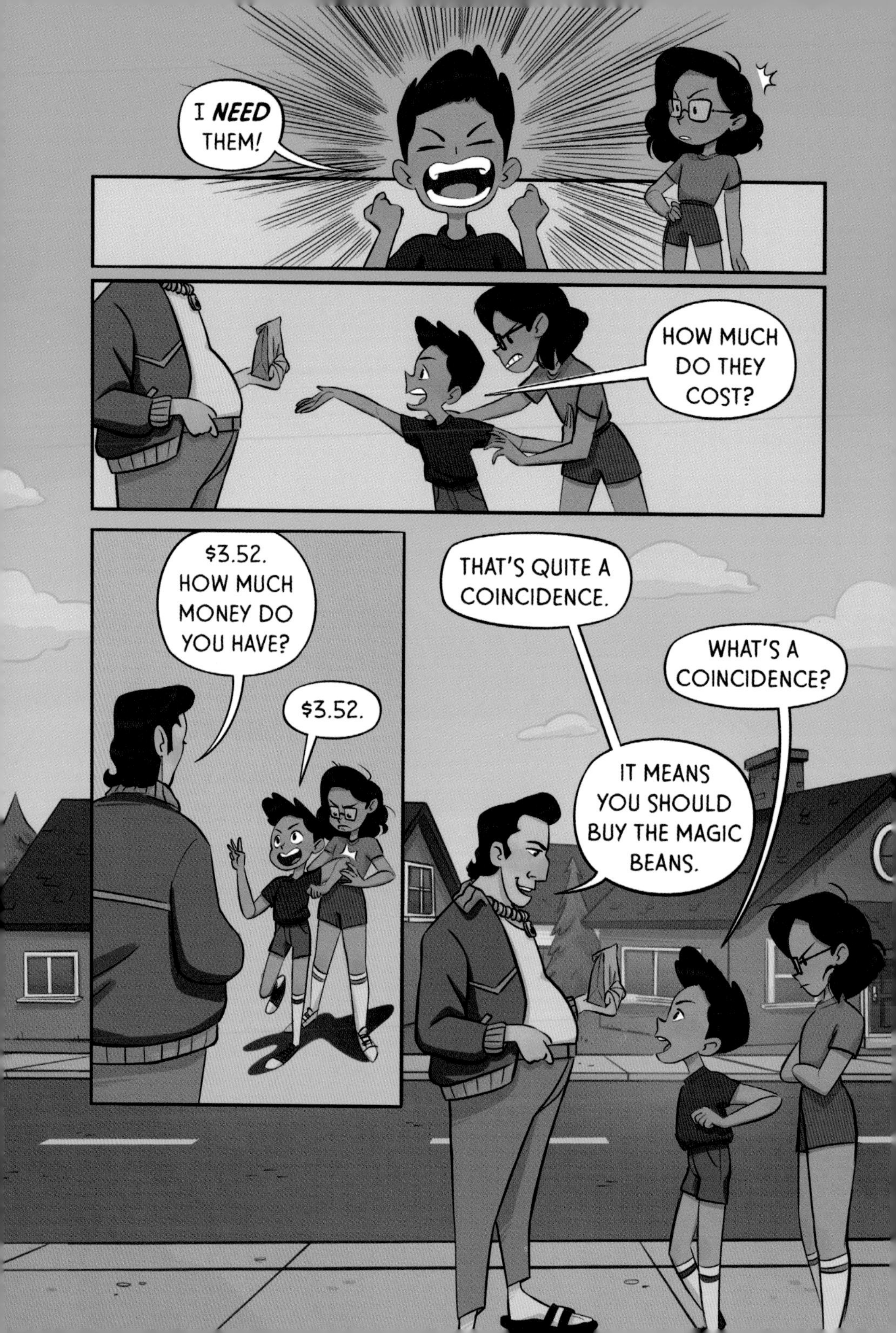
I NEED THEM!
HOW MUCH DO THEY COST?
$3.52. HOW MUCH MONEY DO YOU HAVE?
$3.52.
THAT'S QUITE A COINCIDENCE.
WHAT'S A COINCIDENCE?
IT MEANS YOU SHOULD BUY THE MAGIC BEANS.

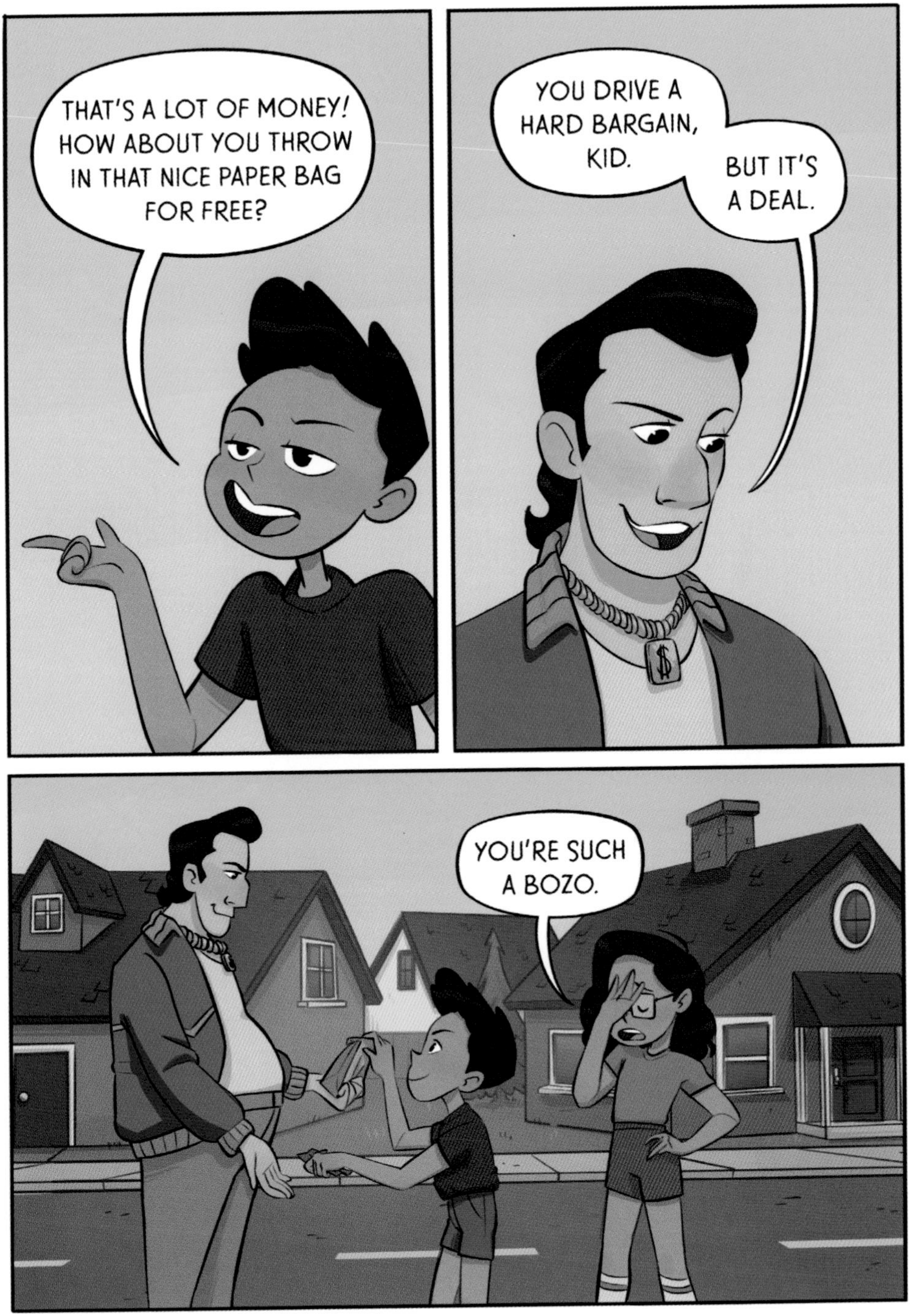
THAT'S A LOT OF MONEY! HOW ABOUT YOU THROW IN THAT NICE PAPER BAG FOR FREE?
YOU DRIVE A HARD BARGAIN, KID.
BUT IT'S A DEAL.
YOU'RE SUCH A BOZO.

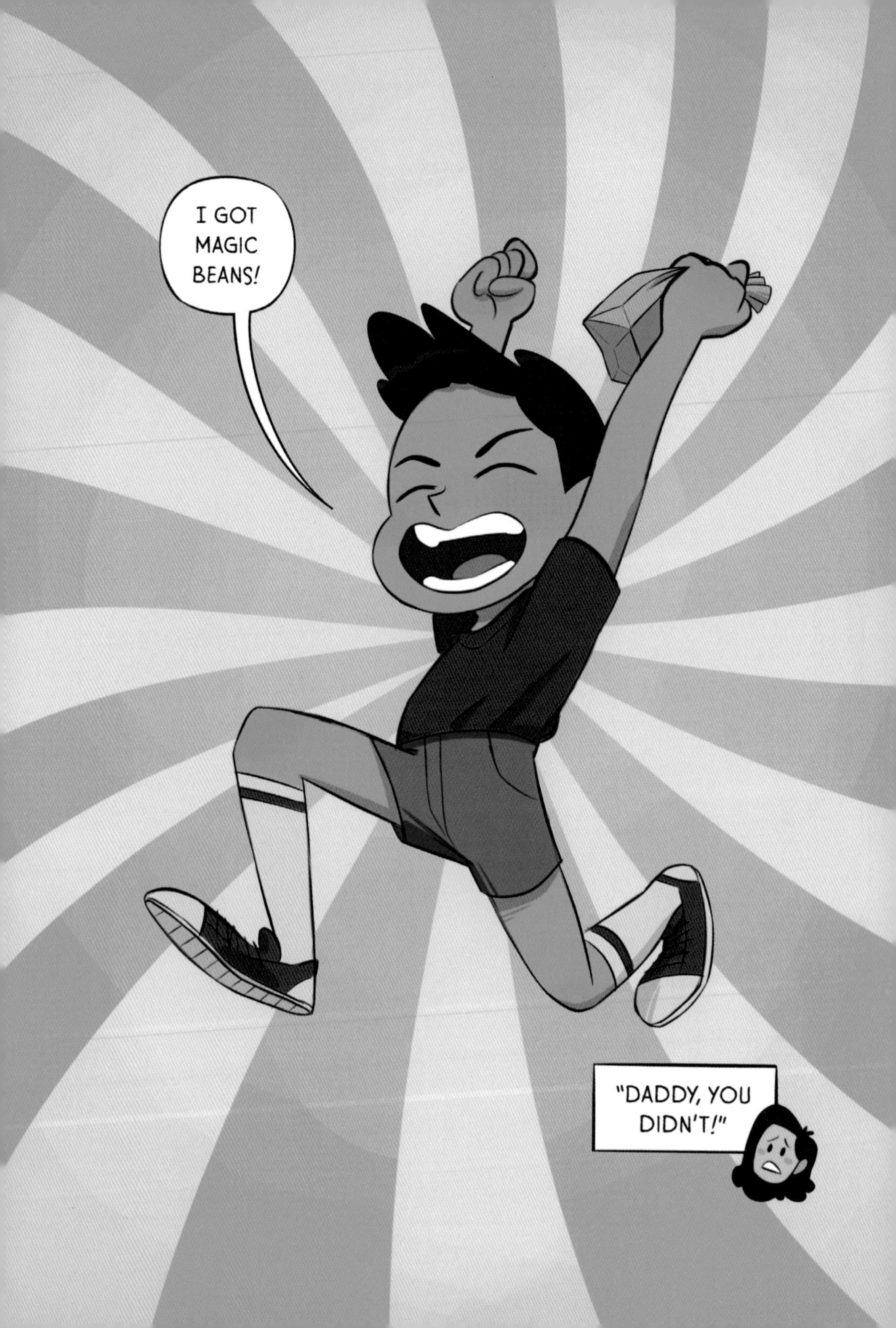
I GOT MAGIC BEANS!
"DADDY, YOU DIDN'T!"

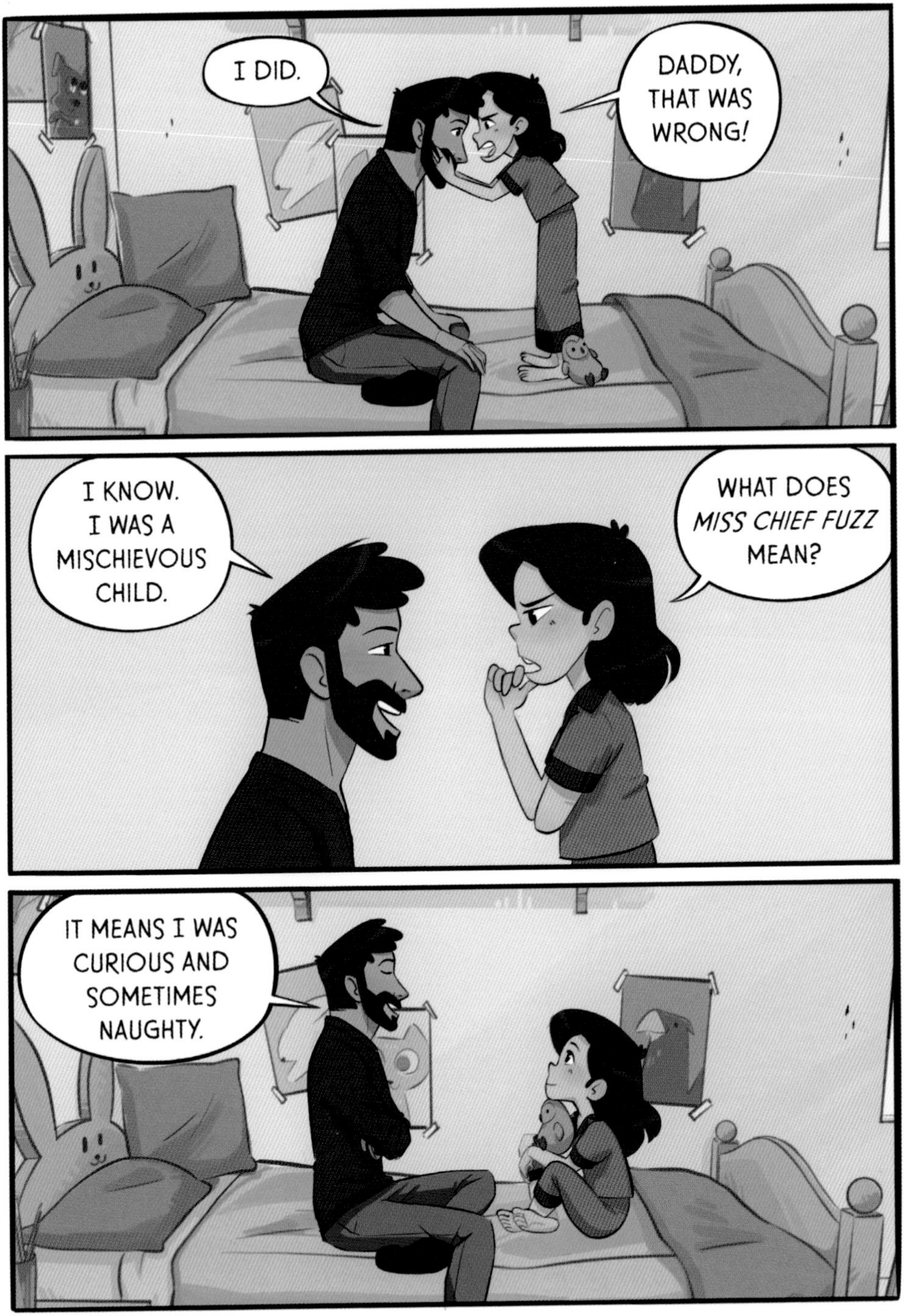
DADDY, THAT WAS WRONG!
I DID.
WHAT DOES *MISS CHIEF FUZZ* MEAN?
I KNOW. I WAS A MISCHIEVOUS CHILD.
IT MEANS I WAS CURIOUS AND SOMETIMES NAUGHTY.

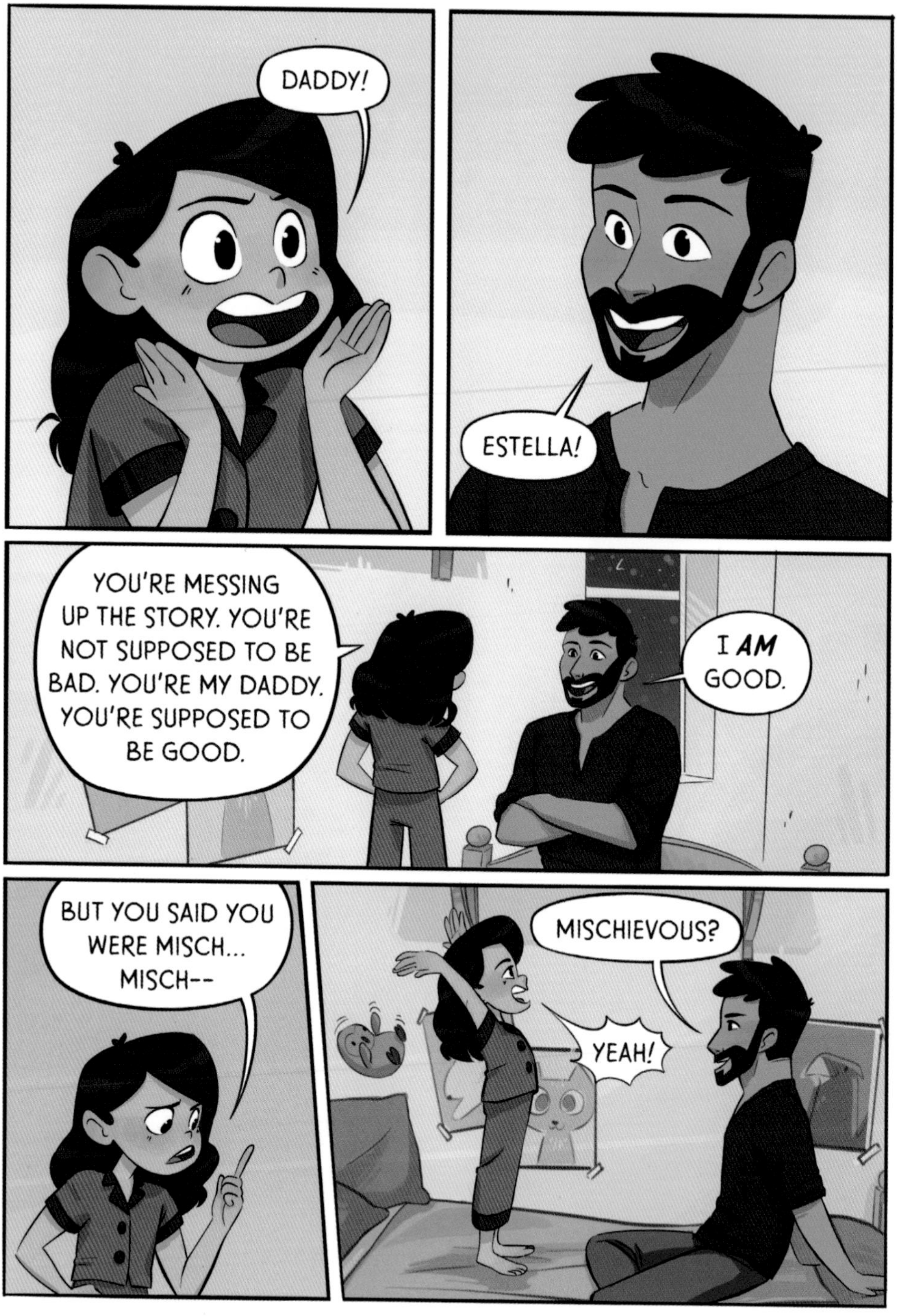
DADDY!
ESTELLA!
YOU'RE MESSING UP THE STORY. YOU'RE NOT SUPPOSED TO BE BAD. YOU'RE MY DADDY. YOU'RE SUPPOSED TO BE GOOD.
I *AM* GOOD.
BUT YOU SAID YOU WERE MISCH... MISCH--
MISCHIEVOUS?
YEAH!

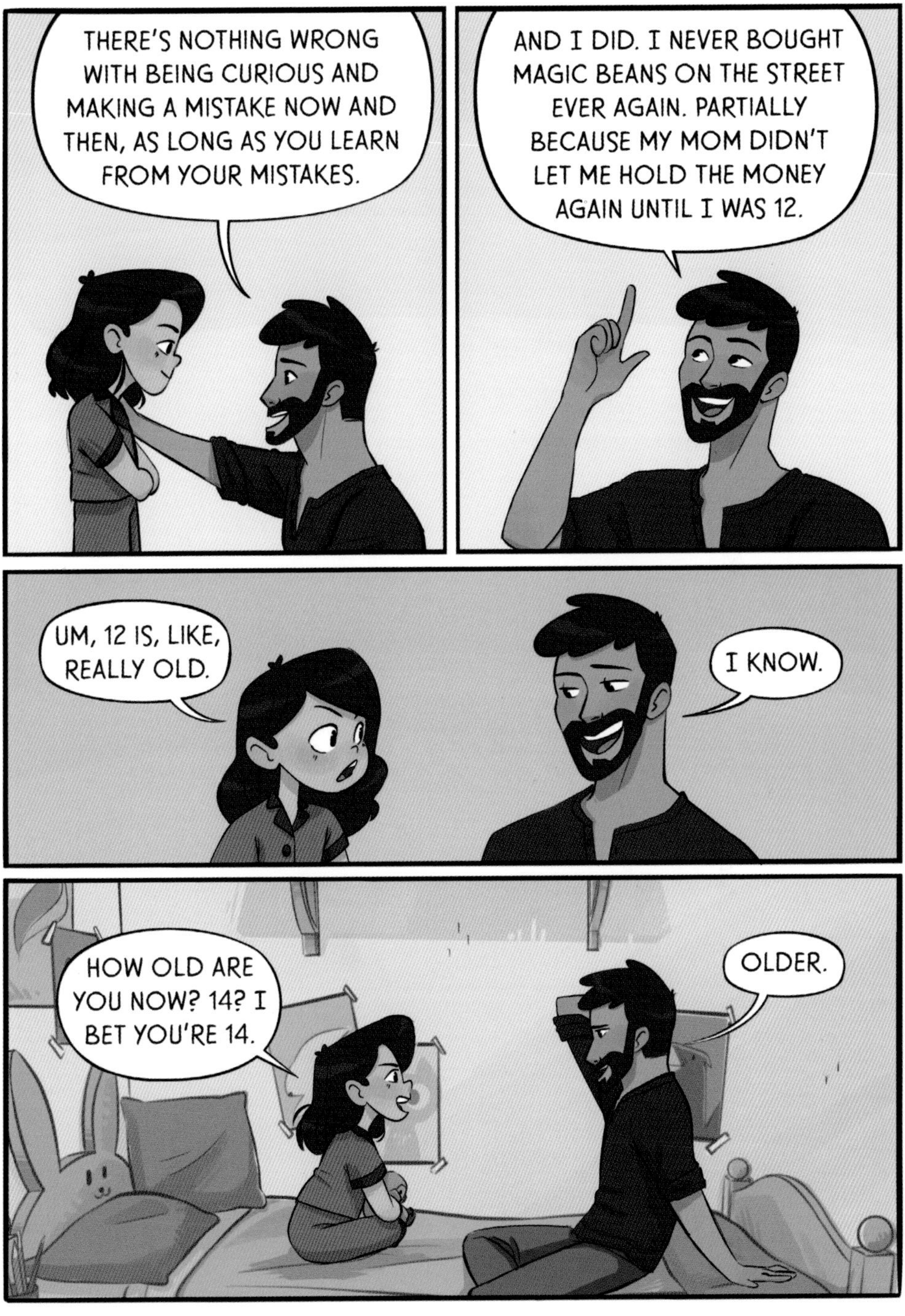
THERE'S NOTHING WRONG WITH BEING CURIOUS AND MAKING A MISTAKE NOW AND THEN, AS LONG AS YOU LEARN FROM YOUR MISTAKES.
AND I DID. I NEVER BOUGHT MAGIC BEANS ON THE STREET EVER AGAIN. PARTIALLY BECAUSE MY MOM DIDN'T LET ME HOLD THE MONEY AGAIN UNTIL I WAS 12.
UM, 12 IS, LIKE, REALLY OLD.
I KNOW.
HOW OLD ARE YOU NOW? 14? I BET YOU'RE 14.
OLDER.

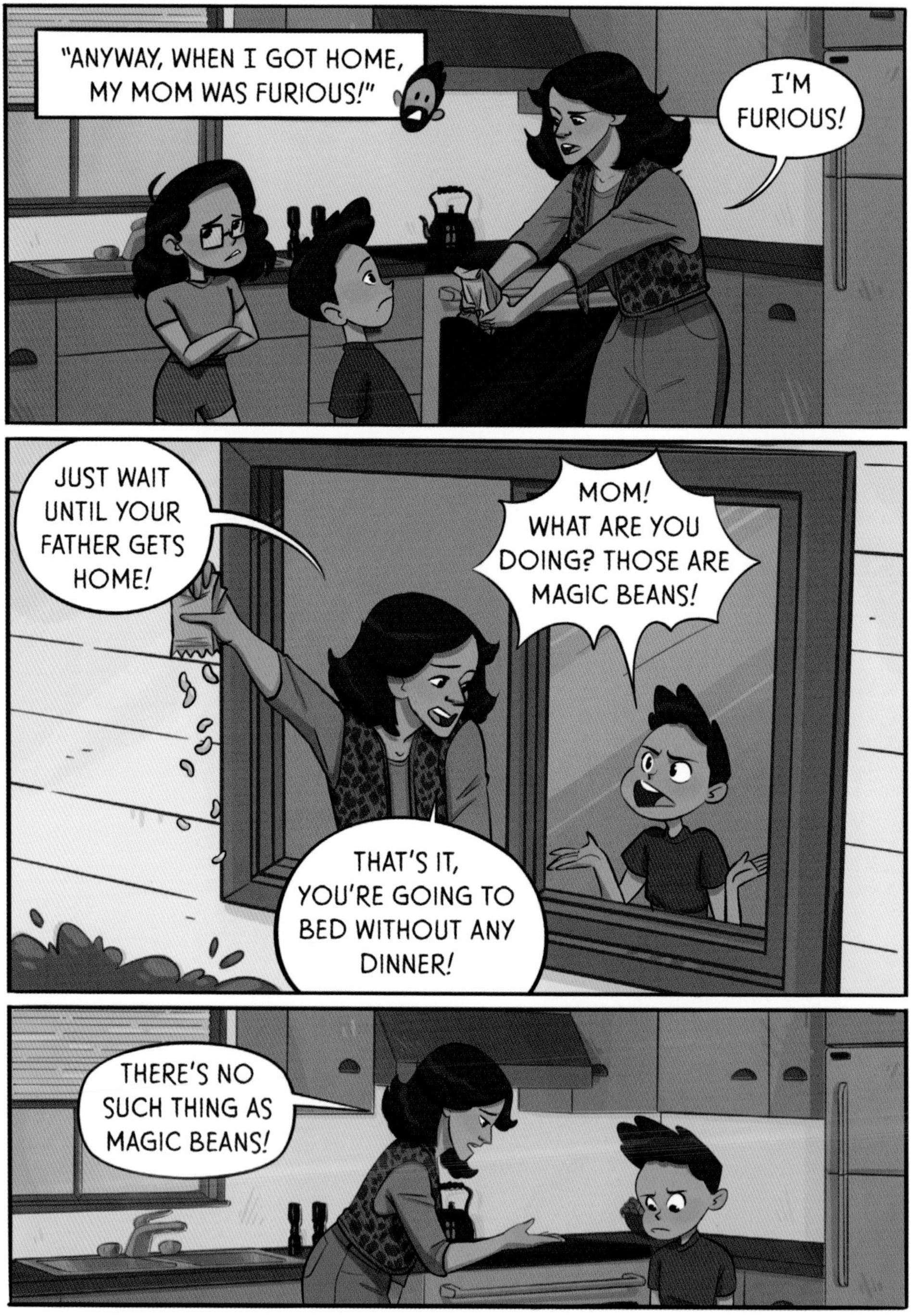
"ANYWAY, WHEN I GOT HOME, MY MOM WAS FURIOUS!"
I'M FURIOUS!
JUST WAIT UNTIL YOUR FATHER GETS HOME!
MOM! WHAT ARE YOU DOING? THOSE ARE MAGIC BEANS!
THAT'S IT, YOU'RE GOING TO BED WITHOUT ANY DINNER!
THERE'S NO SUCH THING AS MAGIC BEANS!

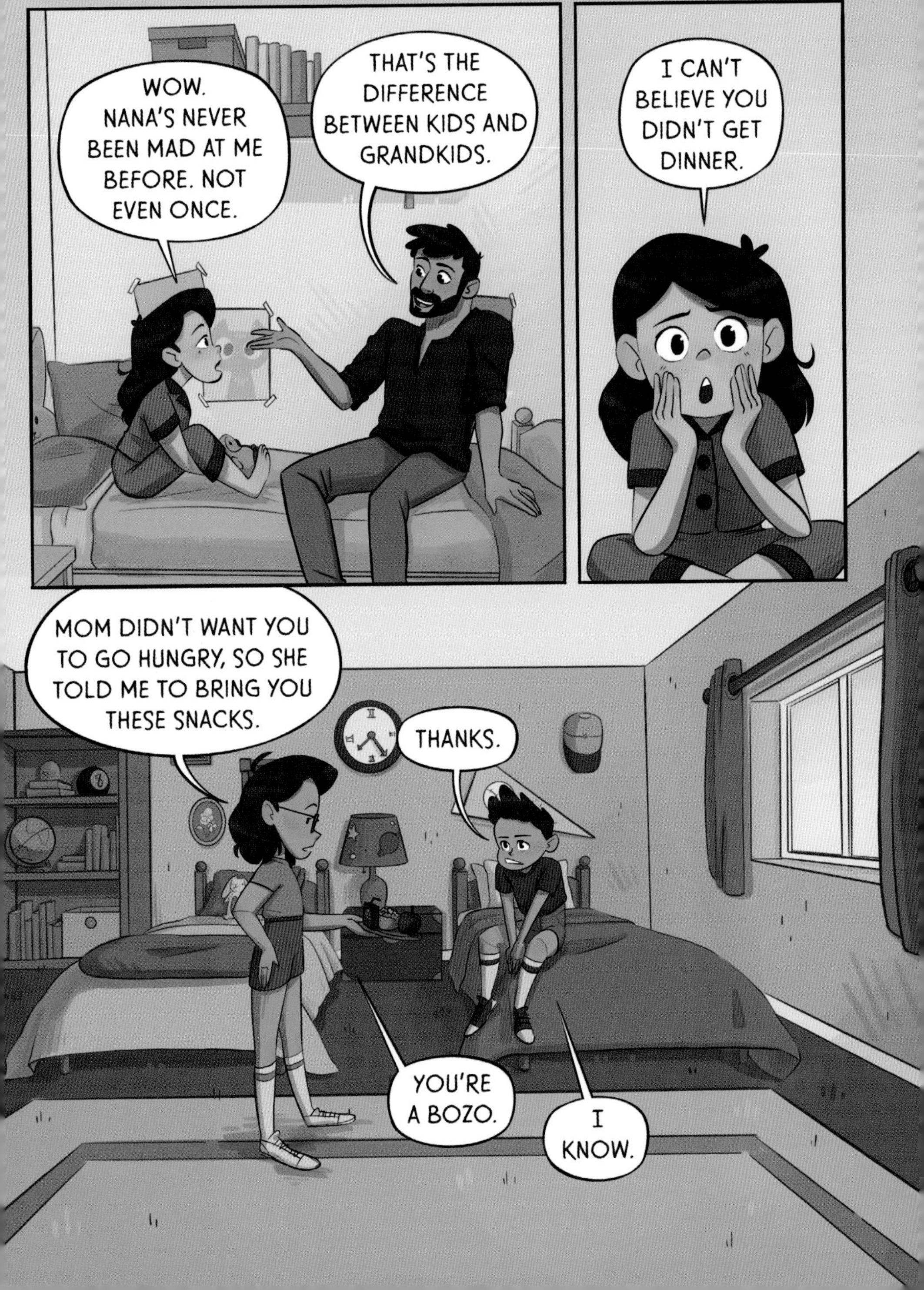
WOW. NANA'S NEVER BEEN MAD AT ME BEFORE. NOT EVEN ONCE.
THAT'S THE DIFFERENCE BETWEEN KIDS AND GRANDKIDS.
I CAN'T BELIEVE YOU DIDN'T GET DINNER.
MOM DIDN'T WANT YOU TO GO HUNGRY, SO SHE TOLD ME TO BRING YOU THESE SNACKS.
THANKS.
YOU'RE A BOZO.
I KNOW.

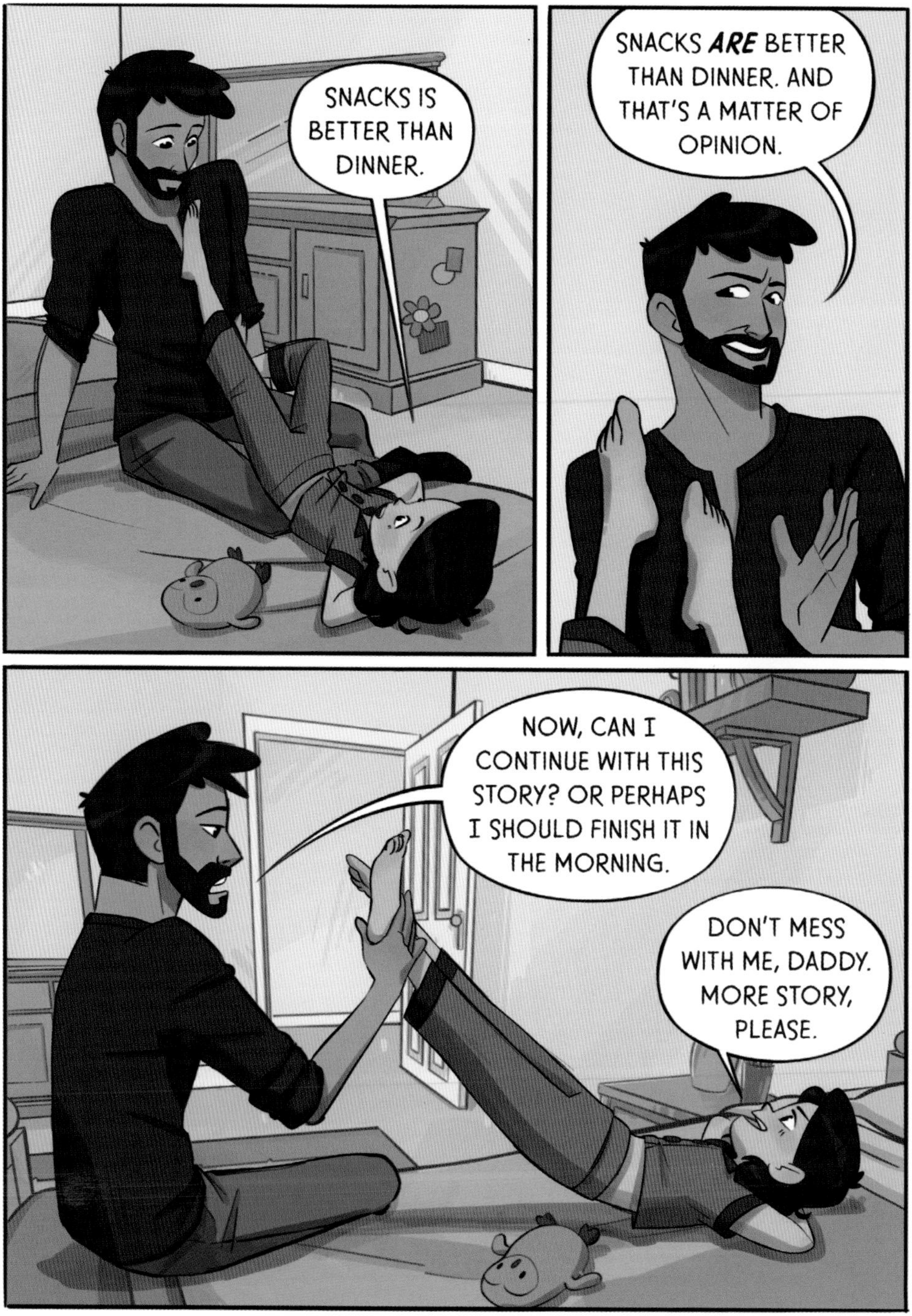
SNACKS IS BETTER THAN DINNER.
SNACKS ARE BETTER THAN DINNER. AND THAT'S A MATTER OF OPINION.
NOW, CAN I CONTINUE WITH THIS STORY? OR PERHAPS I SHOULD FINISH IT IN THE MORNING.
DON'T MESS WITH ME, DADDY. MORE STORY, PLEASE.

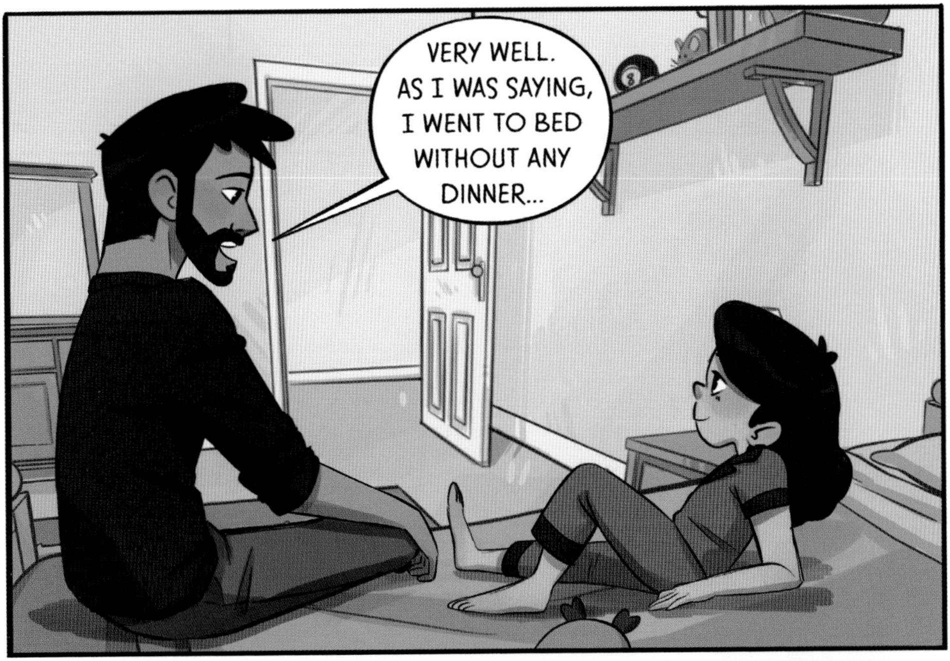
VERY WELL. AS I WAS SAYING, I WENT TO BED WITHOUT ANY DINNER...

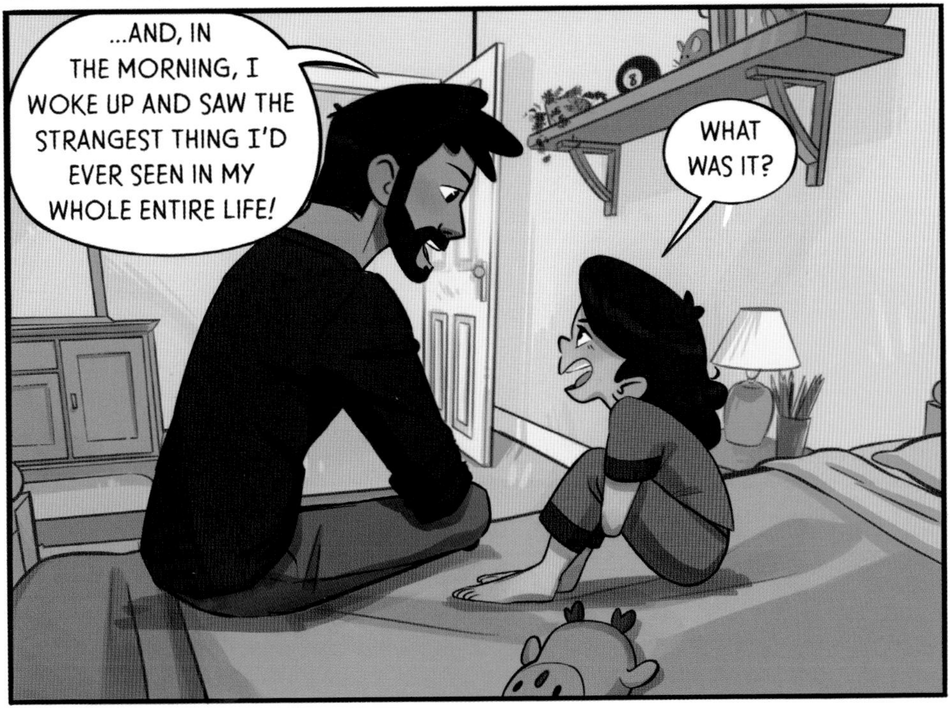
...AND, IN THE MORNING, I WOKE UP AND SAW THE STRANGEST THING I'D EVER SEEN IN MY WHOLE ENTIRE LIFE!
WHAT WAS IT?

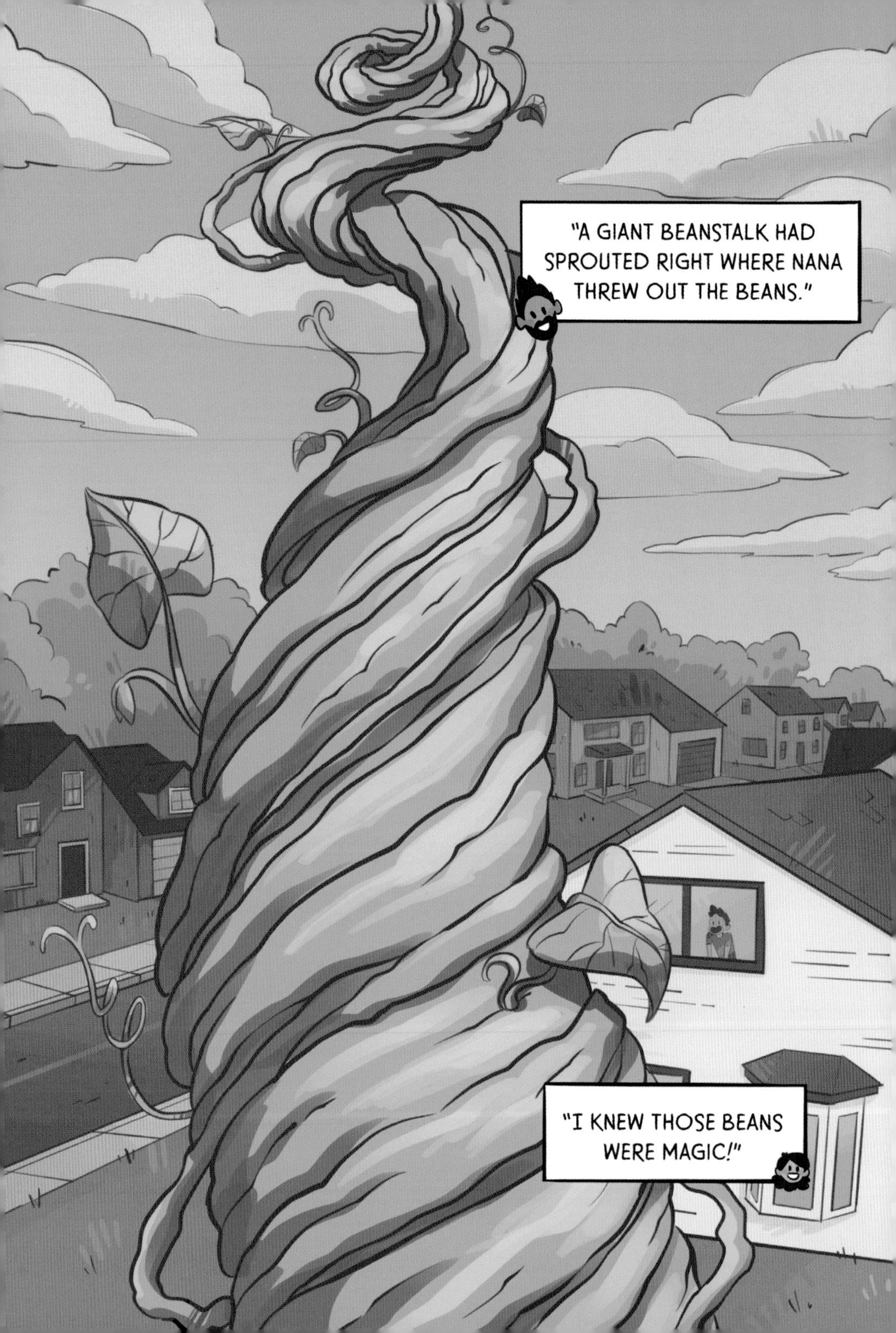
"A GIANT BEANSTALK HAD SPROUTED RIGHT WHERE NANA THREW OUT THE BEANS."
"I KNEW THOSE BEANS WERE MAGIC!"

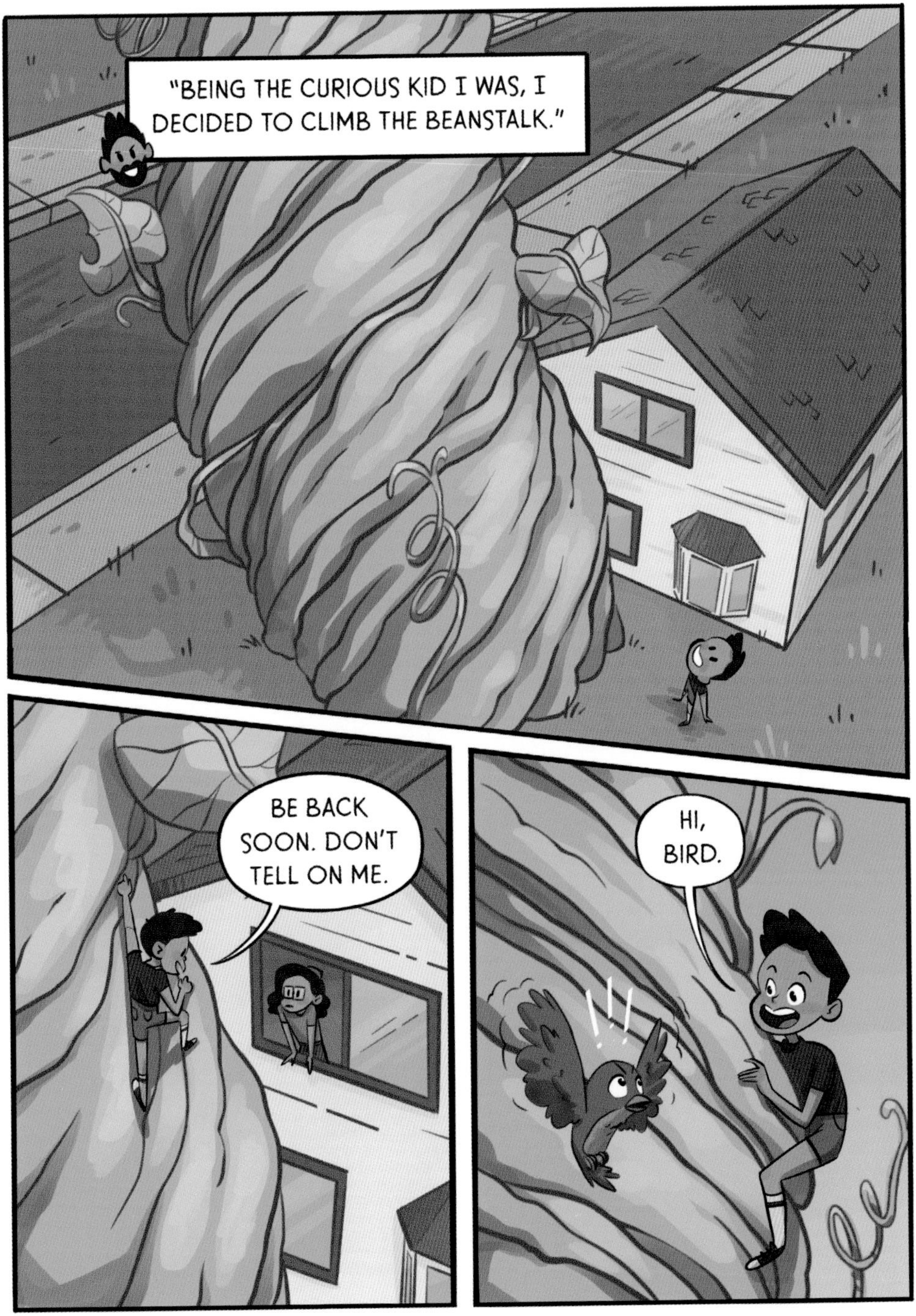
"BEING THE CURIOUS KID I WAS, I DECIDED TO CLIMB THE BEANSTALK."
BE BACK SOON. DON'T TELL ON ME.
HI, BIRD.
!!

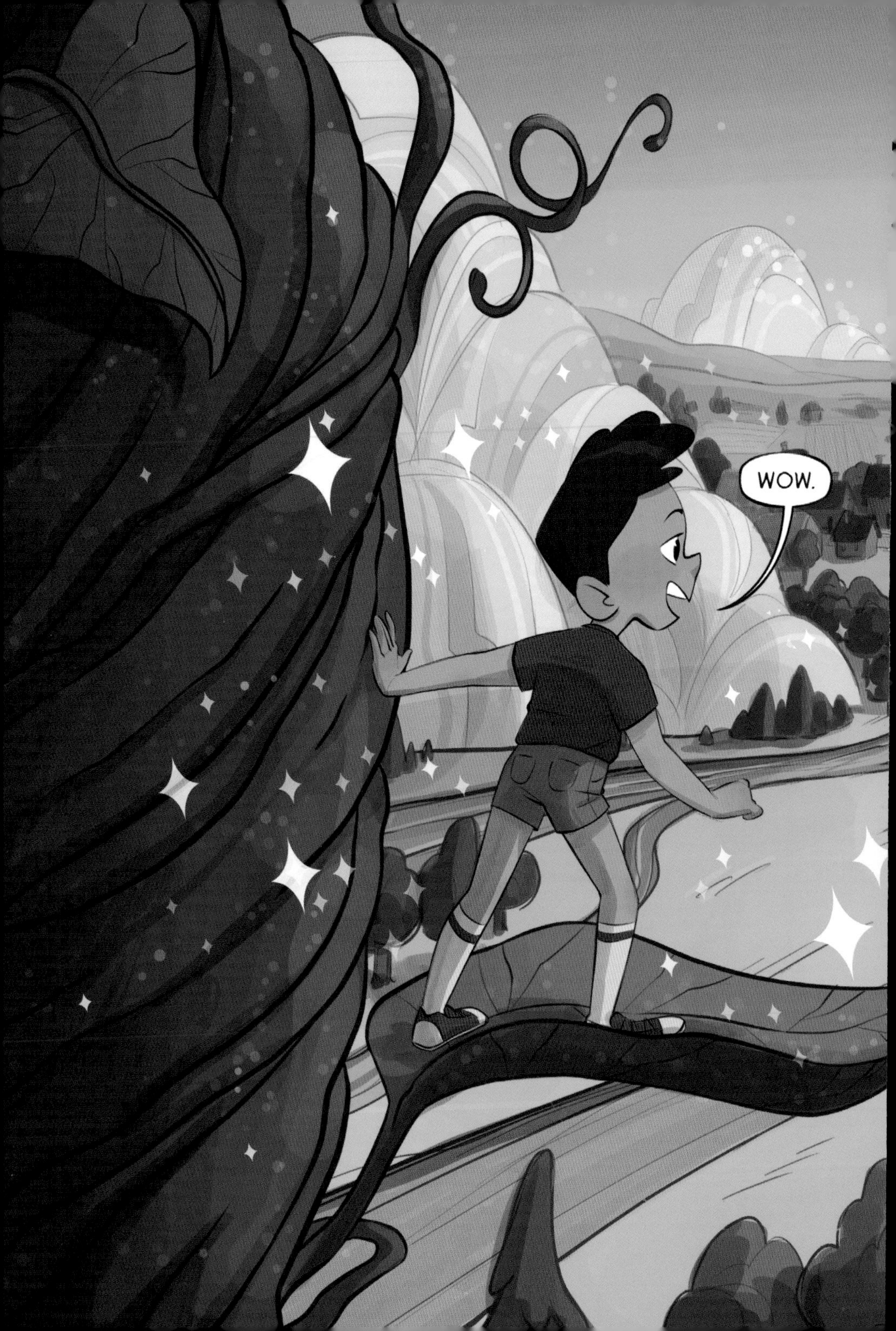
WOW.

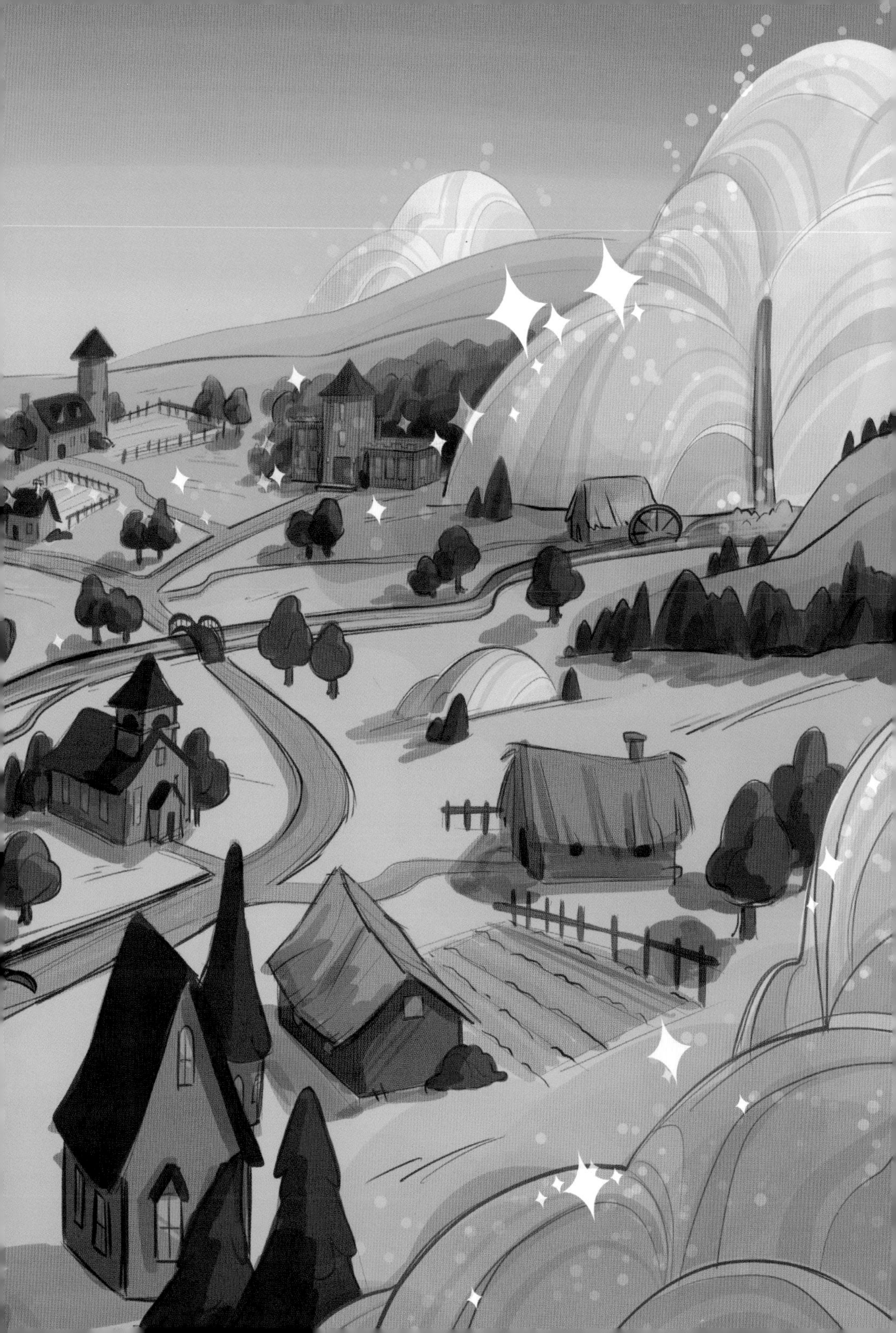

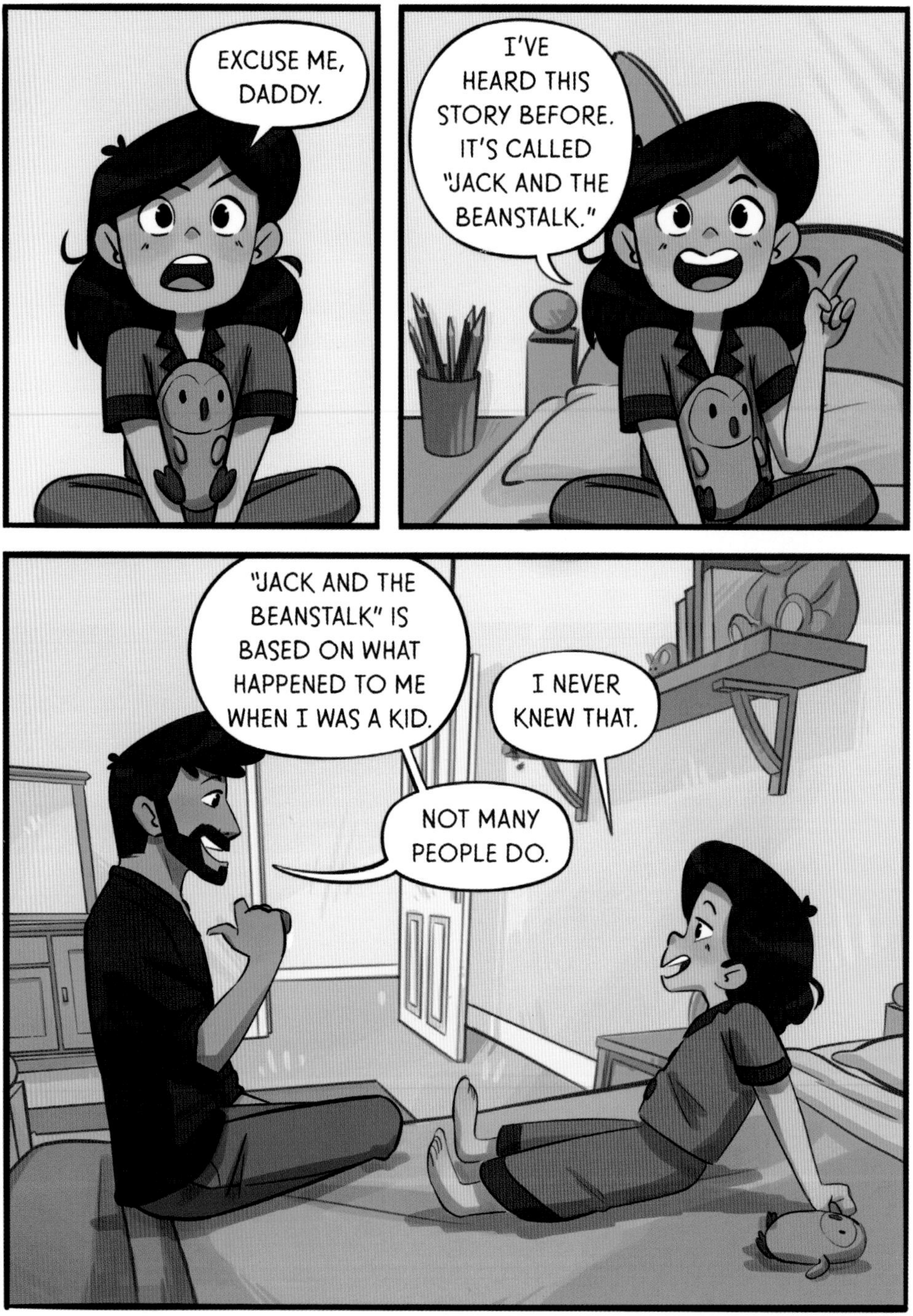
EXCUSE ME, DADDY.
I'VE HEARD THIS STORY BEFORE. IT'S CALLED "JACK AND THE BEANSTALK."
"JACK AND THE BEANSTALK" IS BASED ON WHAT HAPPENED TO ME WHEN I WAS A KID.
I NEVER KNEW THAT.
NOT MANY PEOPLE DO.

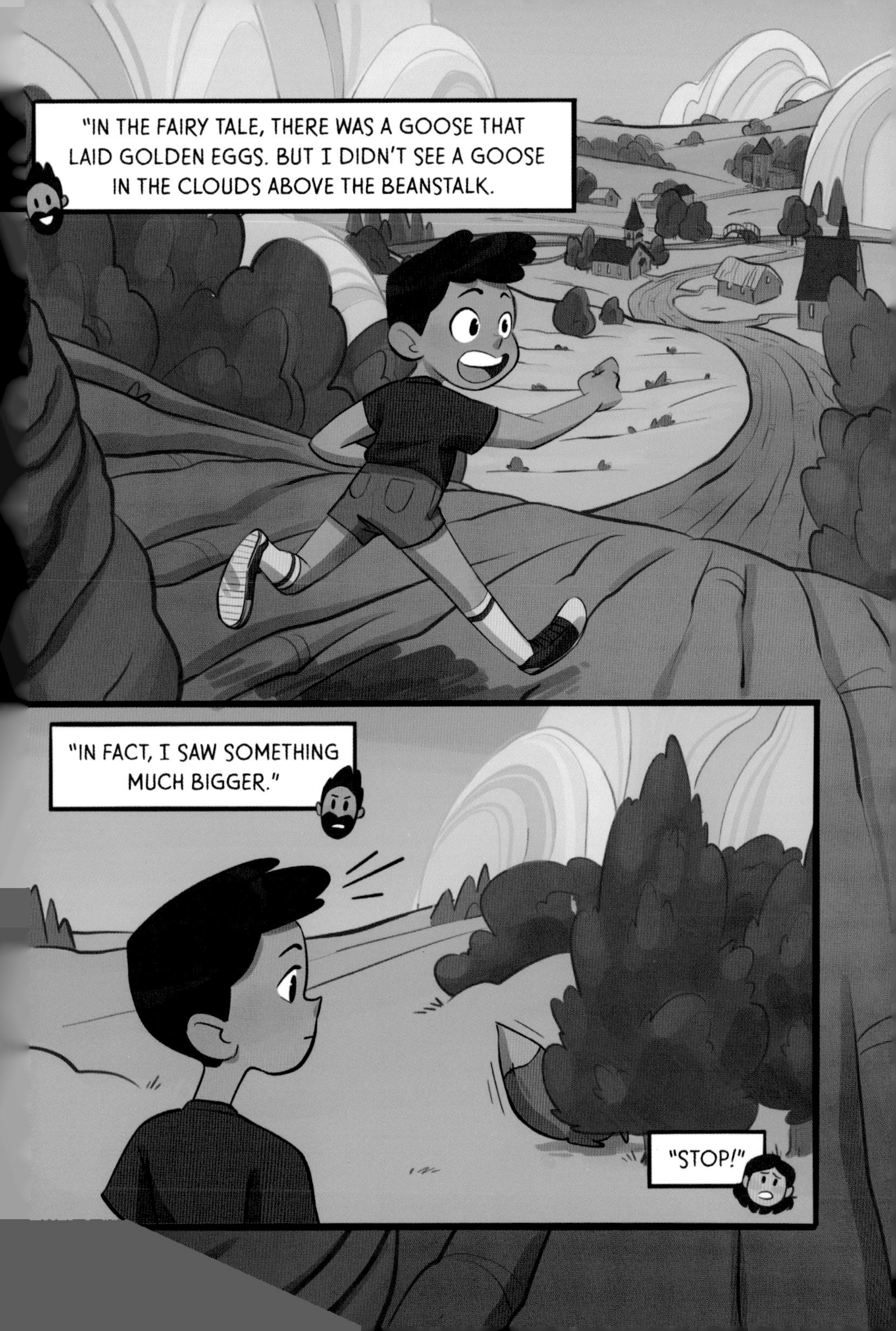
"IN THE FAIRY TALE, THERE WAS A GOOSE THAT LAID GOLDEN EGGS. BUT I DIDN'T SEE A GOOSE IN THE CLOUDS ABOVE THE BEANSTALK.
"IN FACT, I SAW SOMETHING MUCH BIGGER."
"STOP!"

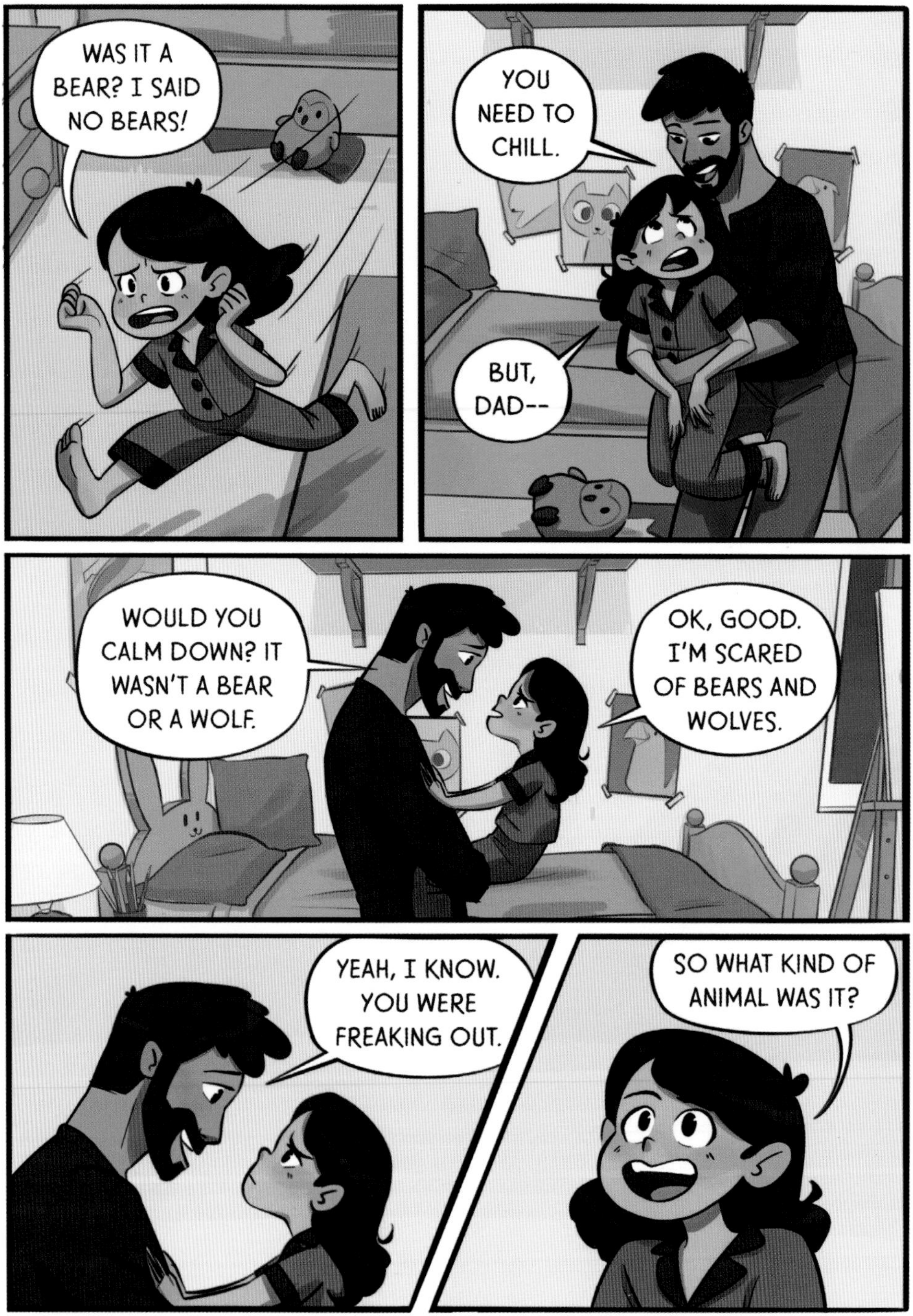
WAS IT A BEAR? I SAID NO BEARS!
YOU NEED TO CHILL.
BUT, DAD--
WOULD YOU CALM DOWN? IT WASN'T A BEAR OR A WOLF.
OK, GOOD. I'M SCARED OF BEARS AND WOLVES.
YEAH, I KNOW. YOU WERE FREAKING OUT.
SO WHAT KIND OF ANIMAL WAS IT?

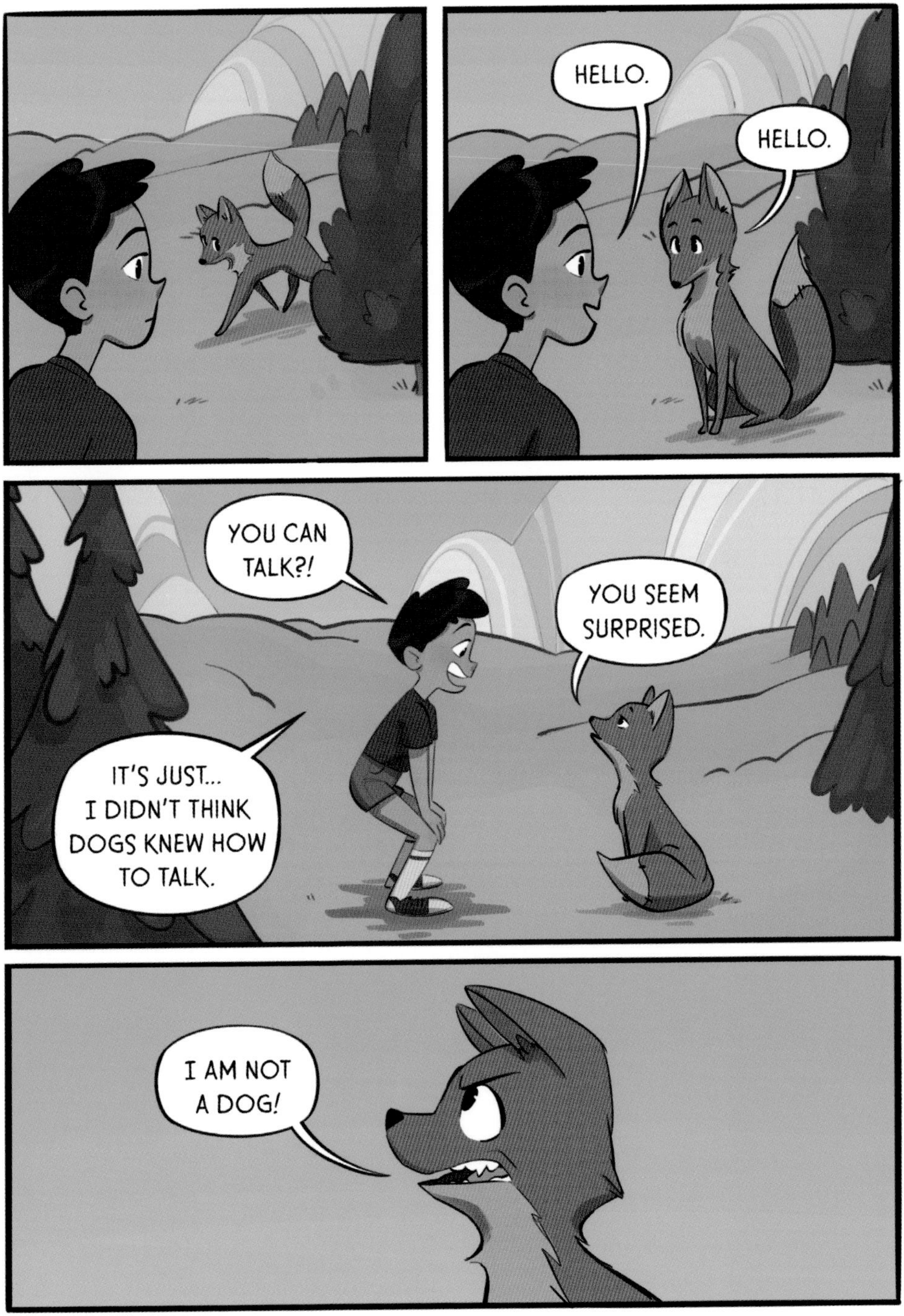
HELLO.
HELLO.
YOU CAN TALK?!
YOU SEEM SURPRISED.
IT'S JUST... I DIDN'T THINK DOGS KNEW HOW TO TALK.
I AM NOT A DOG!

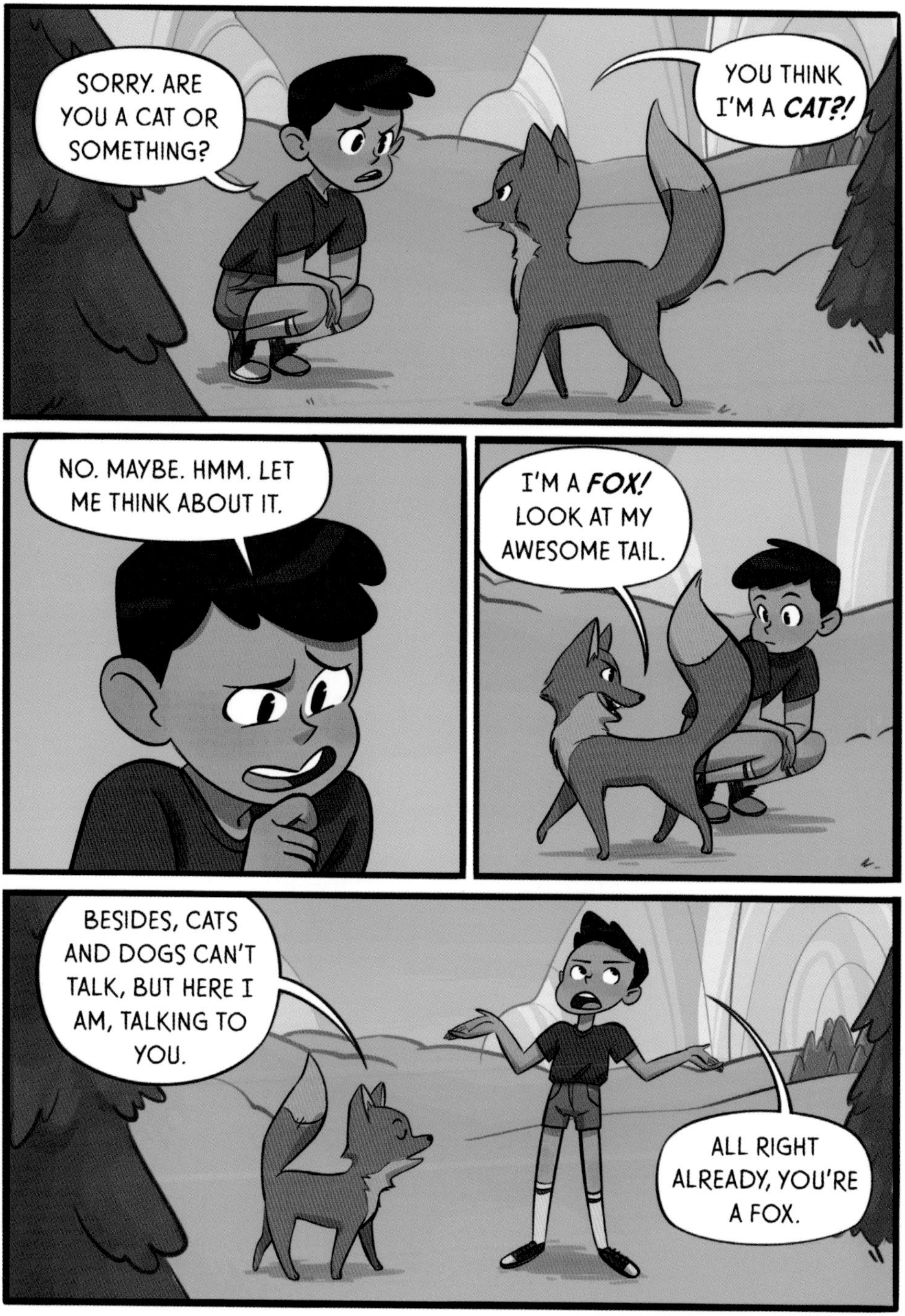
SORRY. ARE YOU A CAT OR SOMETHING?
YOU THINK I'M A ***CAT?!***
NO. MAYBE. HMM. LET ME THINK ABOUT IT.
I'M A ***FOX!*** LOOK AT MY AWESOME TAIL.
BESIDES, CATS AND DOGS CAN'T TALK, BUT HERE I AM, TALKING TO YOU.
ALL RIGHT ALREADY, YOU'RE A FOX.

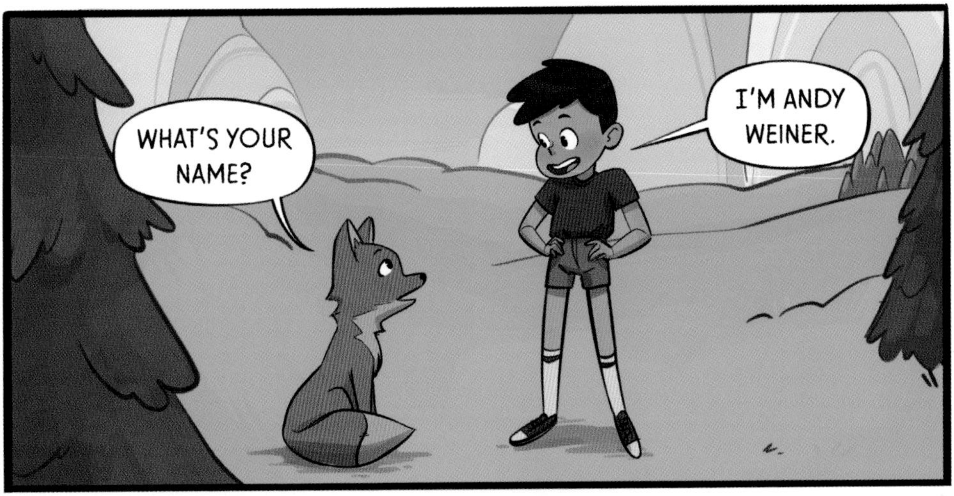
WHAT'S YOUR NAME?
I'M ANDY WEINER.

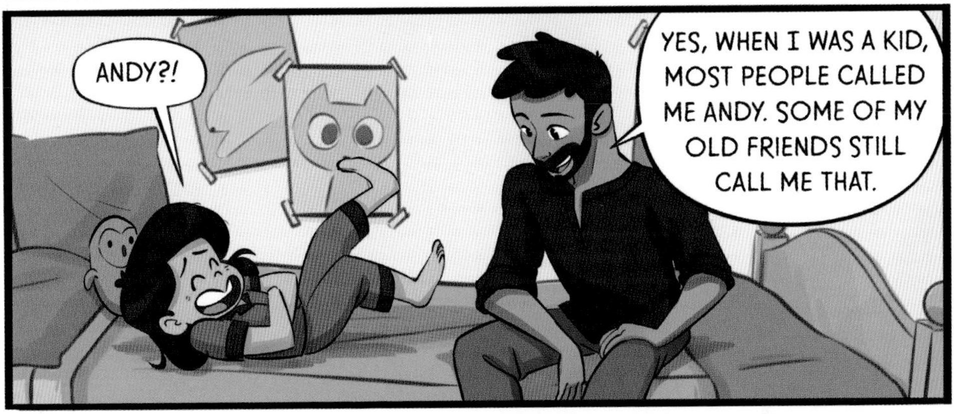
ANDY?!
YES, WHEN I WAS A KID, MOST PEOPLE CALLED ME ANDY. SOME OF MY OLD FRIENDS STILL CALL ME THAT.

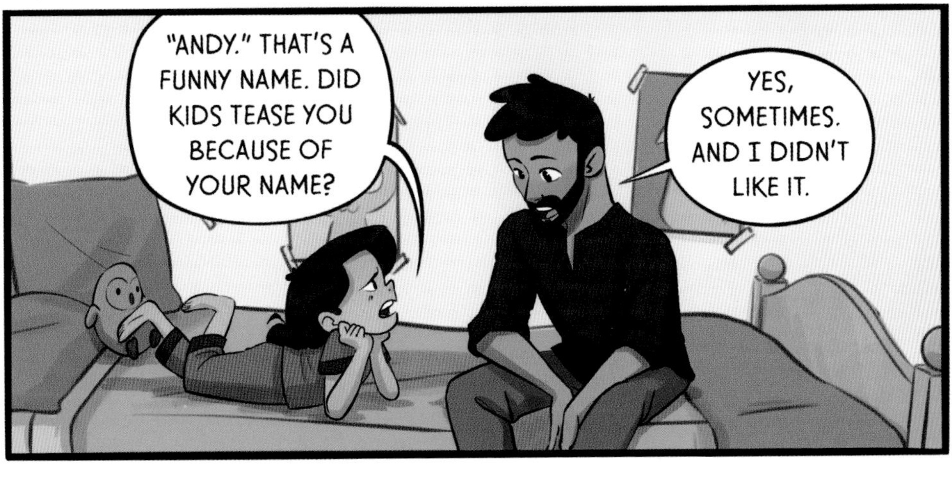
"ANDY." THAT'S A FUNNY NAME. DID KIDS TEASE YOU BECAUSE OF YOUR NAME?
YES, SOMETIMES. AND I DIDN'T LIKE IT.

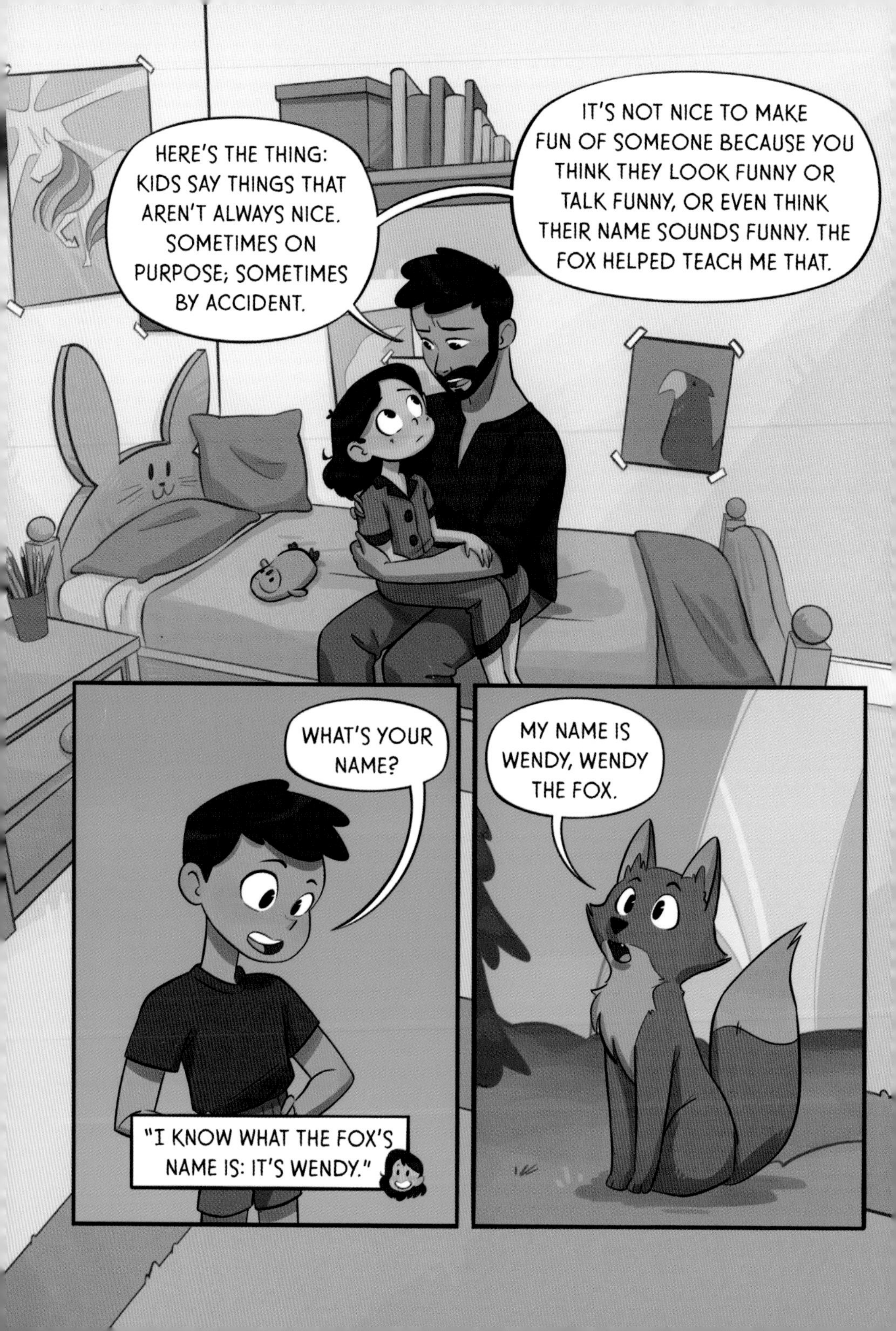
HERE'S THE THING: KIDS SAY THINGS THAT AREN'T ALWAYS NICE. SOMETIMES ON PURPOSE; SOMETIMES BY ACCIDENT.
IT'S NOT NICE TO MAKE FUN OF SOMEONE BECAUSE YOU THINK THEY LOOK FUNNY OR TALK FUNNY, OR EVEN THINK THEIR NAME SOUNDS FUNNY. THE FOX HELPED TEACH ME THAT.
WHAT'S YOUR NAME?
"I KNOW WHAT THE FOX'S NAME IS: IT'S WENDY."
MY NAME IS WENDY, WENDY THE FOX.

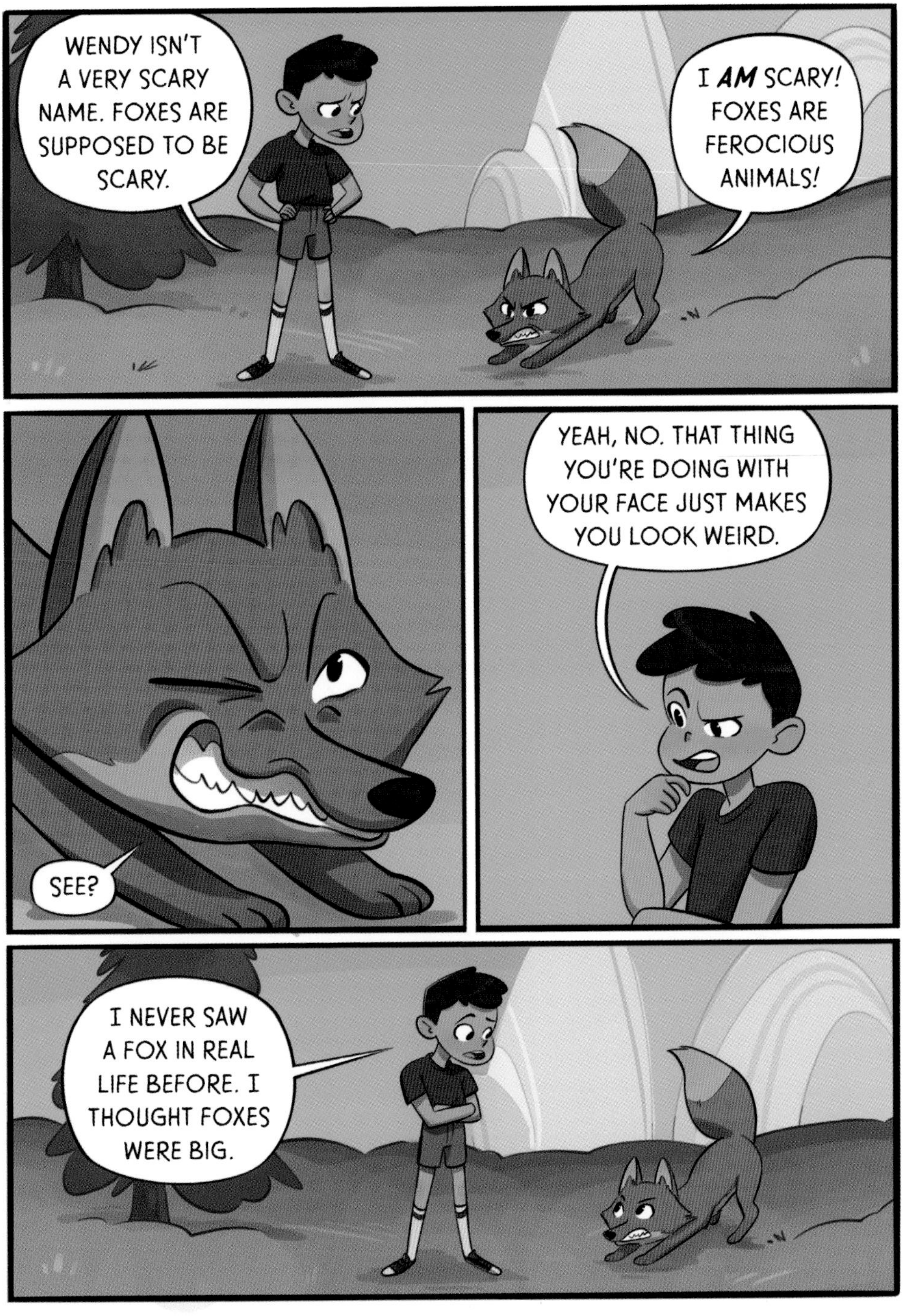
WENDY ISN'T A VERY SCARY NAME. FOXES ARE SUPPOSED TO BE SCARY.
I **AM** SCARY! FOXES ARE FEROCIOUS ANIMALS!
SEE?
YEAH, NO. THAT THING YOU'RE DOING WITH YOUR FACE JUST MAKES YOU LOOK WEIRD.
I NEVER SAW A FOX IN REAL LIFE BEFORE. I THOUGHT FOXES WERE BIG.

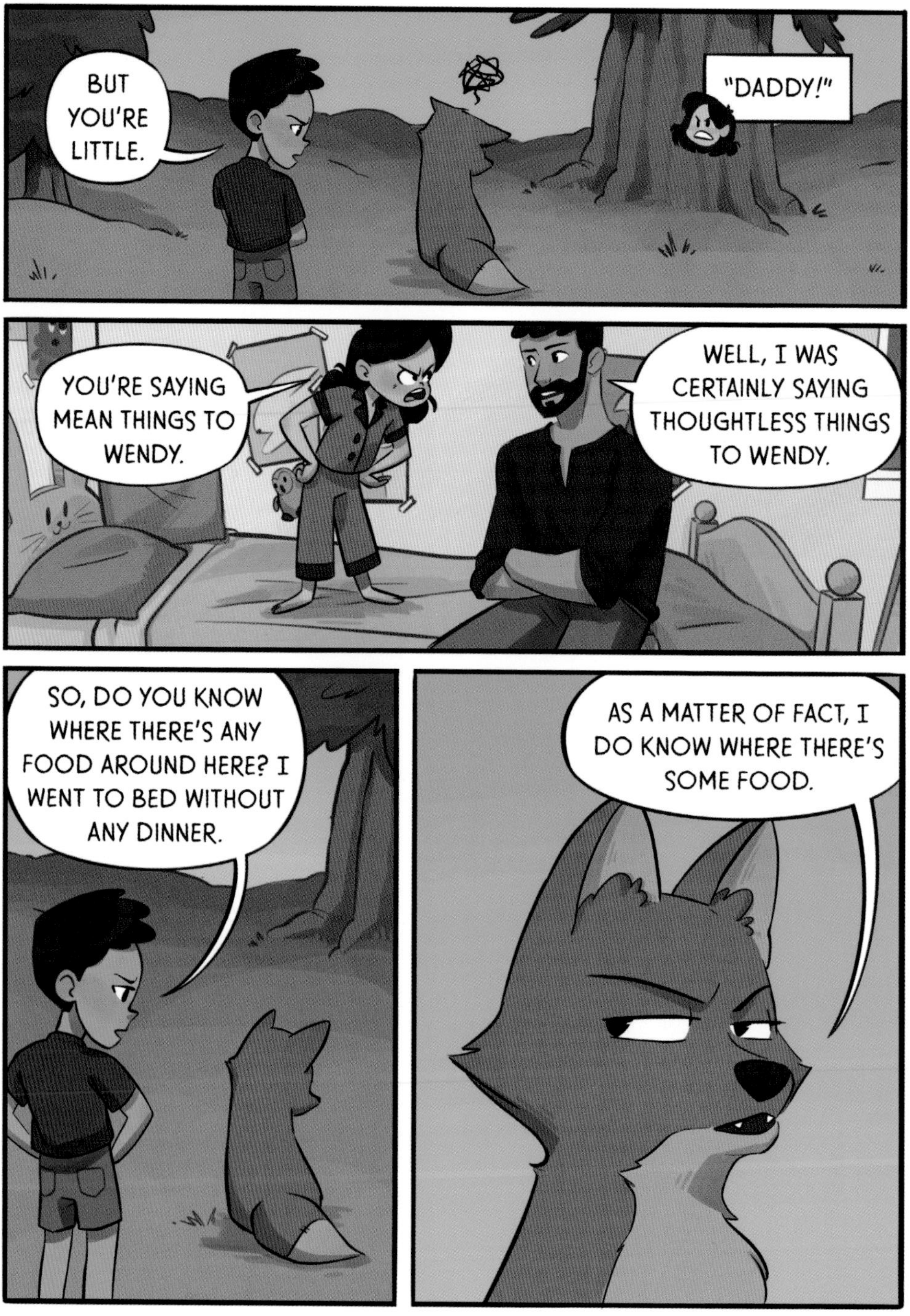
BUT YOU'RE LITTLE.
"DADDY!"
YOU'RE SAYING MEAN THINGS TO WENDY.
WELL, I WAS CERTAINLY SAYING THOUGHTLESS THINGS TO WENDY.
SO, DO YOU KNOW WHERE THERE'S ANY FOOD AROUND HERE? I WENT TO BED WITHOUT ANY DINNER.
AS A MATTER OF FACT, I DO KNOW WHERE THERE'S SOME FOOD.

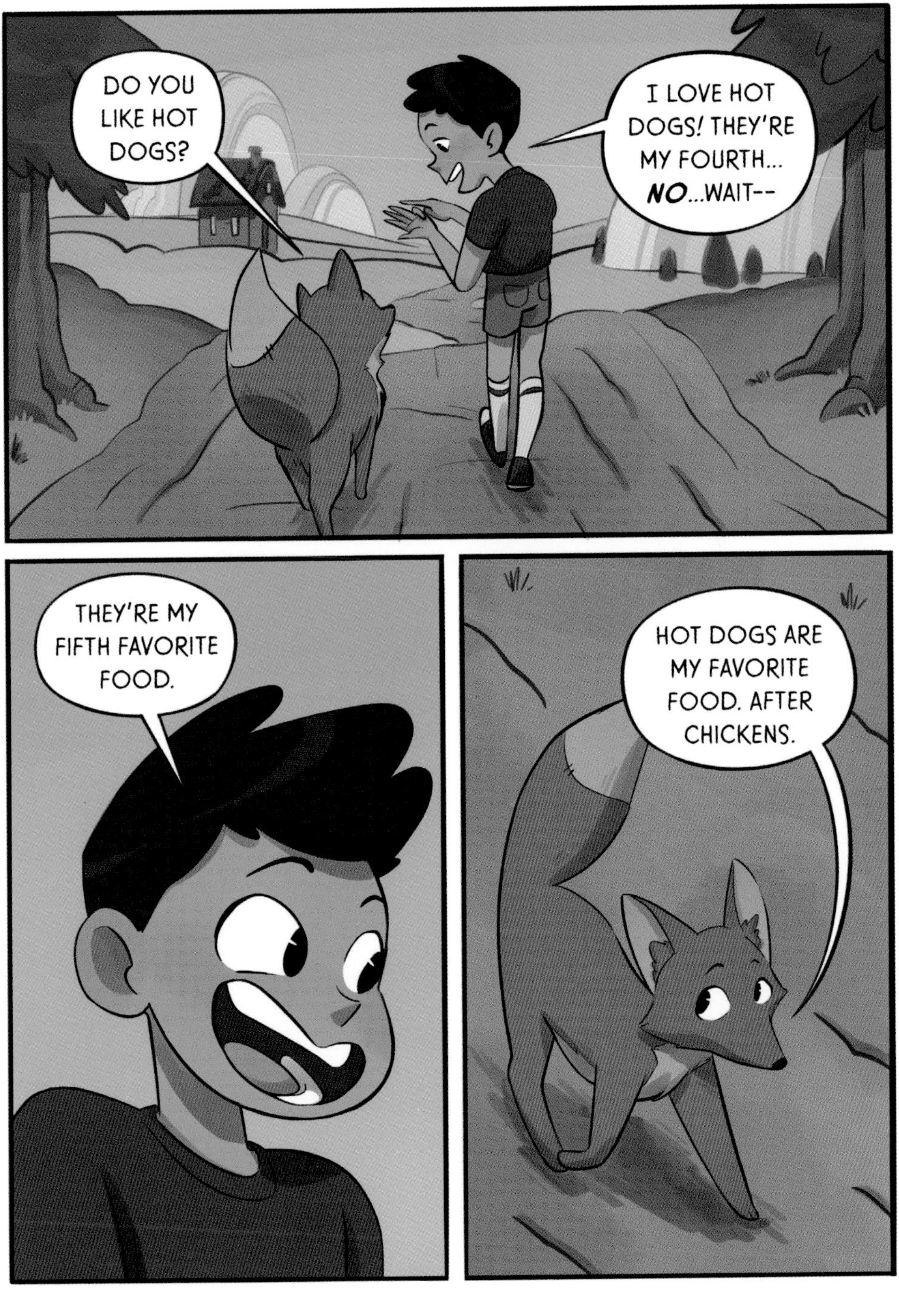
DO YOU LIKE HOT DOGS?
I LOVE HOT DOGS! THEY'RE MY FOURTH... **NO**...WAIT--
THEY'RE MY FIFTH FAVORITE FOOD.
HOT DOGS ARE MY FAVORITE FOOD. AFTER CHICKENS.

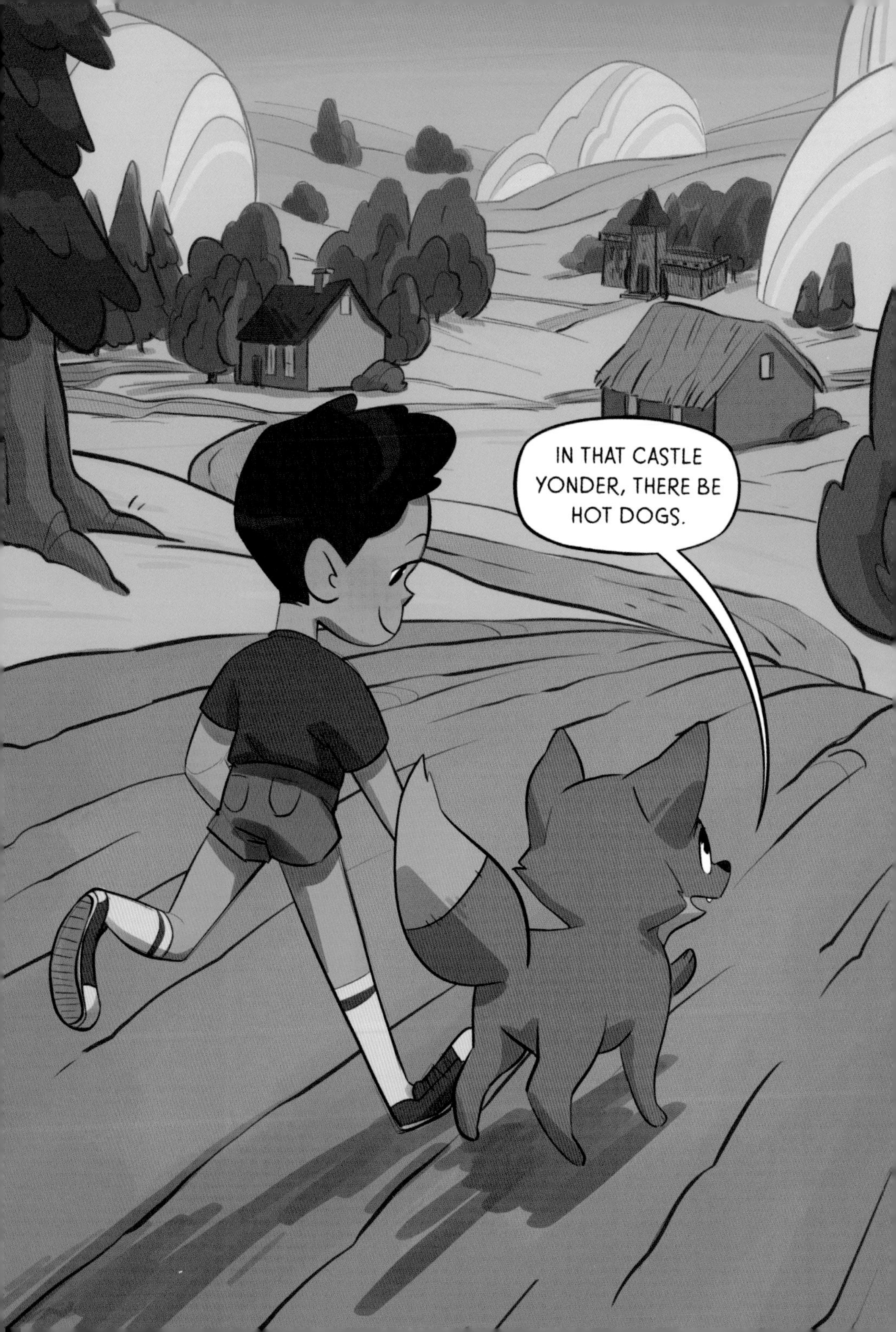
IN THAT CASTLE YONDER, THERE BE HOT DOGS.

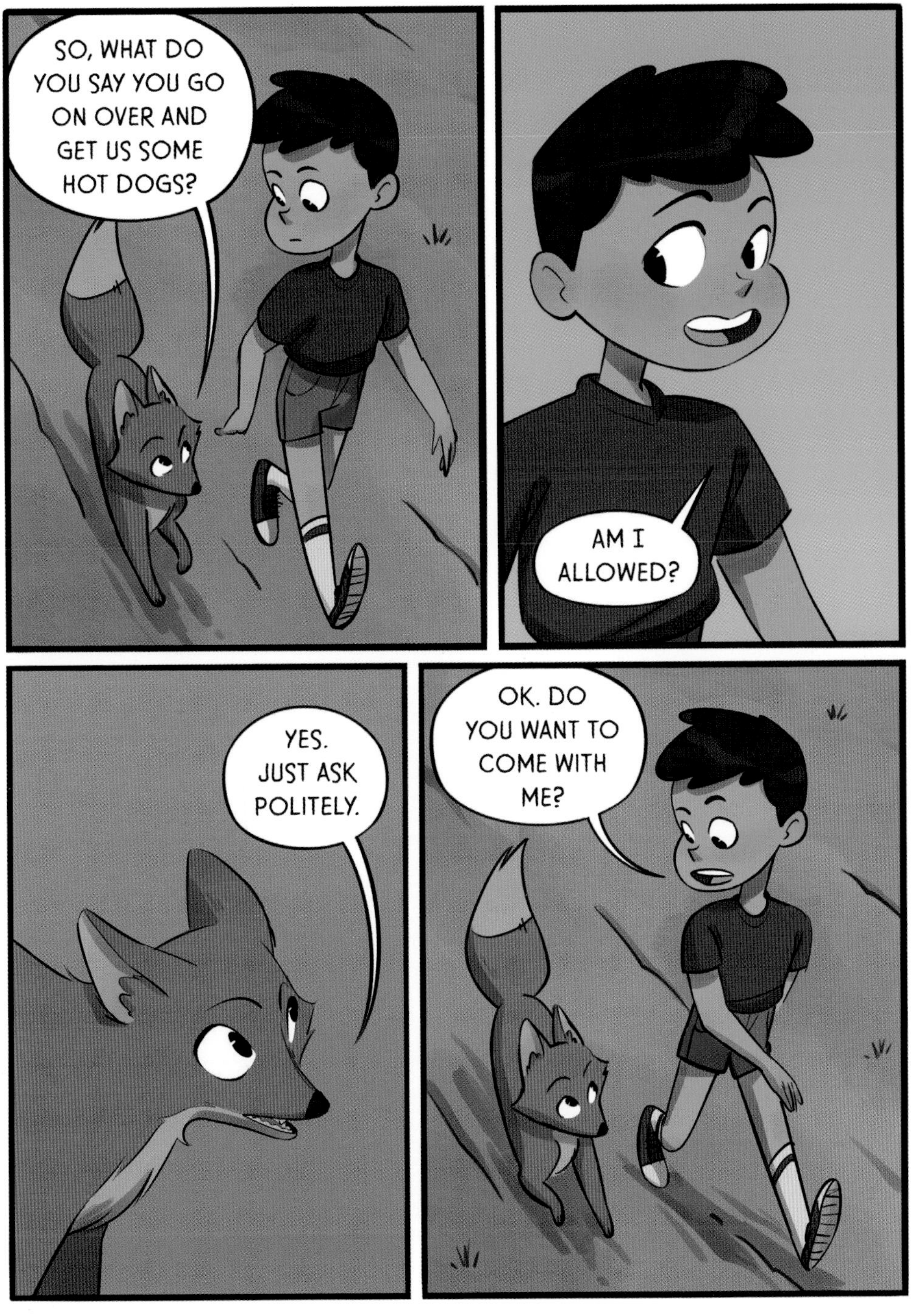
SO, WHAT DO YOU SAY YOU GO ON OVER AND GET US SOME HOT DOGS?
AM I ALLOWED?
YES. JUST ASK POLITELY.
OK. DO YOU WANT TO COME WITH ME?

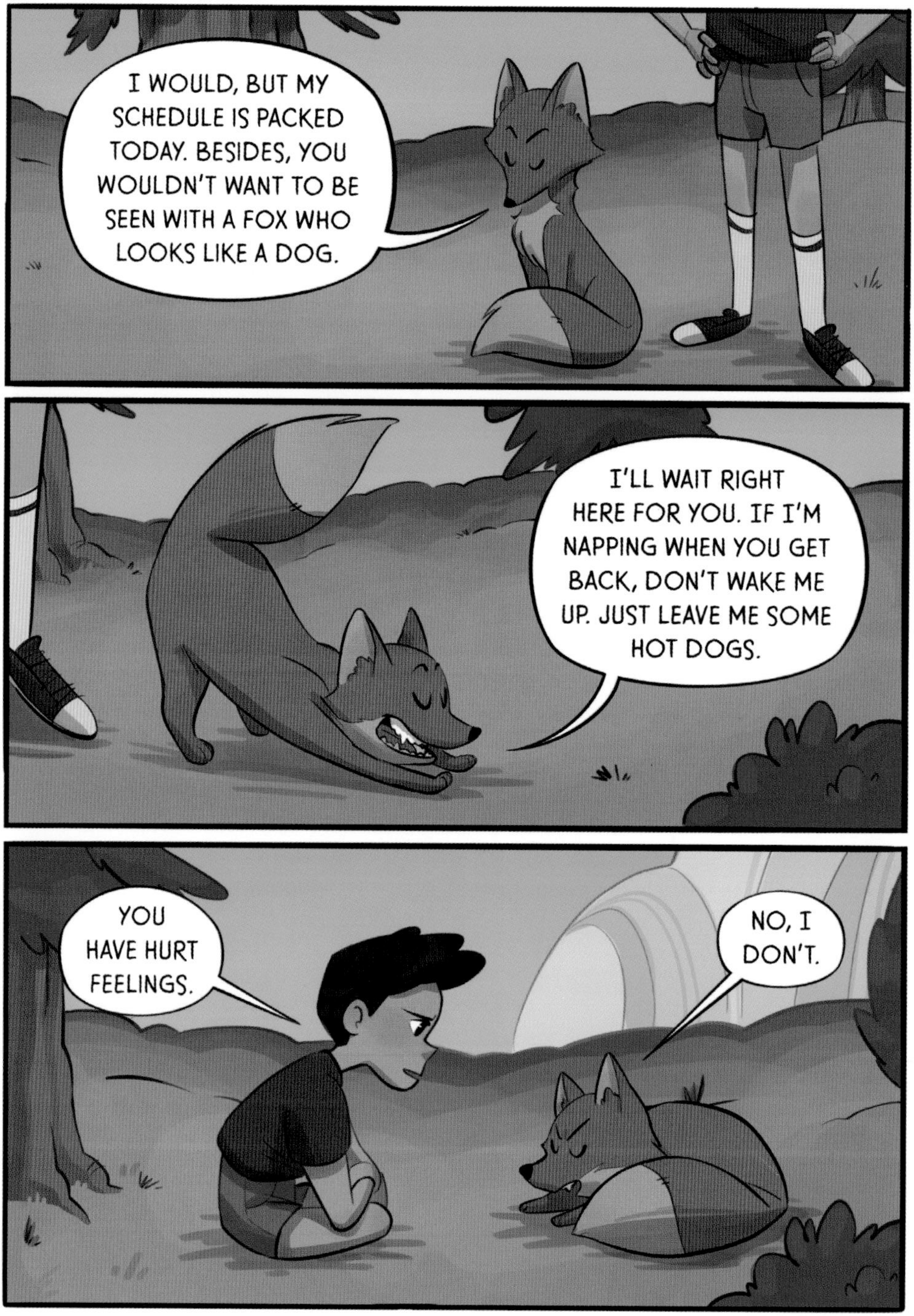
I WOULD, BUT MY SCHEDULE IS PACKED TODAY. BESIDES, YOU WOULDN'T WANT TO BE SEEN WITH A FOX WHO LOOKS LIKE A DOG.
I'LL WAIT RIGHT HERE FOR YOU. IF I'M NAPPING WHEN YOU GET BACK, DON'T WAKE ME UP. JUST LEAVE ME SOME HOT DOGS.
YOU HAVE HURT FEELINGS.
NO, I DON'T.

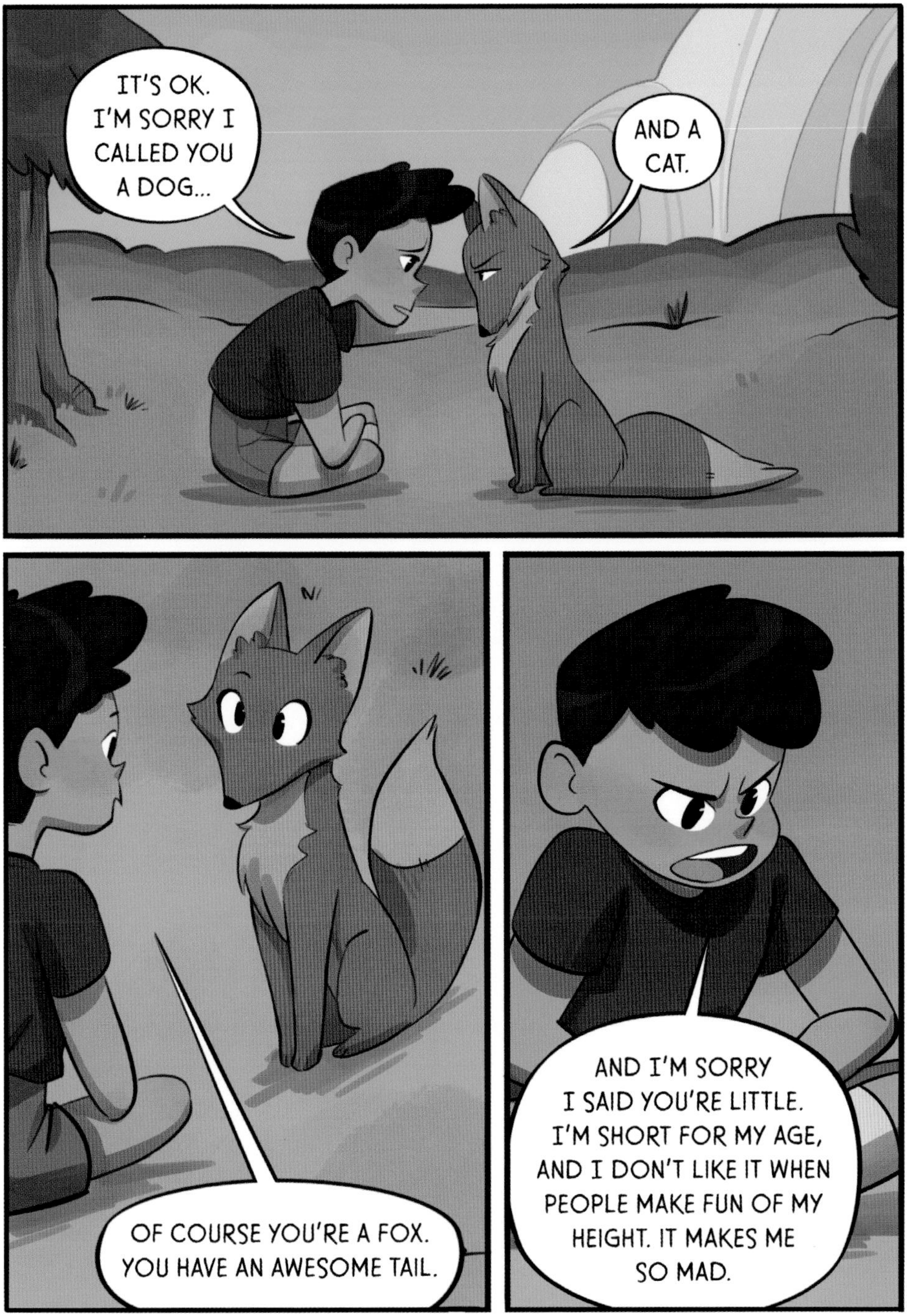
IT'S OK. I'M SORRY I CALLED YOU A DOG...
AND A CAT.
OF COURSE YOU'RE A FOX. YOU HAVE AN AWESOME TAIL.
AND I'M SORRY I SAID YOU'RE LITTLE. I'M SHORT FOR MY AGE, AND I DON'T LIKE IT WHEN PEOPLE MAKE FUN OF MY HEIGHT. IT MAKES ME SO MAD.

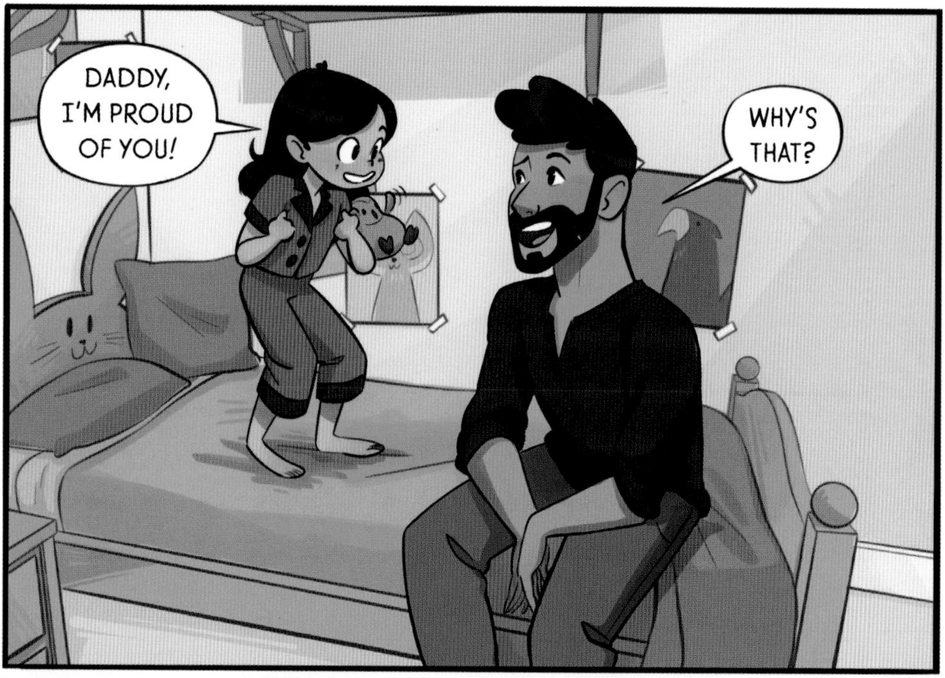
DADDY, I'M PROUD OF YOU!
WHY'S THAT?

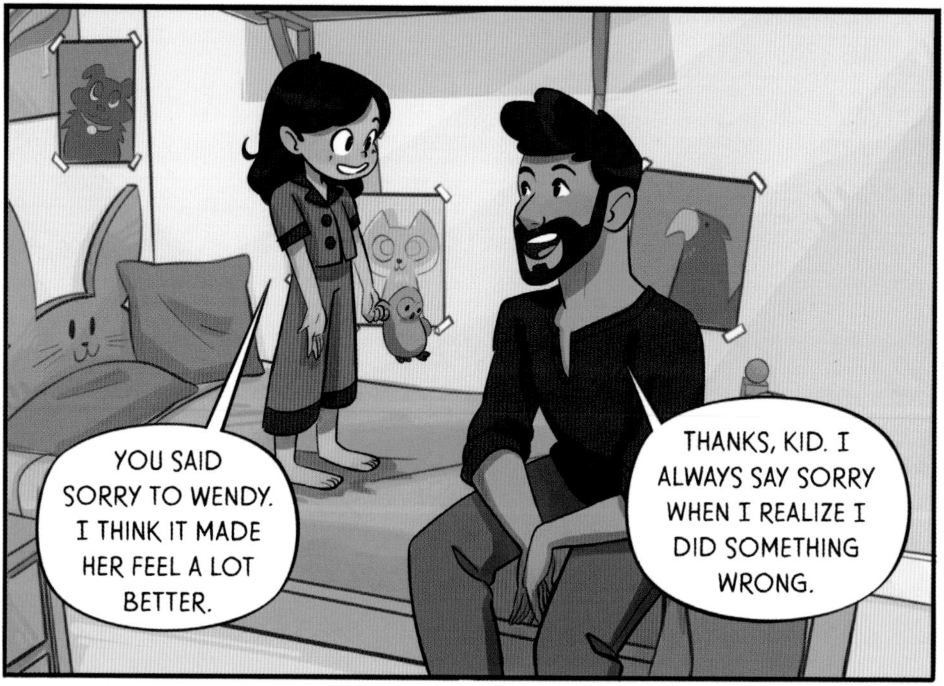
YOU SAID SORRY TO WENDY. I THINK IT MADE HER FEEL A LOT BETTER.
THANKS, KID. I ALWAYS SAY SORRY WHEN I REALIZE I DID SOMETHING WRONG.

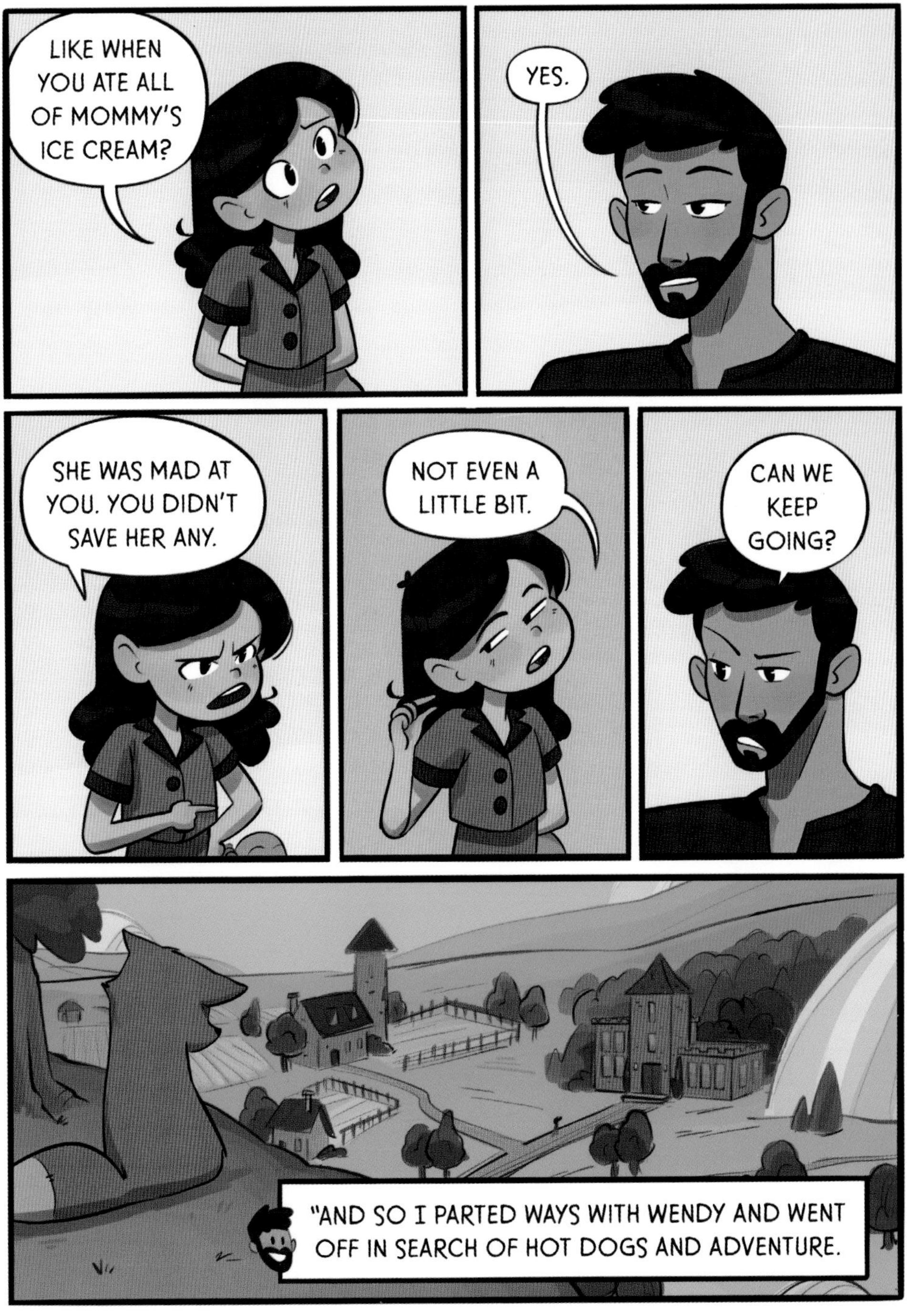

LIKE WHEN YOU ATE ALL OF MOMMY'S ICE CREAM?
YES.
SHE WAS MAD AT YOU. YOU DIDN'T SAVE HER ANY.
NOT EVEN A LITTLE BIT.
CAN WE KEEP GOING?
"AND SO I PARTED WAYS WITH WENDY AND WENT OFF IN SEARCH OF HOT DOGS AND ADVENTURE.

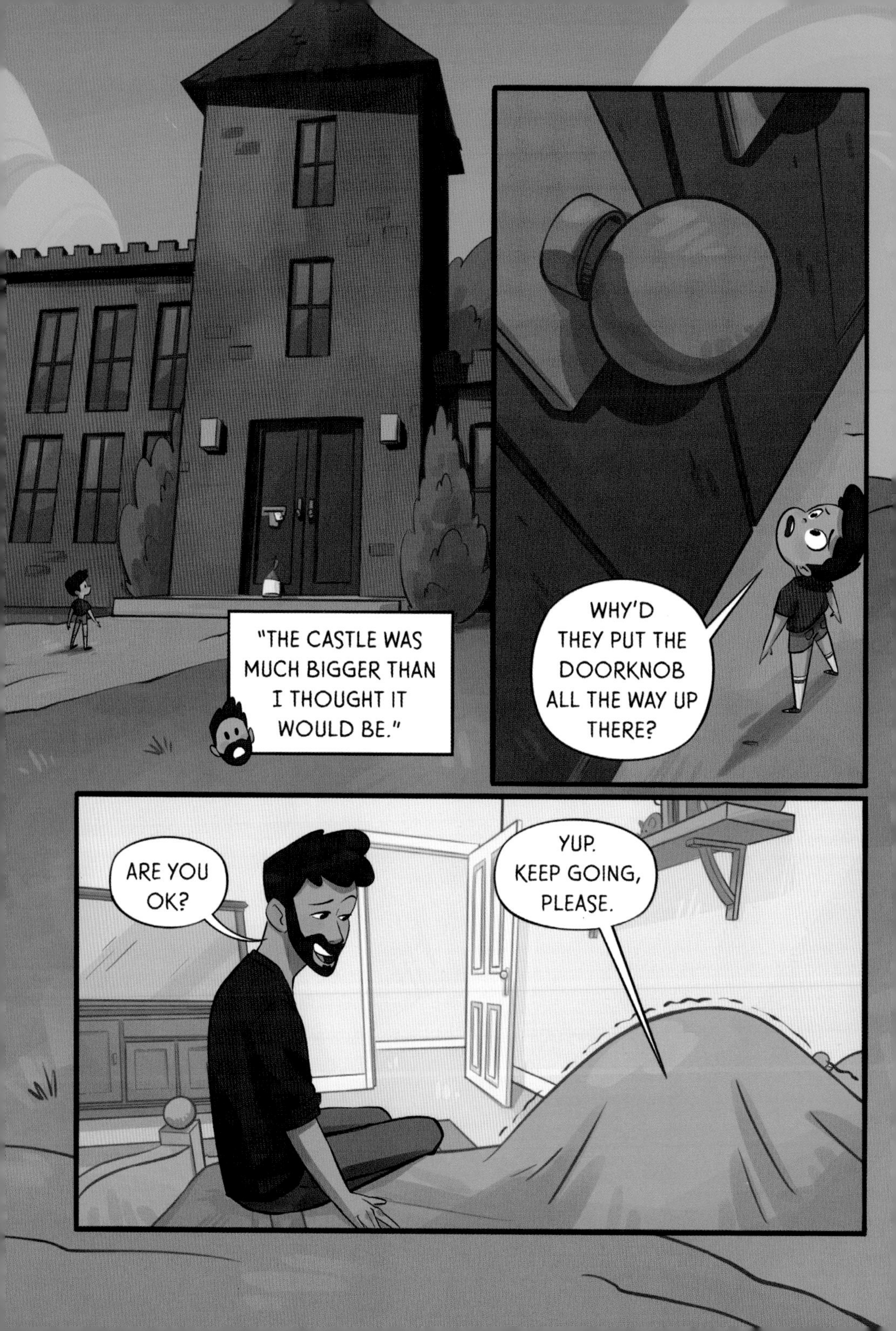
"THE CASTLE WAS MUCH BIGGER THAN I THOUGHT IT WOULD BE."
WHY'D THEY PUT THE DOORKNOB ALL THE WAY UP THERE?
ARE YOU OK?
YUP. KEEP GOING, PLEASE.

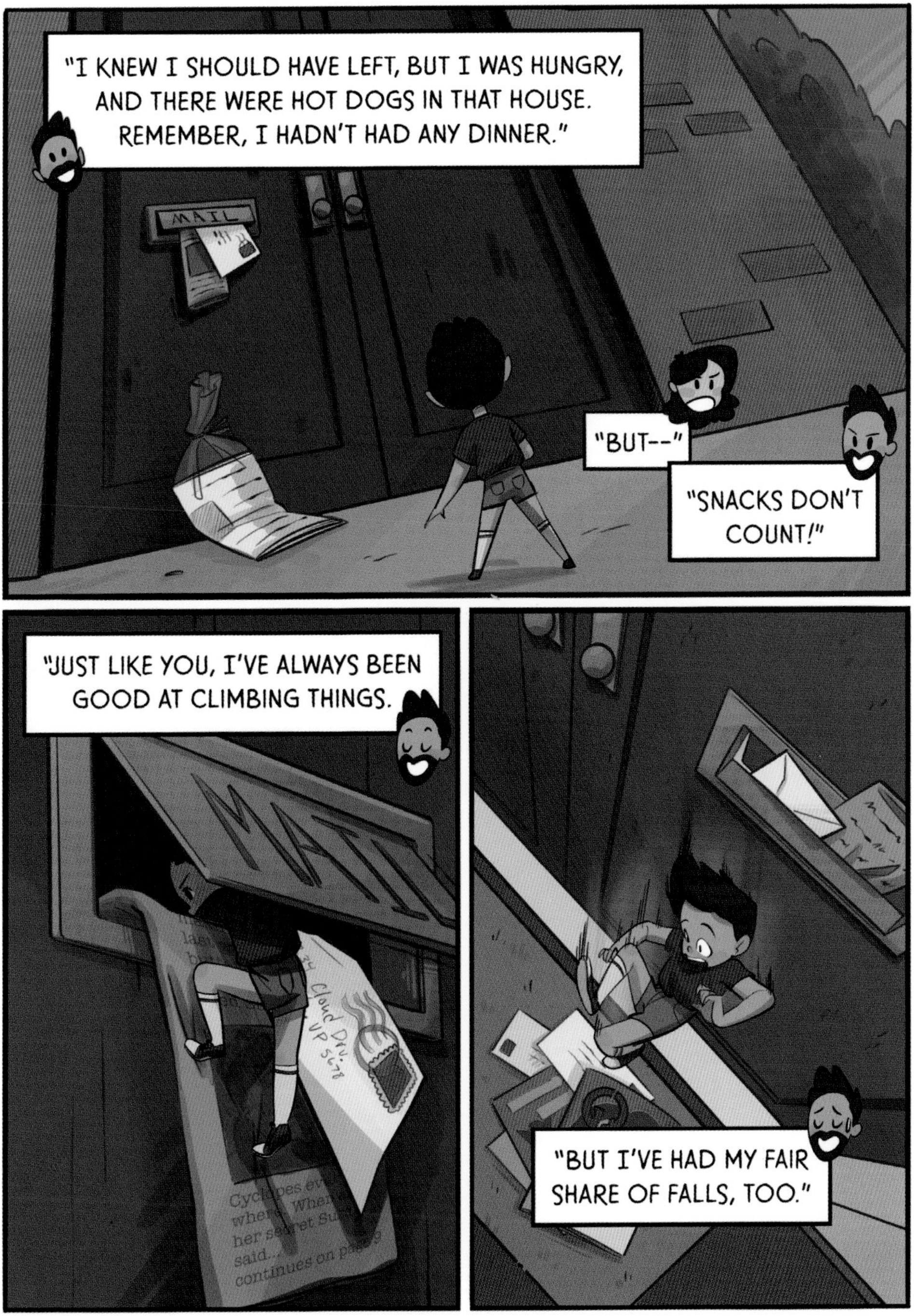
"I KNEW I SHOULD HAVE LEFT, BUT I WAS HUNGRY, AND THERE WERE HOT DOGS IN THAT HOUSE. REMEMBER, I HADN'T HAD ANY DINNER."
MAIL
"BUT--"
"SNACKS DON'T COUNT!"
"JUST LIKE YOU, I'VE ALWAYS BEEN GOOD AT CLIMBING THINGS.
"BUT I'VE HAD MY FAIR SHARE OF FALLS, TOO."

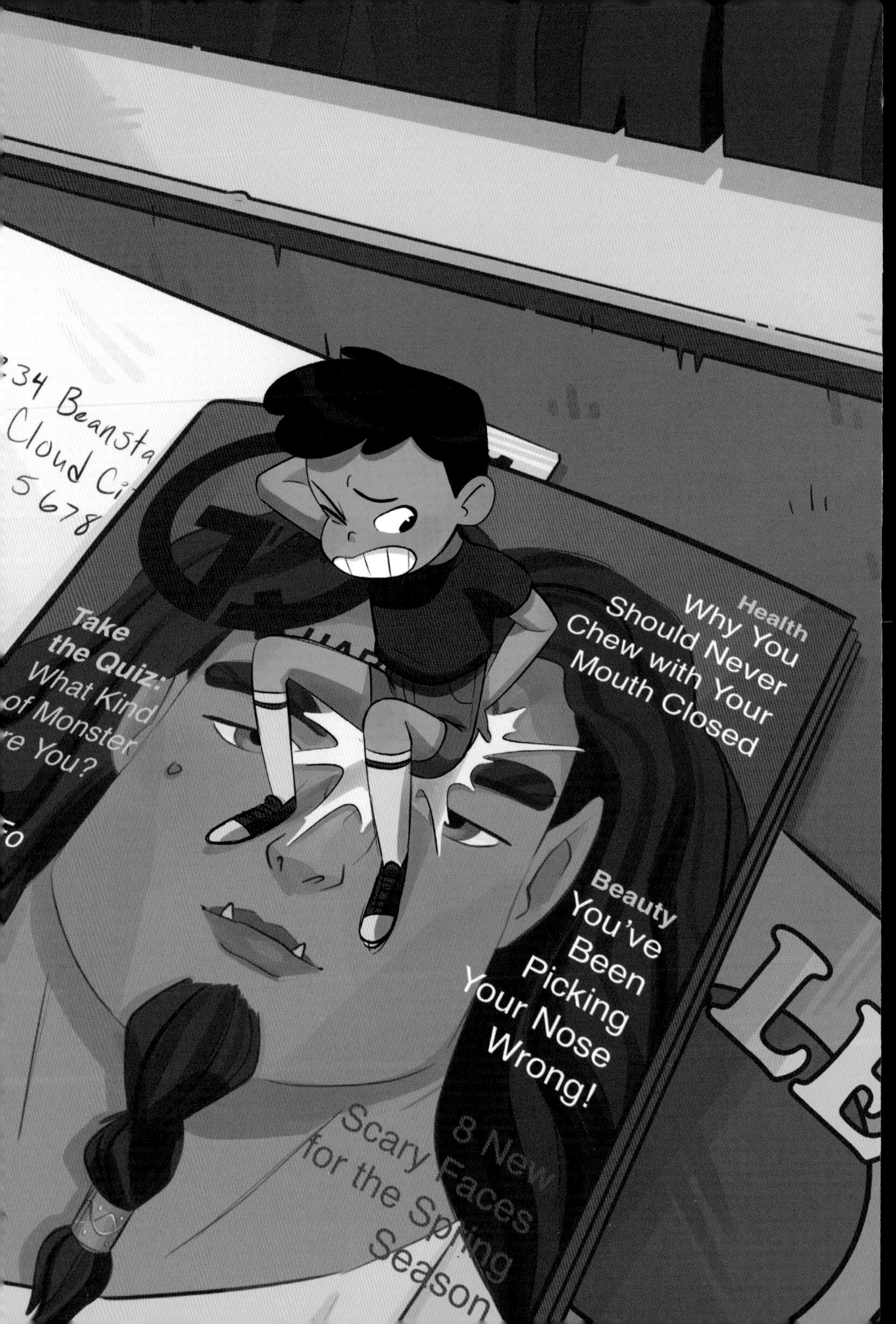

234 Beansta
Cloud Ci
5678
Take the Quiz: What Kind of Monster re You?
Fo
Health
Why You Should Never Chew with Your Mouth Closed
Beauty
You've Been Picking Your Nose Wrong!
8 New Scary Faces for the Spring Season

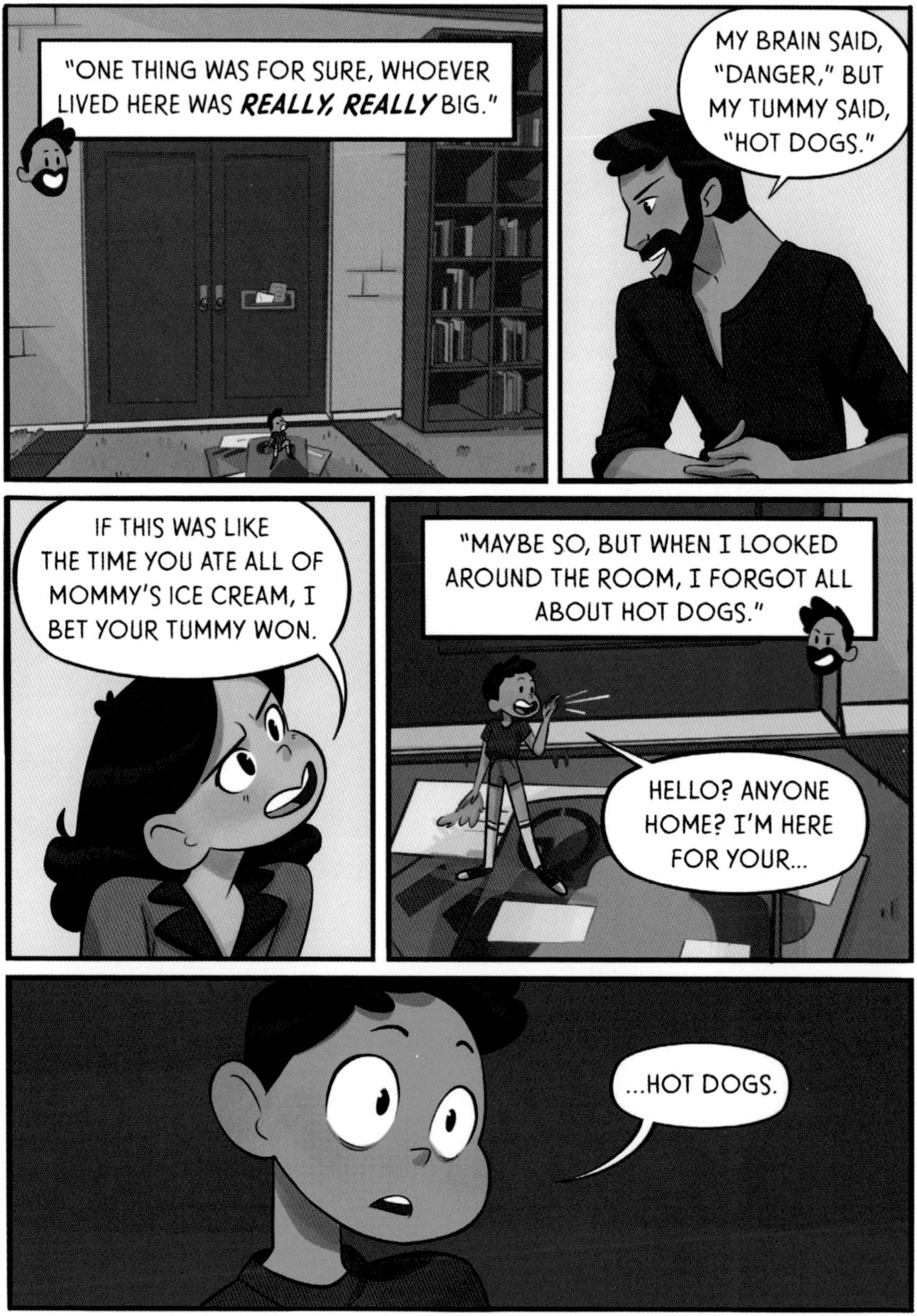
"ONE THING WAS FOR SURE, WHOEVER LIVED HERE WAS ***REALLY, REALLY*** BIG."
MY BRAIN SAID, "DANGER," BUT MY TUMMY SAID, "HOT DOGS."
IF THIS WAS LIKE THE TIME YOU ATE ALL OF MOMMY'S ICE CREAM, I BET YOUR TUMMY WON.
"MAYBE SO, BUT WHEN I LOOKED AROUND THE ROOM, I FORGOT ALL ABOUT HOT DOGS."
HELLO? ANYONE HOME? I'M HERE FOR YOUR...
...HOT DOGS.

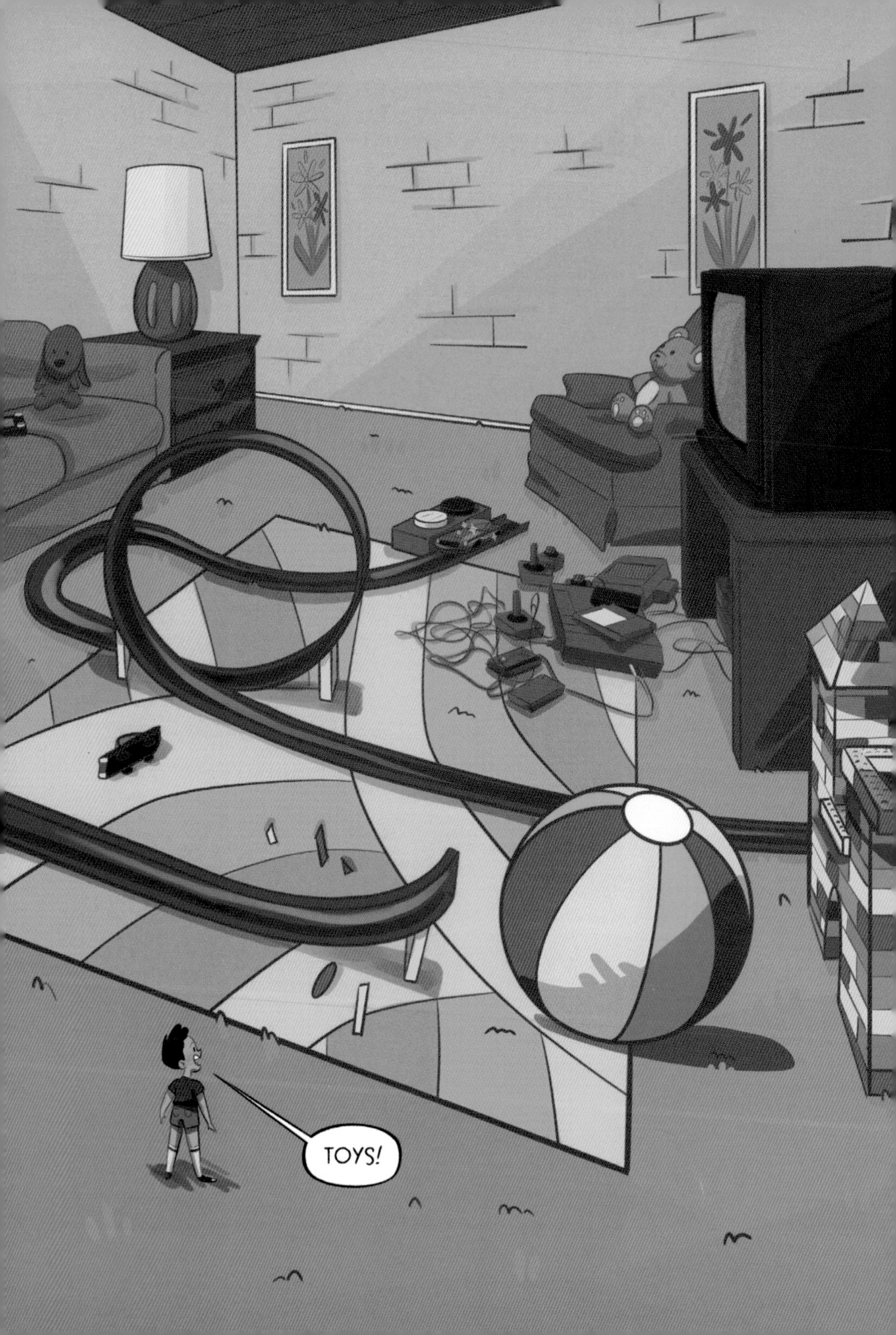
TOYS!

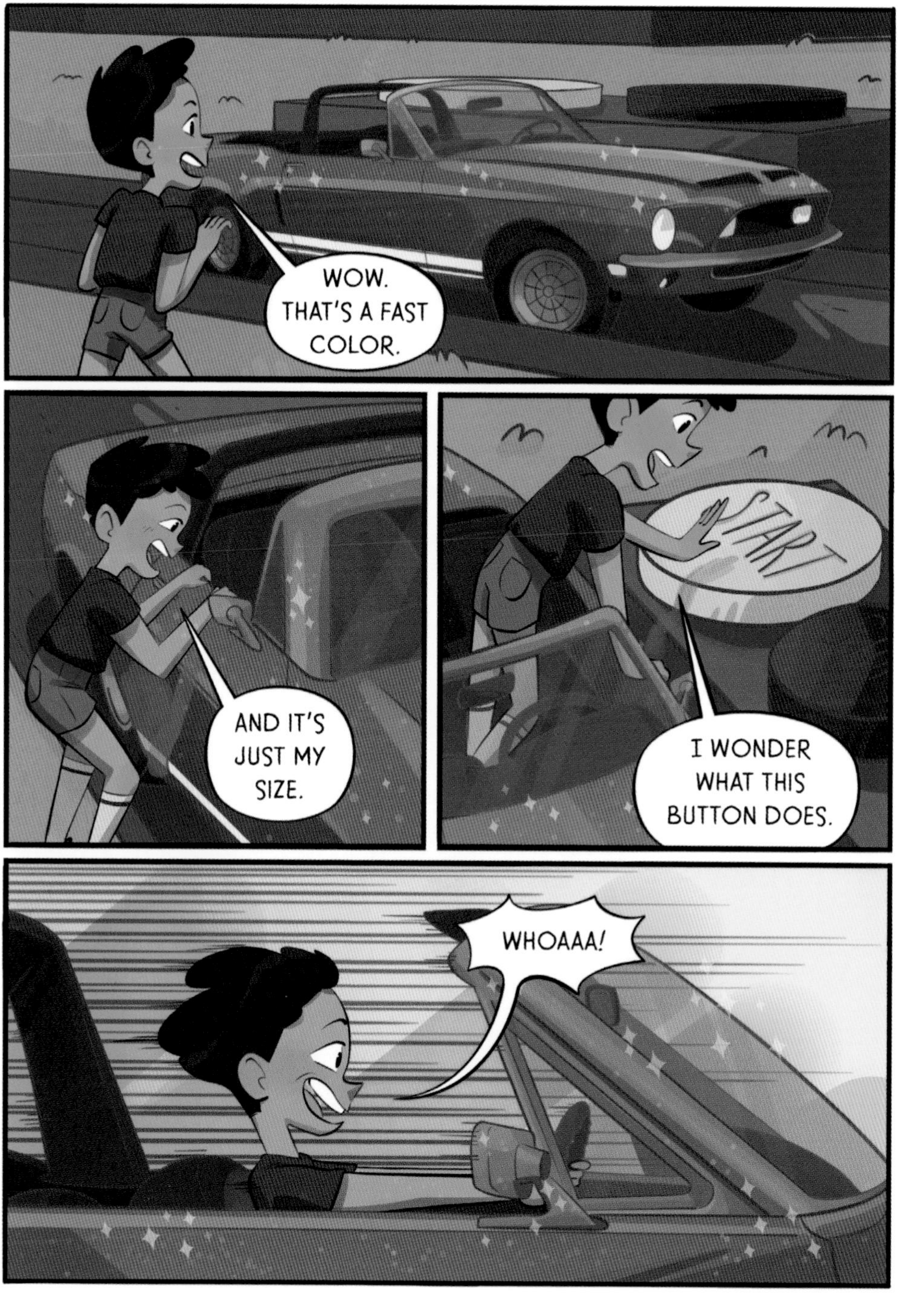
WOW. THAT'S A FAST COLOR.
AND IT'S JUST MY SIZE.
START
I WONDER WHAT THIS BUTTON DOES.
WHOAAA!

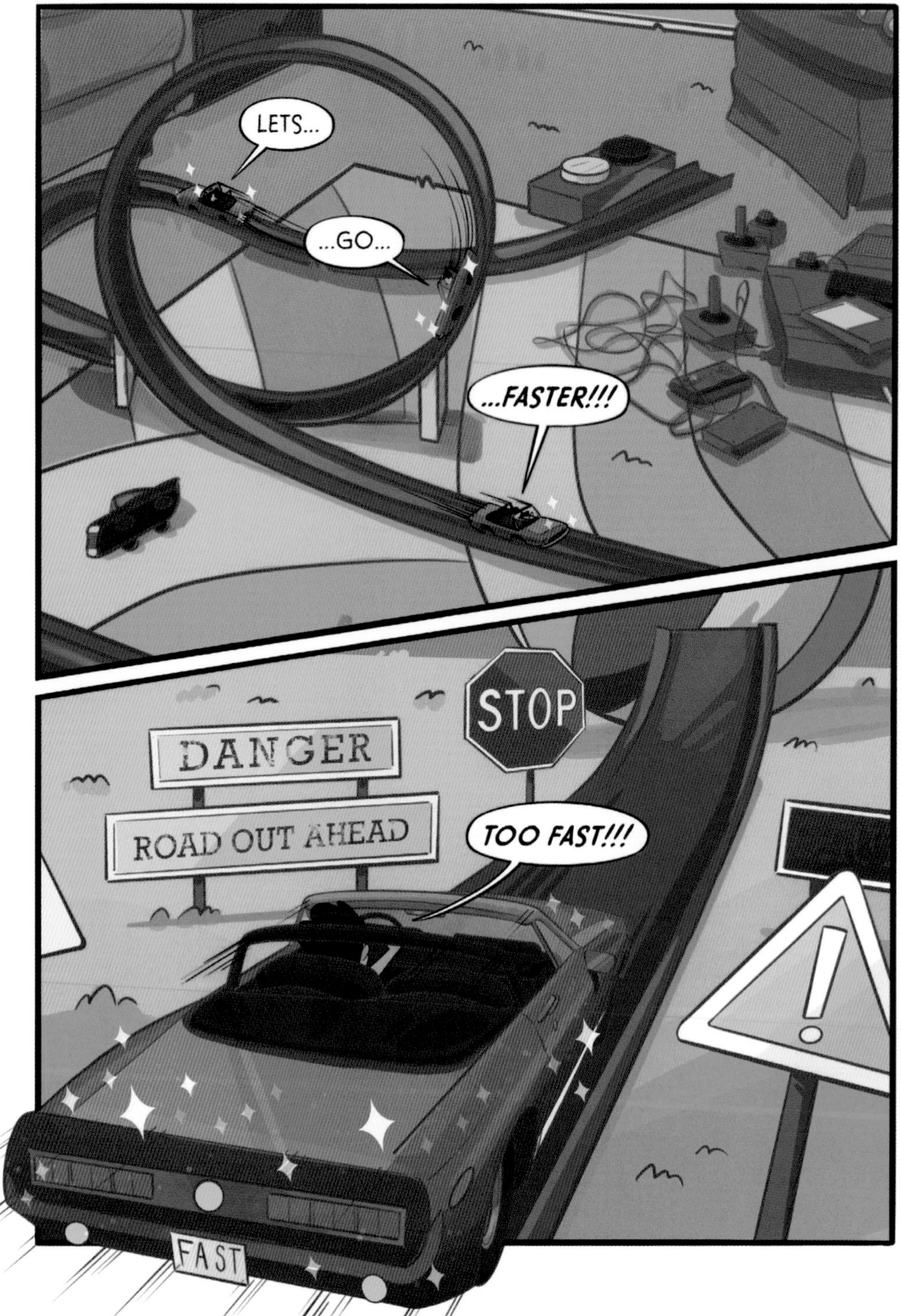
LETS...
...GO...
...FASTER!!!
DANGER
ROAD OUT AHEAD
STOP
TOO FAST!!!
FAST

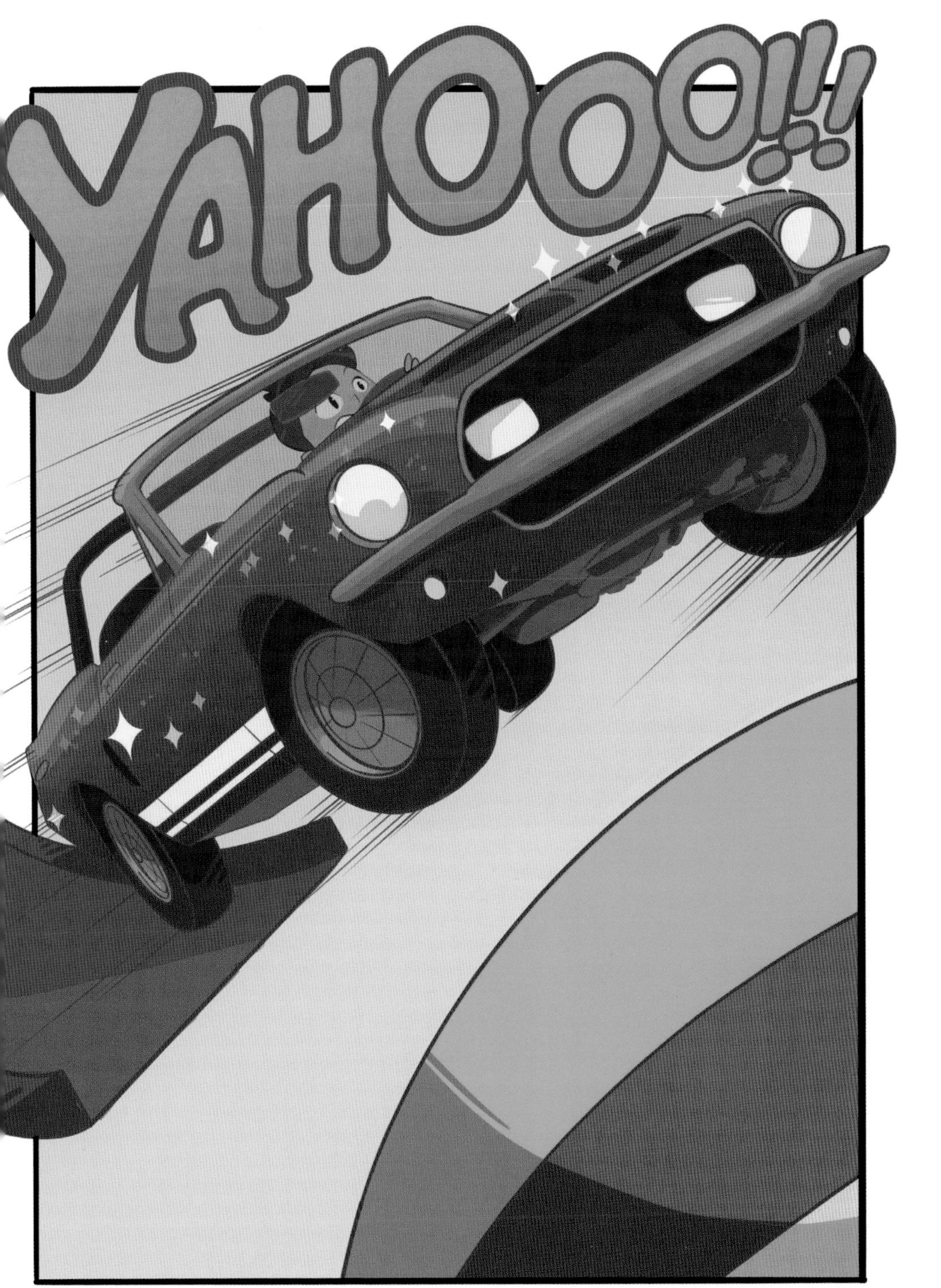
YAHOOO!!!

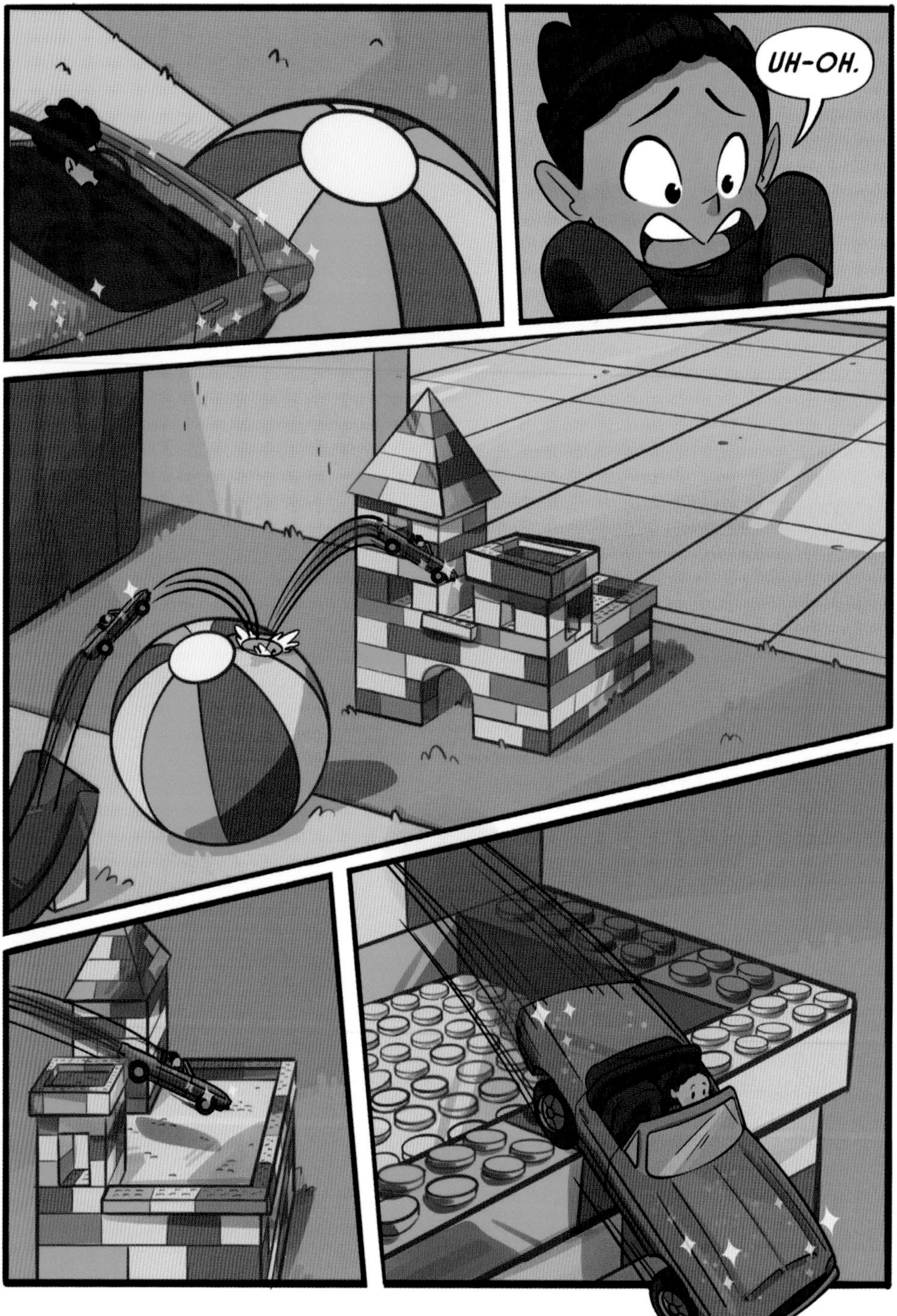
UH-OH.

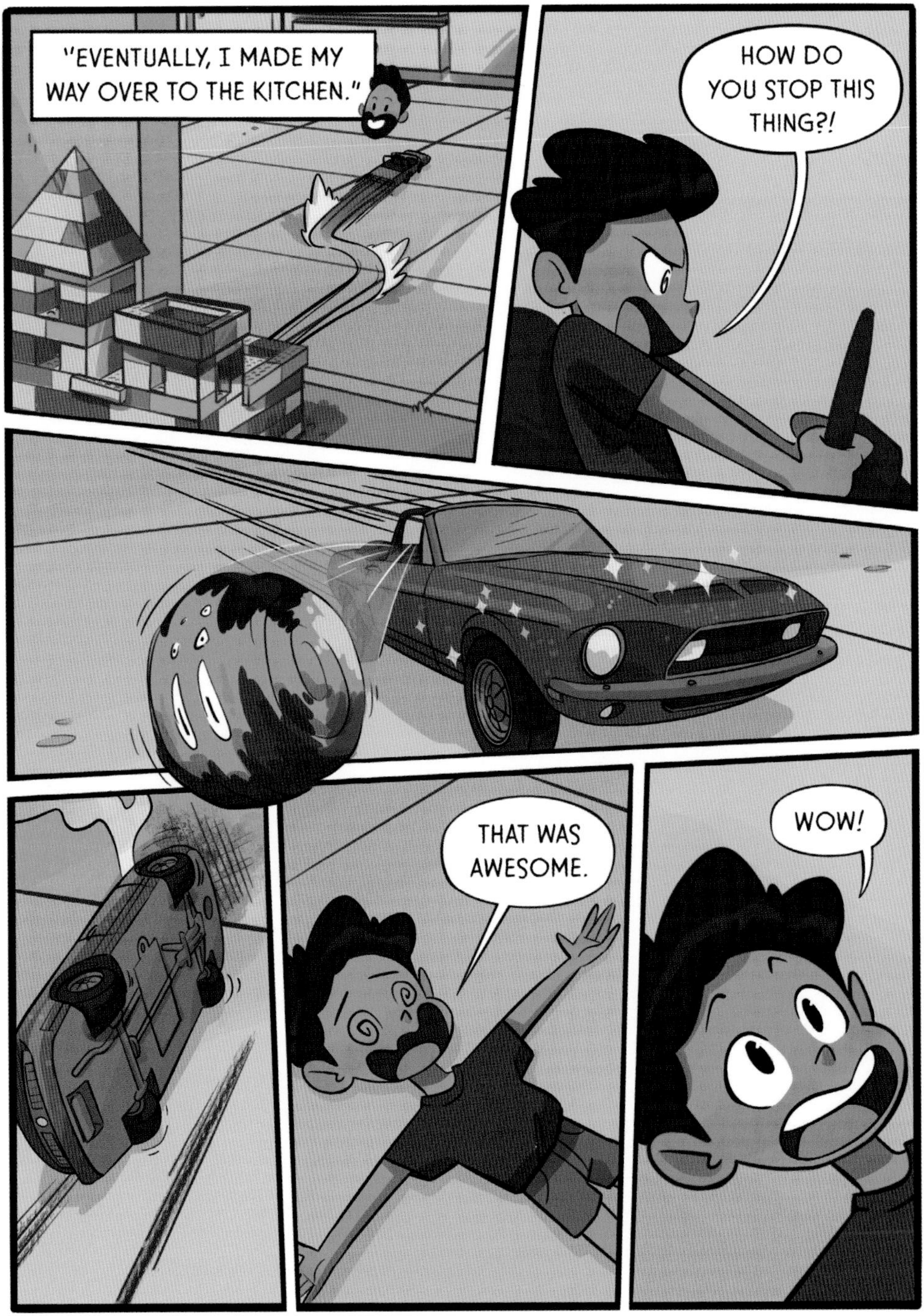
"EVENTUALLY, I MADE MY WAY OVER TO THE KITCHEN."
HOW DO YOU STOP THIS THING?!
THAT WAS AWESOME.
WOW!

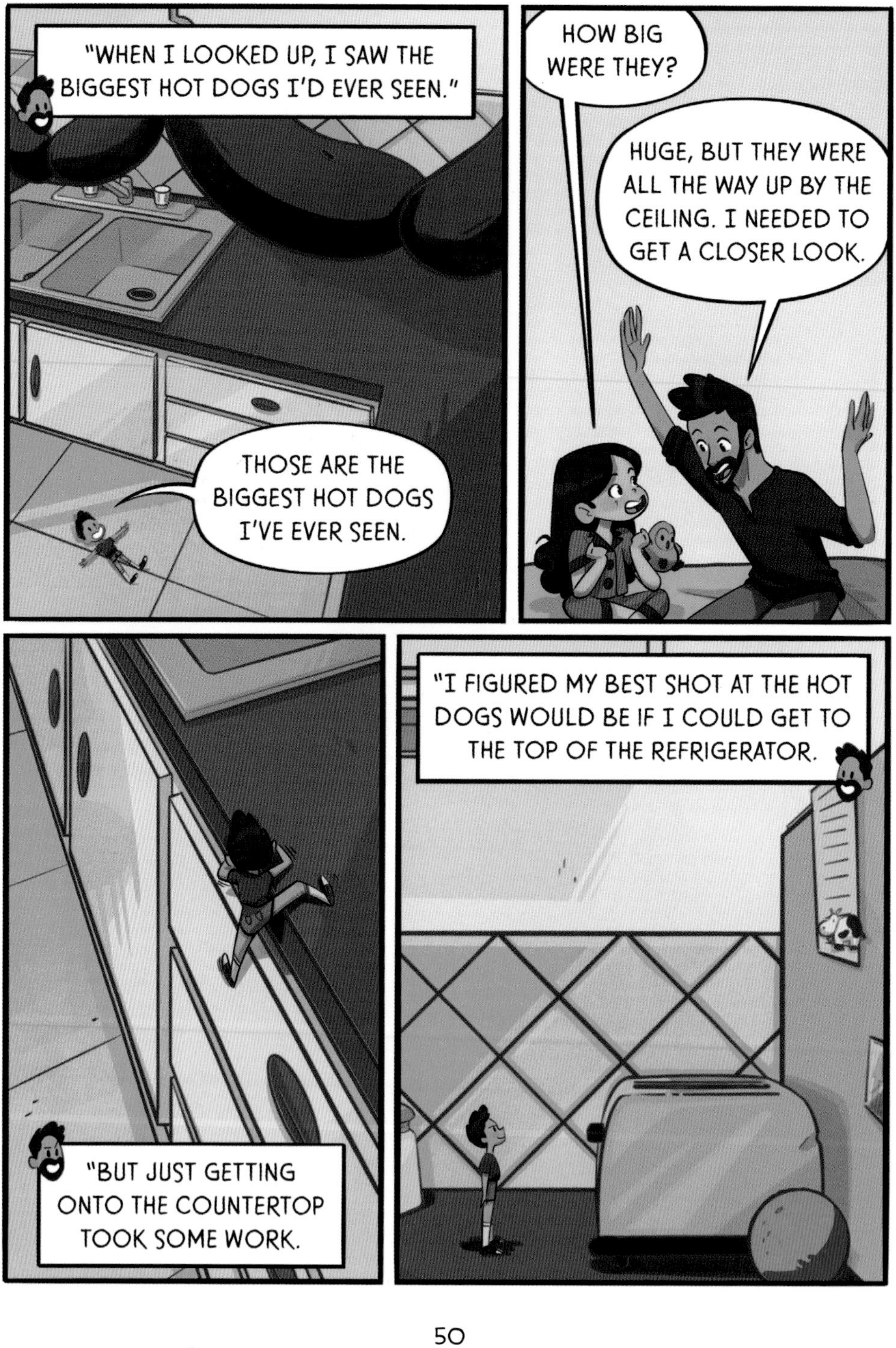
"WHEN I LOOKED UP, I SAW THE BIGGEST HOT DOGS I'D EVER SEEN."
THOSE ARE THE BIGGEST HOT DOGS I'VE EVER SEEN.
HOW BIG WERE THEY?
HUGE, BUT THEY WERE ALL THE WAY UP BY THE CEILING. I NEEDED TO GET A CLOSER LOOK.
"BUT JUST GETTING ONTO THE COUNTERTOP TOOK SOME WORK.
"I FIGURED MY BEST SHOT AT THE HOT DOGS WOULD BE IF I COULD GET TO THE TOP OF THE REFRIGERATOR.

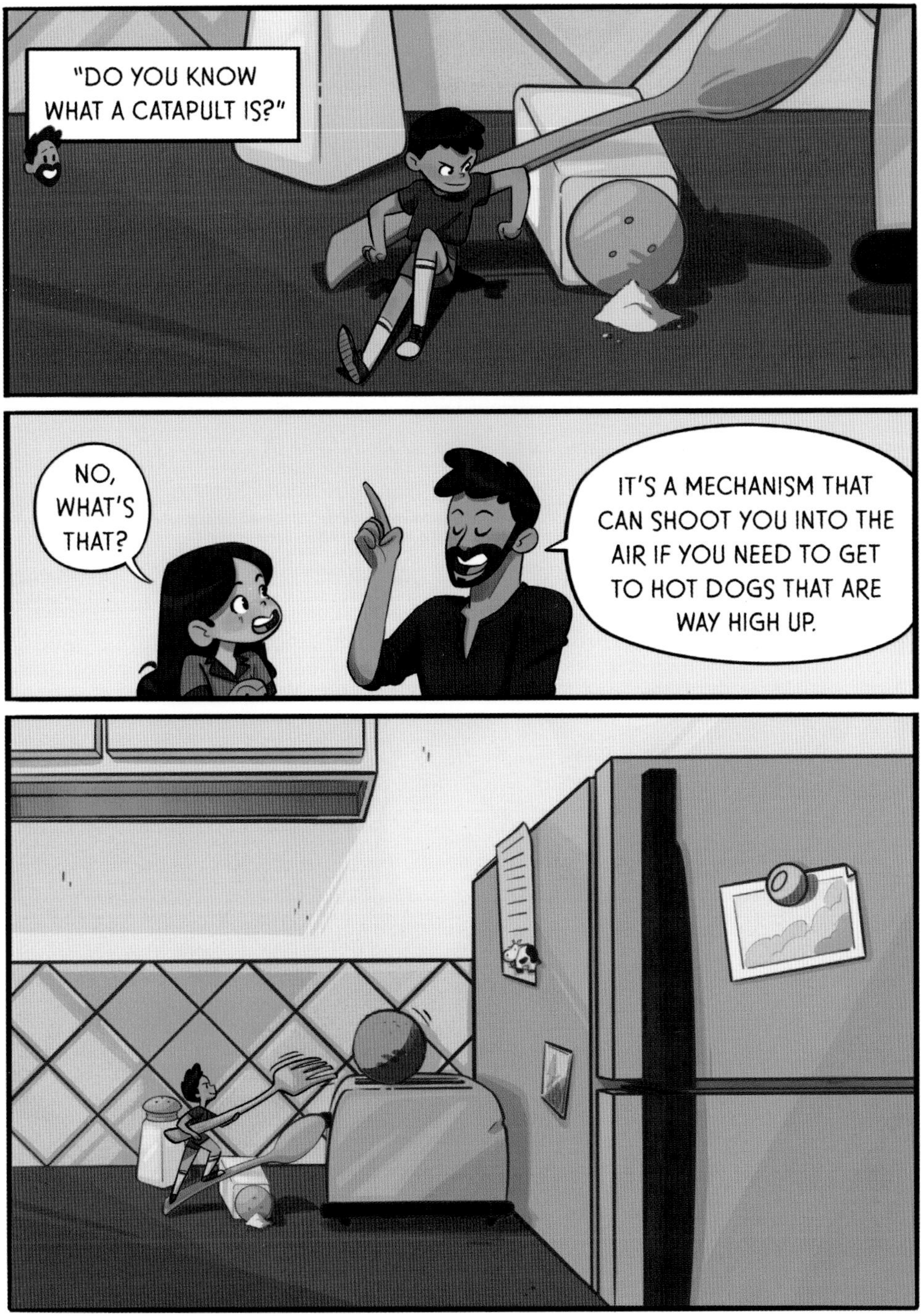
"DO YOU KNOW WHAT A CATAPULT IS?"
NO, WHAT'S THAT?
IT'S A MECHANISM THAT CAN SHOOT YOU INTO THE AIR IF YOU NEED TO GET TO HOT DOGS THAT ARE WAY HIGH UP.

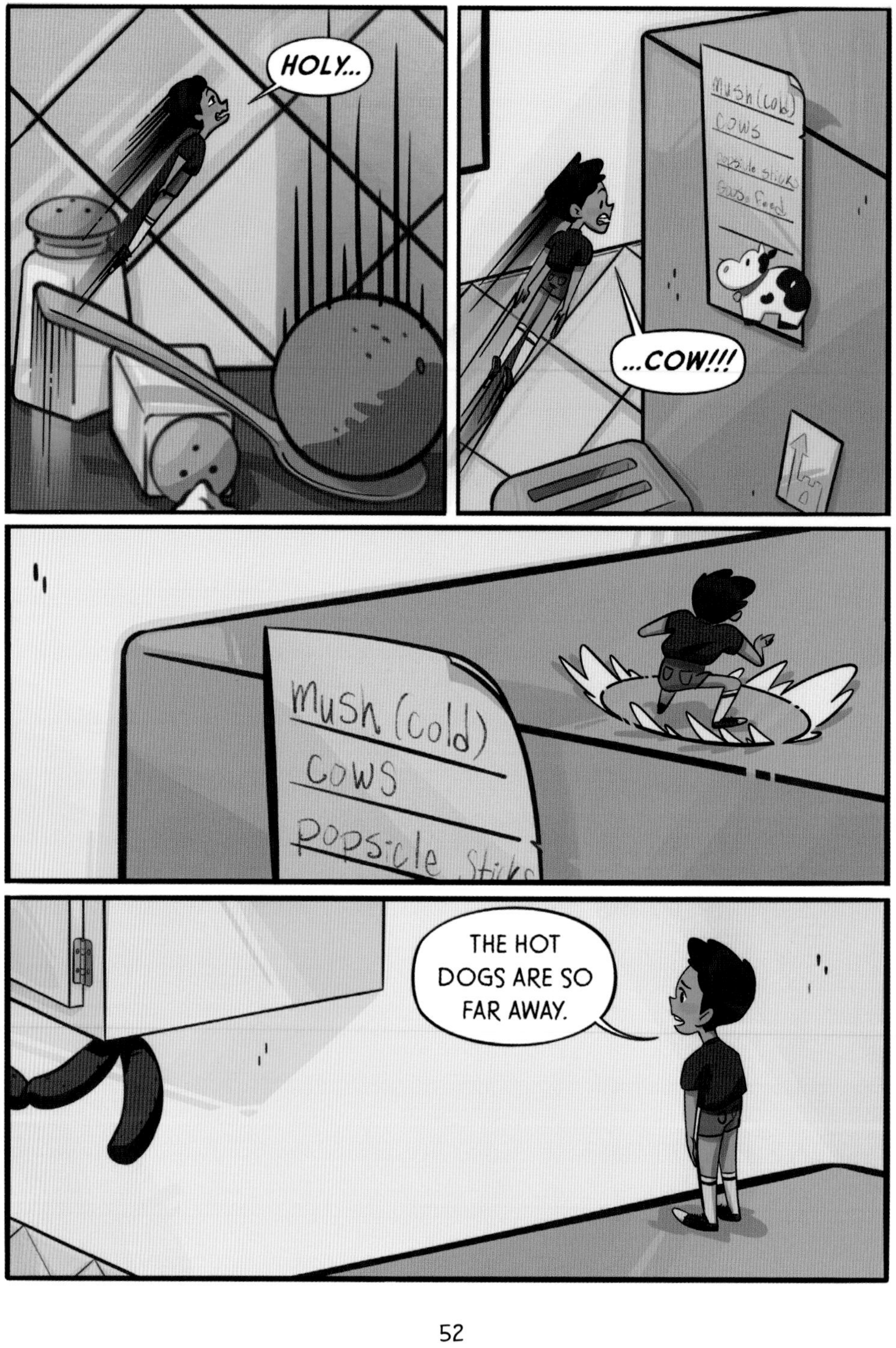
HOLY...
...COW!!!
mush (cold)
cows
popsicle
THE HOT DOGS ARE SO FAR AWAY.

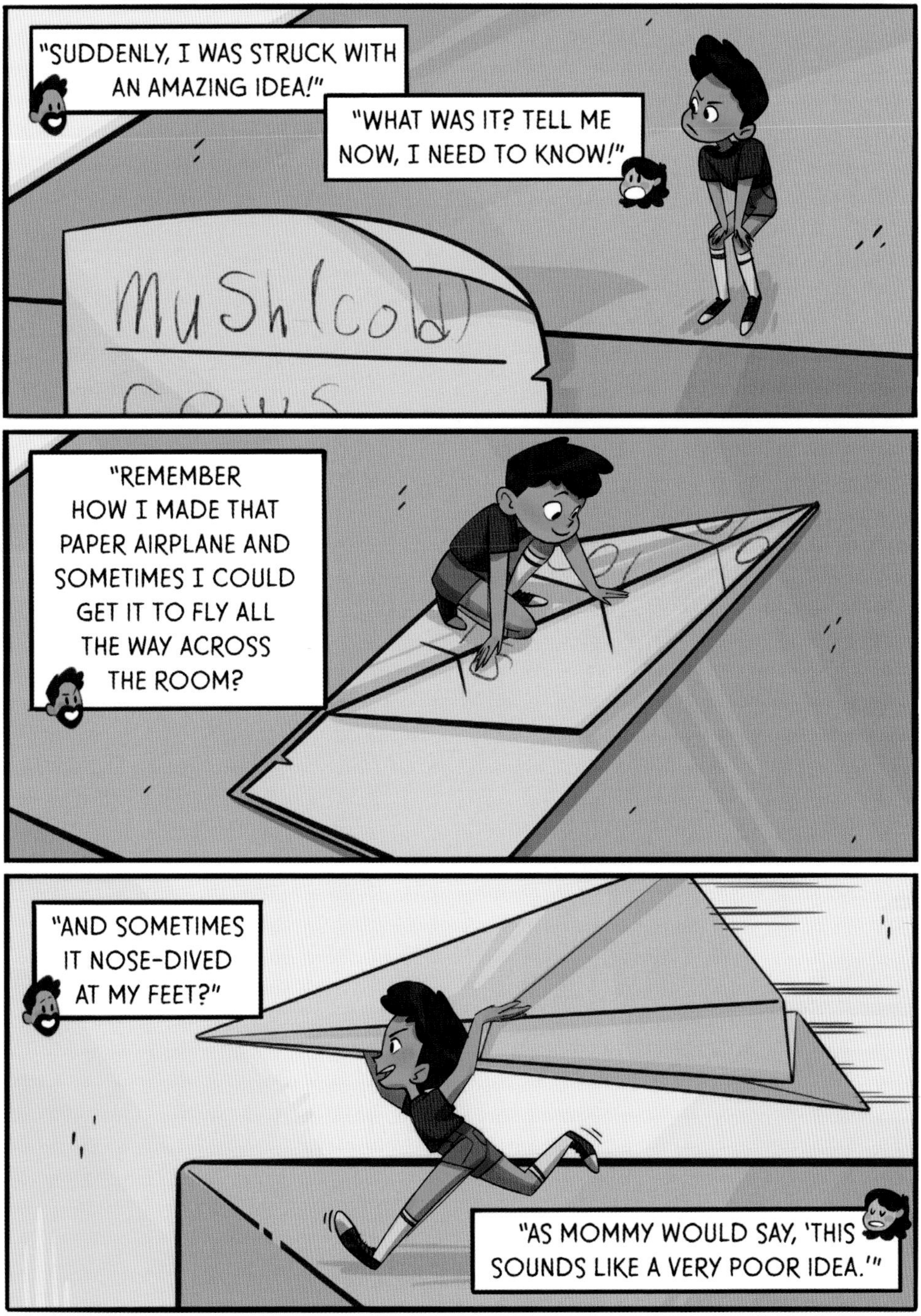
"SUDDENLY, I WAS STRUCK WITH AN AMAZING IDEA!"
"WHAT WAS IT? TELL ME NOW, I NEED TO KNOW!"
MuSh (cold)
"REMEMBER HOW I MADE THAT PAPER AIRPLANE AND SOMETIMES I COULD GET IT TO FLY ALL THE WAY ACROSS THE ROOM?
"AND SOMETIMES IT NOSE-DIVED AT MY FEET?"
"AS MOMMY WOULD SAY, 'THIS SOUNDS LIKE A VERY POOR IDEA.'"

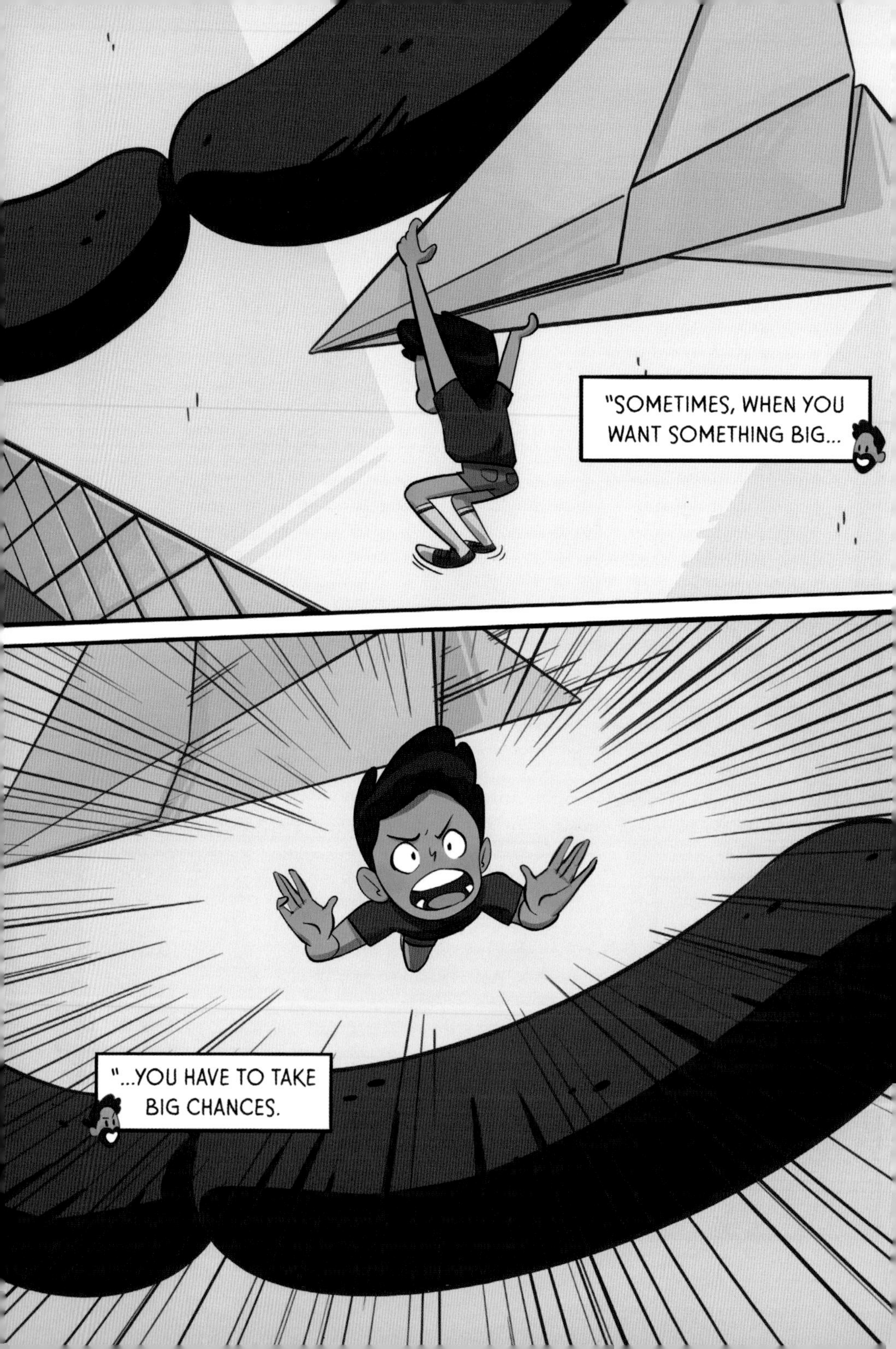
"SOMETIMES, WHEN YOU WANT SOMETHING BIG...
"...YOU HAVE TO TAKE BIG CHANCES.

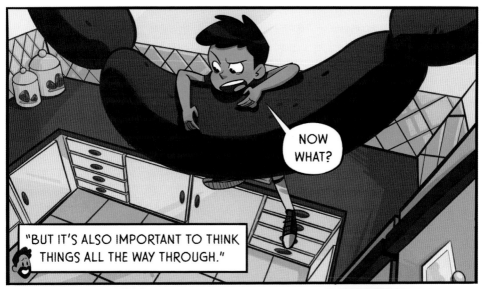

NOW WHAT?

"BUT IT'S ALSO IMPORTANT TO THINK THINGS ALL THE WAY THROUGH."

WHOOPS!

"THAT'S WHEN THE GIANT GRABBED ME!"

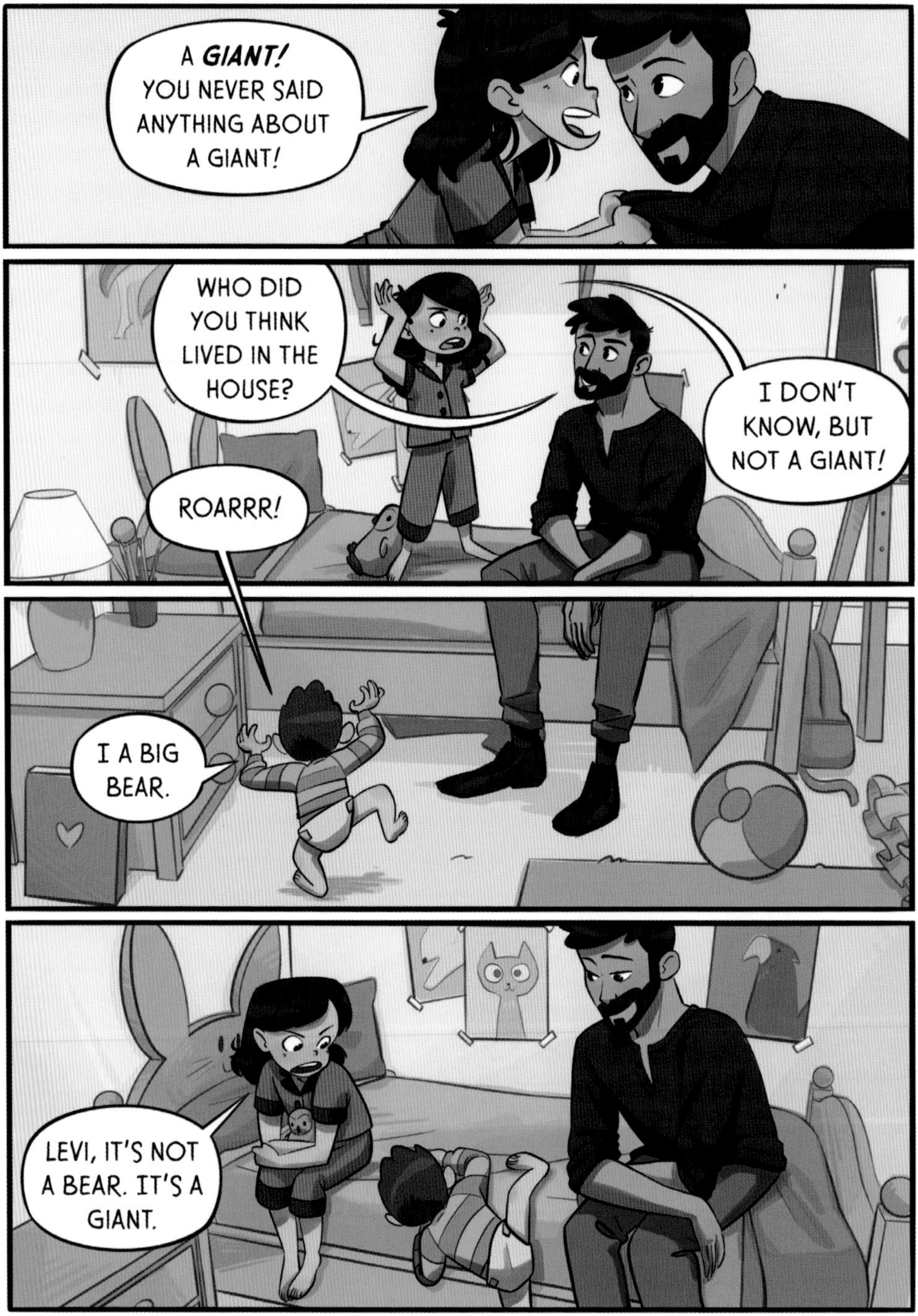
A **GIANT!** YOU NEVER SAID ANYTHING ABOUT A GIANT!
WHO DID YOU THINK LIVED IN THE HOUSE?
I DON'T KNOW, BUT NOT A GIANT!
ROARRR!
I A BIG BEAR.
LEVI, IT'S NOT A BEAR. IT'S A GIANT.

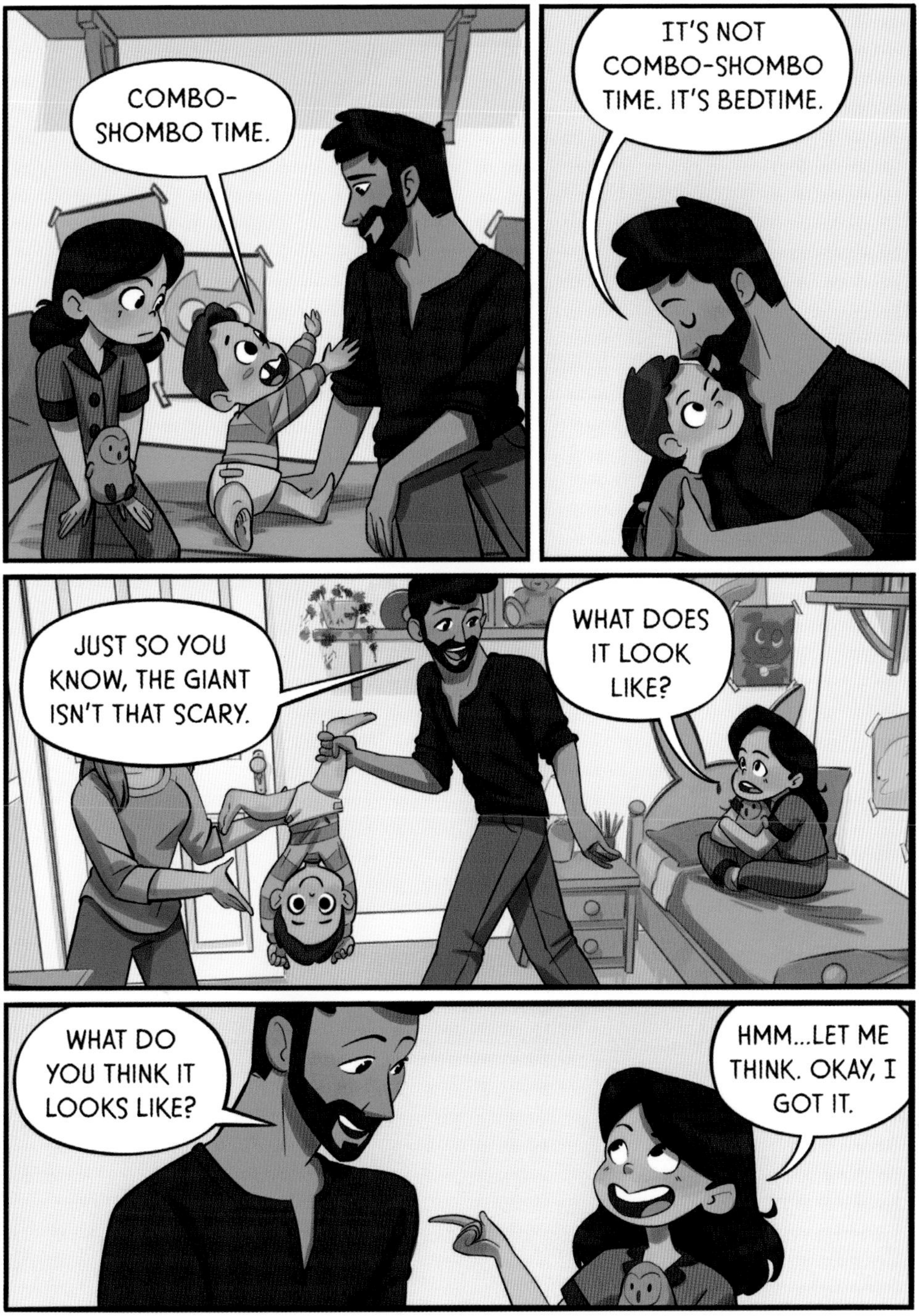
COMBO-SHOMBO TIME.
IT'S NOT COMBO-SHOMBO TIME. IT'S BEDTIME.
JUST SO YOU KNOW, THE GIANT ISN'T THAT SCARY.
WHAT DOES IT LOOK LIKE?
WHAT DO YOU THINK IT LOOKS LIKE?
HMM...LET ME THINK. OKAY, I GOT IT.

BUILD-A-GIANT

"HE'S A KID.

"EXCEPT MUCH BIGGER.

"AND MUCH OLDER THAN ME, LIKE A BIG KID.

"HE'S SUPER TALL. LIKE 5 FEET TALL!"

THAT'S PRETTY SHORT FOR A GIANT.

OK, 1 MILLION FEET TALL!

TOO TALL.

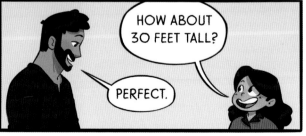

HOW ABOUT 30 FEET TALL?

PERFECT.

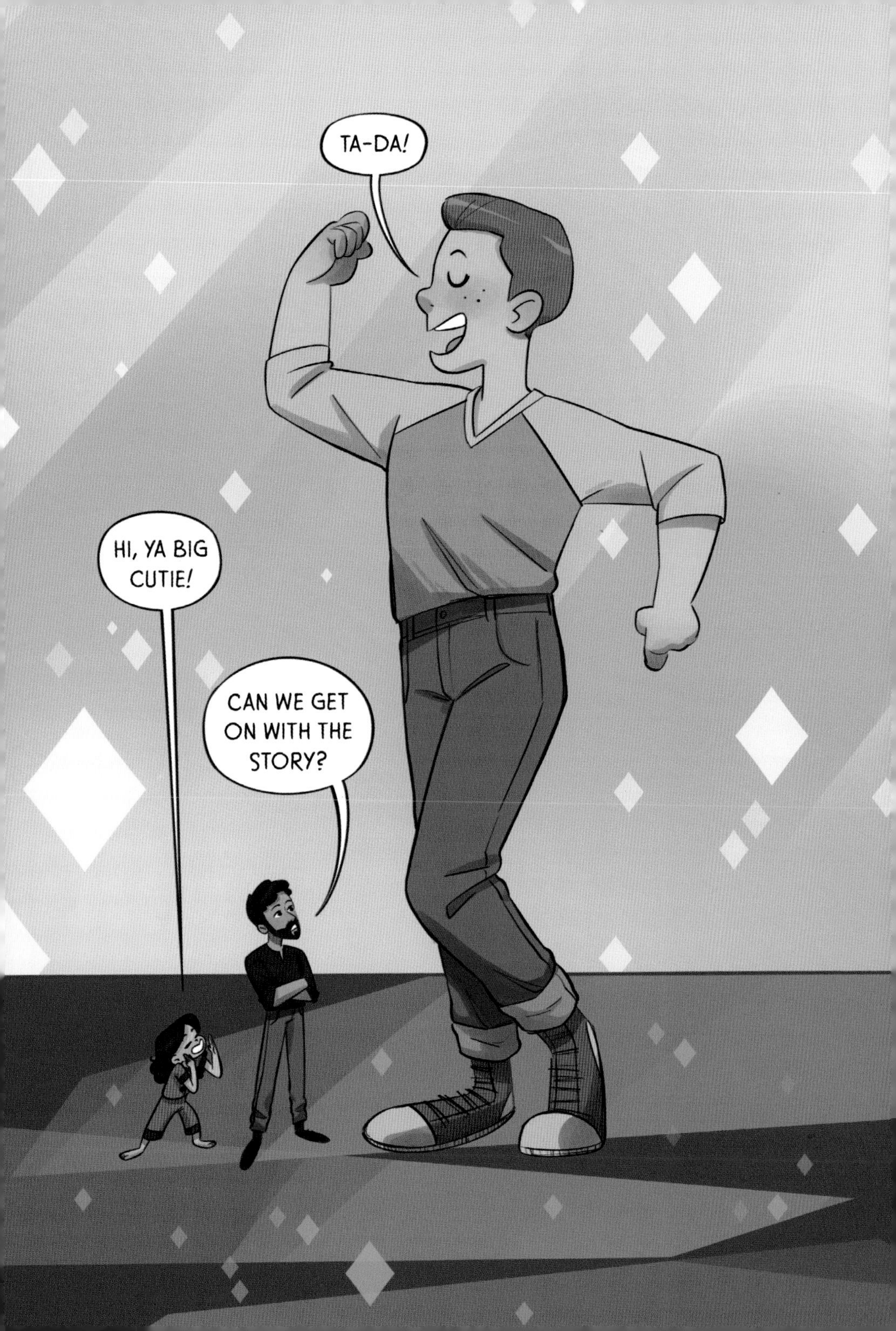
TA-DA!
HI, YA BIG CUTIE!
CAN WE GET ON WITH THE STORY?

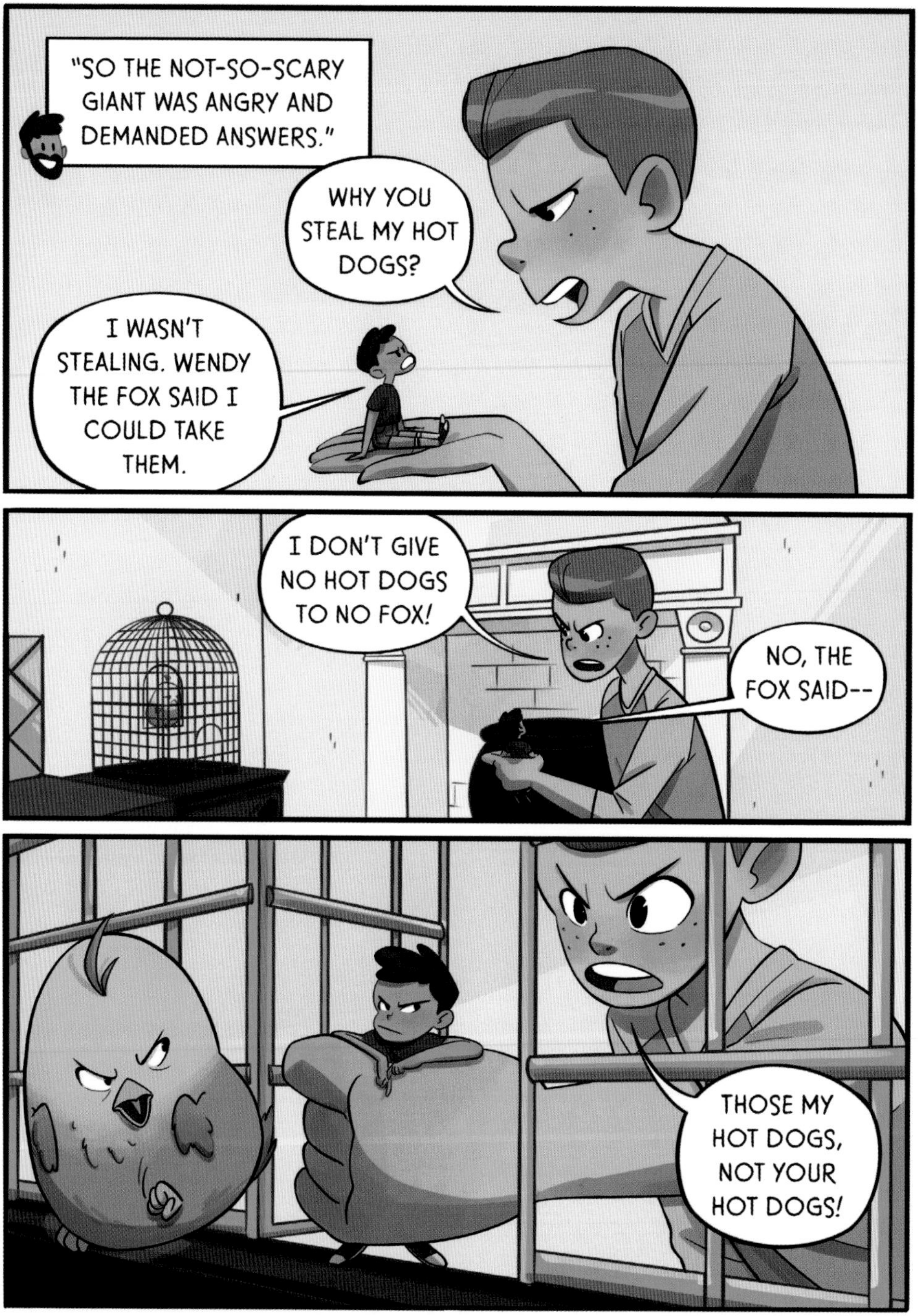
"SO THE NOT-SO-SCARY GIANT WAS ANGRY AND DEMANDED ANSWERS."
WHY YOU STEAL MY HOT DOGS?
I WASN'T STEALING. WENDY THE FOX SAID I COULD TAKE THEM.
I DON'T GIVE NO HOT DOGS TO NO FOX!
NO, THE FOX SAID--
THOSE MY HOT DOGS, NOT YOUR HOT DOGS!

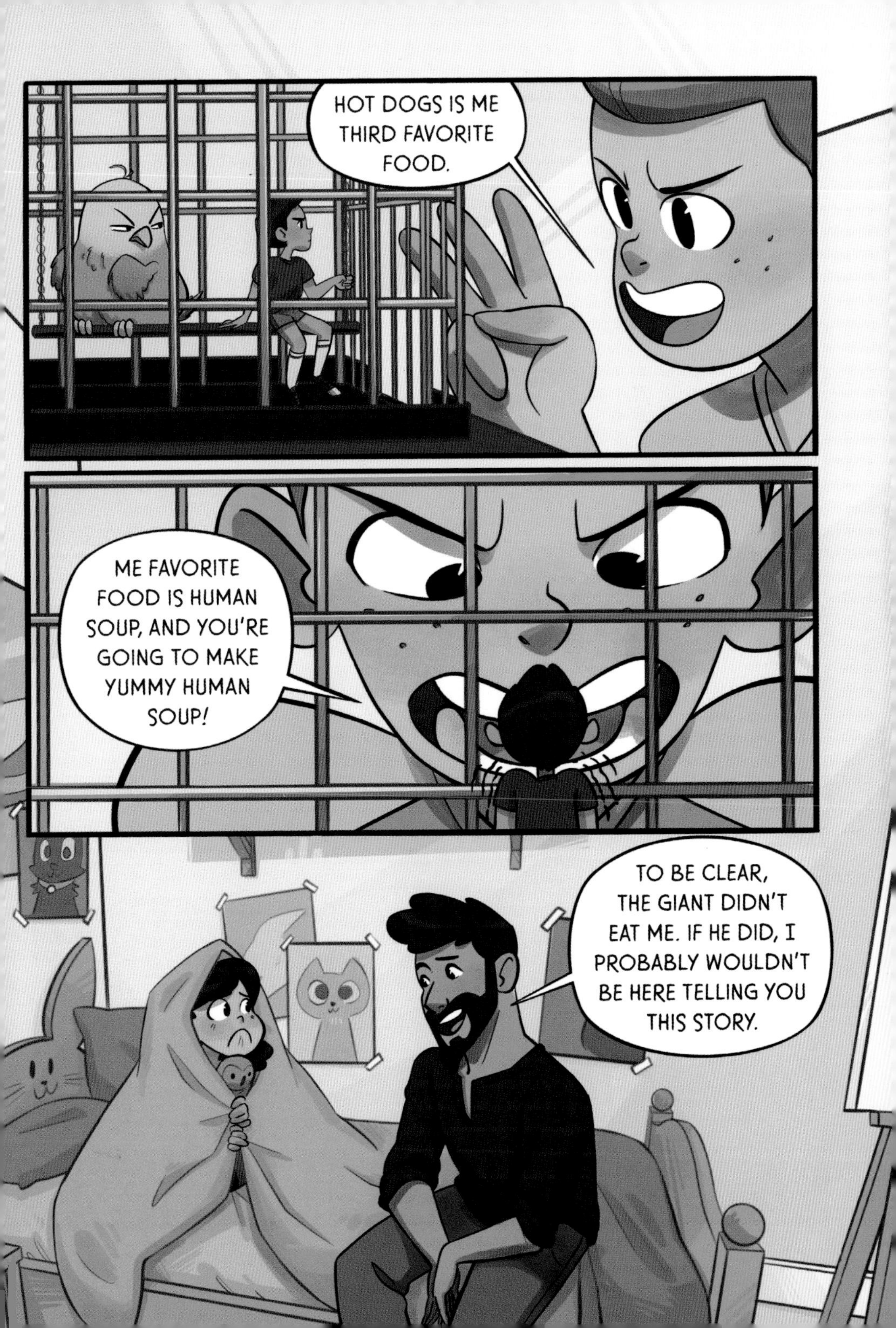
HOT DOGS IS ME THIRD FAVORITE FOOD.
ME FAVORITE FOOD IS HUMAN SOUP, AND YOU'RE GOING TO MAKE YUMMY HUMAN SOUP!
TO BE CLEAR, THE GIANT DIDN'T EAT ME. IF HE DID, I PROBABLY WOULDN'T BE HERE TELLING YOU THIS STORY.

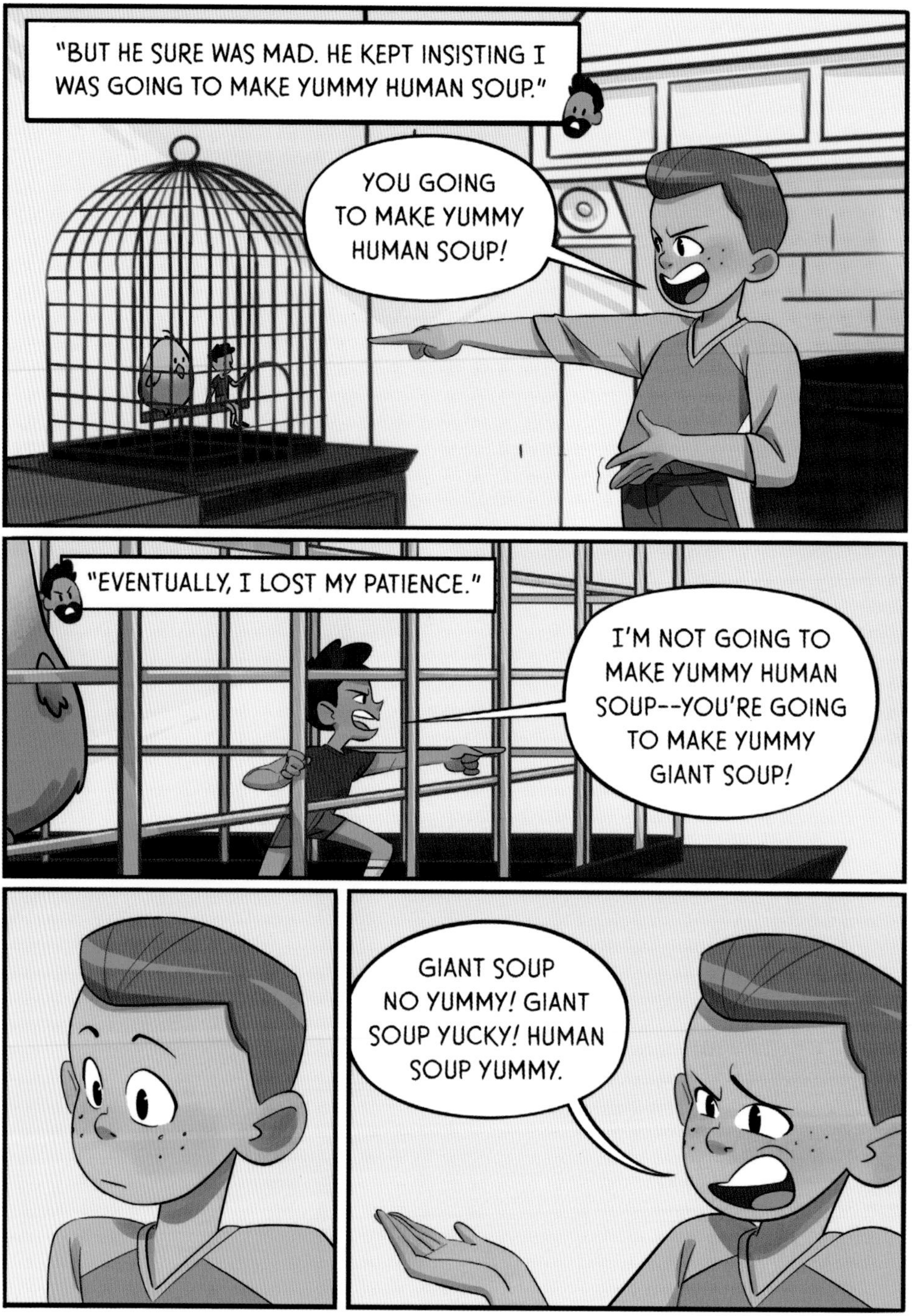
"BUT HE SURE WAS MAD. HE KEPT INSISTING I WAS GOING TO MAKE YUMMY HUMAN SOUP."
YOU GOING TO MAKE YUMMY HUMAN SOUP!
"EVENTUALLY, I LOST MY PATIENCE."
I'M NOT GOING TO MAKE YUMMY HUMAN SOUP--YOU'RE GOING TO MAKE YUMMY GIANT SOUP!
GIANT SOUP NO YUMMY! GIANT SOUP YUCKY! HUMAN SOUP YUMMY.

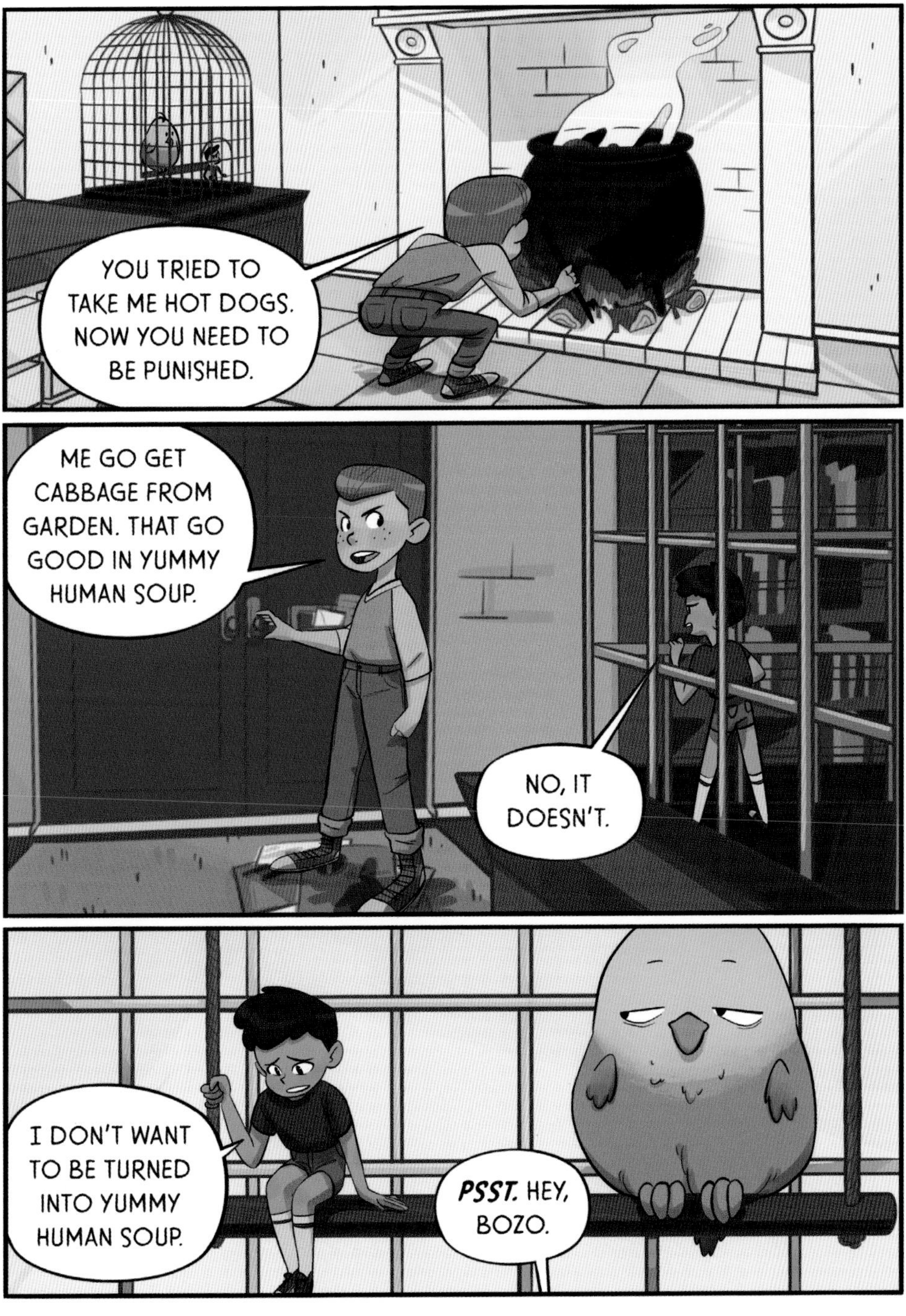
YOU TRIED TO TAKE ME HOT DOGS. NOW YOU NEED TO BE PUNISHED.
ME GO GET CABBAGE FROM GARDEN. THAT GO GOOD IN YUMMY HUMAN SOUP.
NO, IT DOESN'T.
I DON'T WANT TO BE TURNED INTO YUMMY HUMAN SOUP.
PSST. HEY, BOZO.

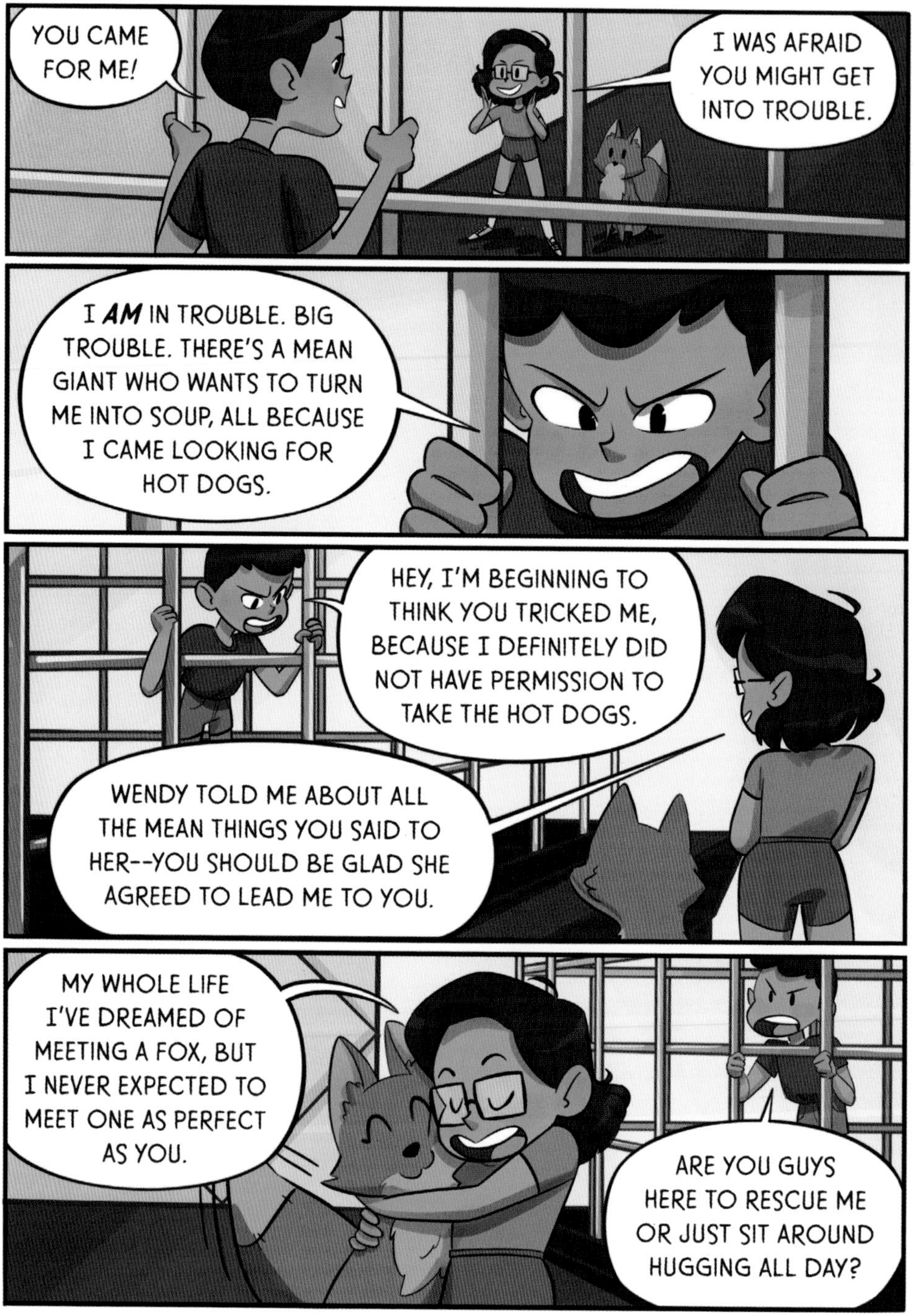
YOU CAME FOR ME!
I WAS AFRAID YOU MIGHT GET INTO TROUBLE.
I **AM** IN TROUBLE. BIG TROUBLE. THERE'S A MEAN GIANT WHO WANTS TO TURN ME INTO SOUP, ALL BECAUSE I CAME LOOKING FOR HOT DOGS.
HEY, I'M BEGINNING TO THINK YOU TRICKED ME, BECAUSE I DEFINITELY DID NOT HAVE PERMISSION TO TAKE THE HOT DOGS.
WENDY TOLD ME ABOUT ALL THE MEAN THINGS YOU SAID TO HER--YOU SHOULD BE GLAD SHE AGREED TO LEAD ME TO YOU.
MY WHOLE LIFE I'VE DREAMED OF MEETING A FOX, BUT I NEVER EXPECTED TO MEET ONE AS PERFECT AS YOU.
ARE YOU GUYS HERE TO RESCUE ME OR JUST SIT AROUND HUGGING ALL DAY?

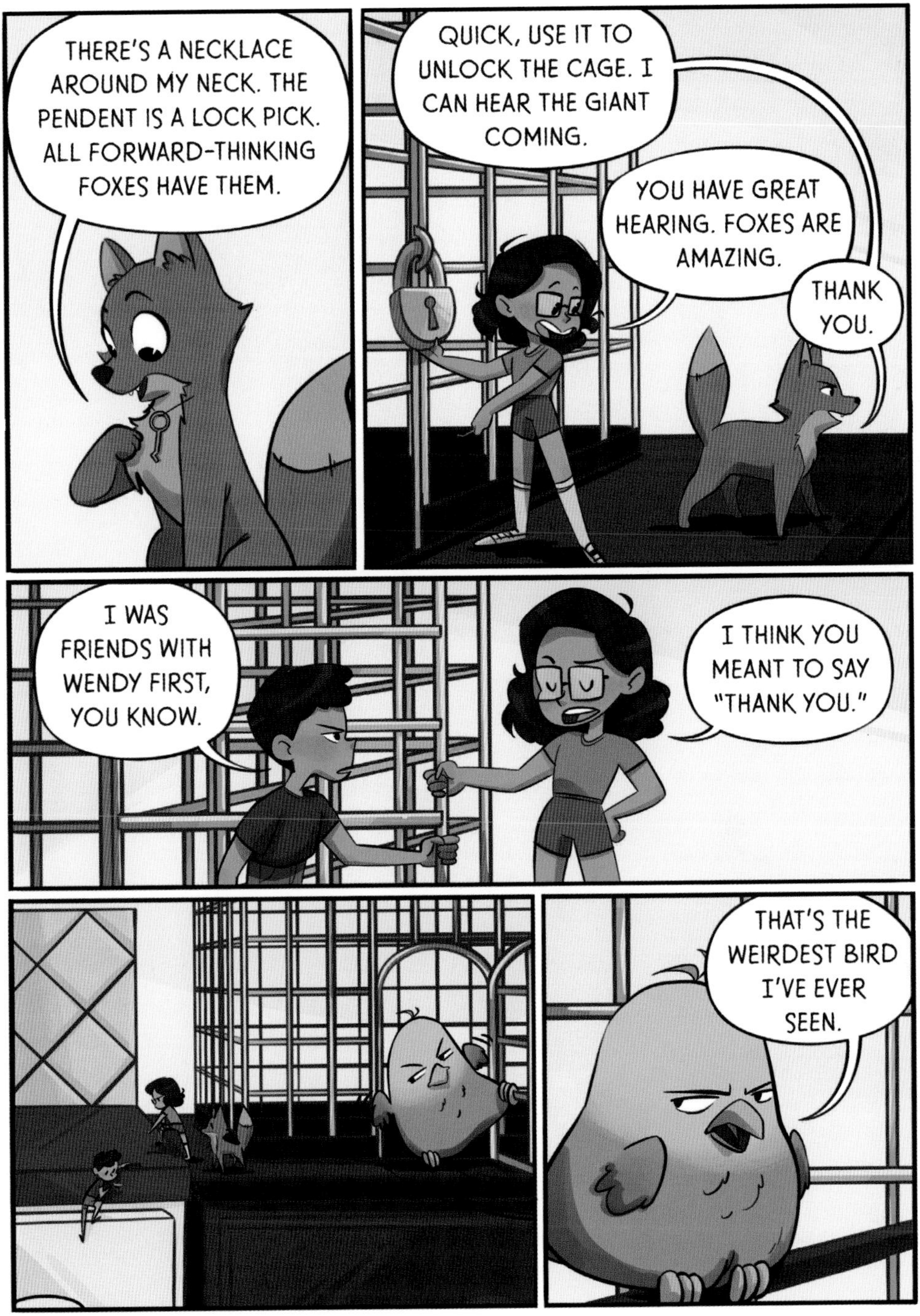
THERE'S A NECKLACE AROUND MY NECK. THE PENDENT IS A LOCK PICK. ALL FORWARD-THINKING FOXES HAVE THEM.
QUICK, USE IT TO UNLOCK THE CAGE. I CAN HEAR THE GIANT COMING.
YOU HAVE GREAT HEARING. FOXES ARE AMAZING.
THANK YOU.
I WAS FRIENDS WITH WENDY FIRST, YOU KNOW.
I THINK YOU MEANT TO SAY "THANK YOU."
THAT'S THE WEIRDEST BIRD I'VE EVER SEEN.

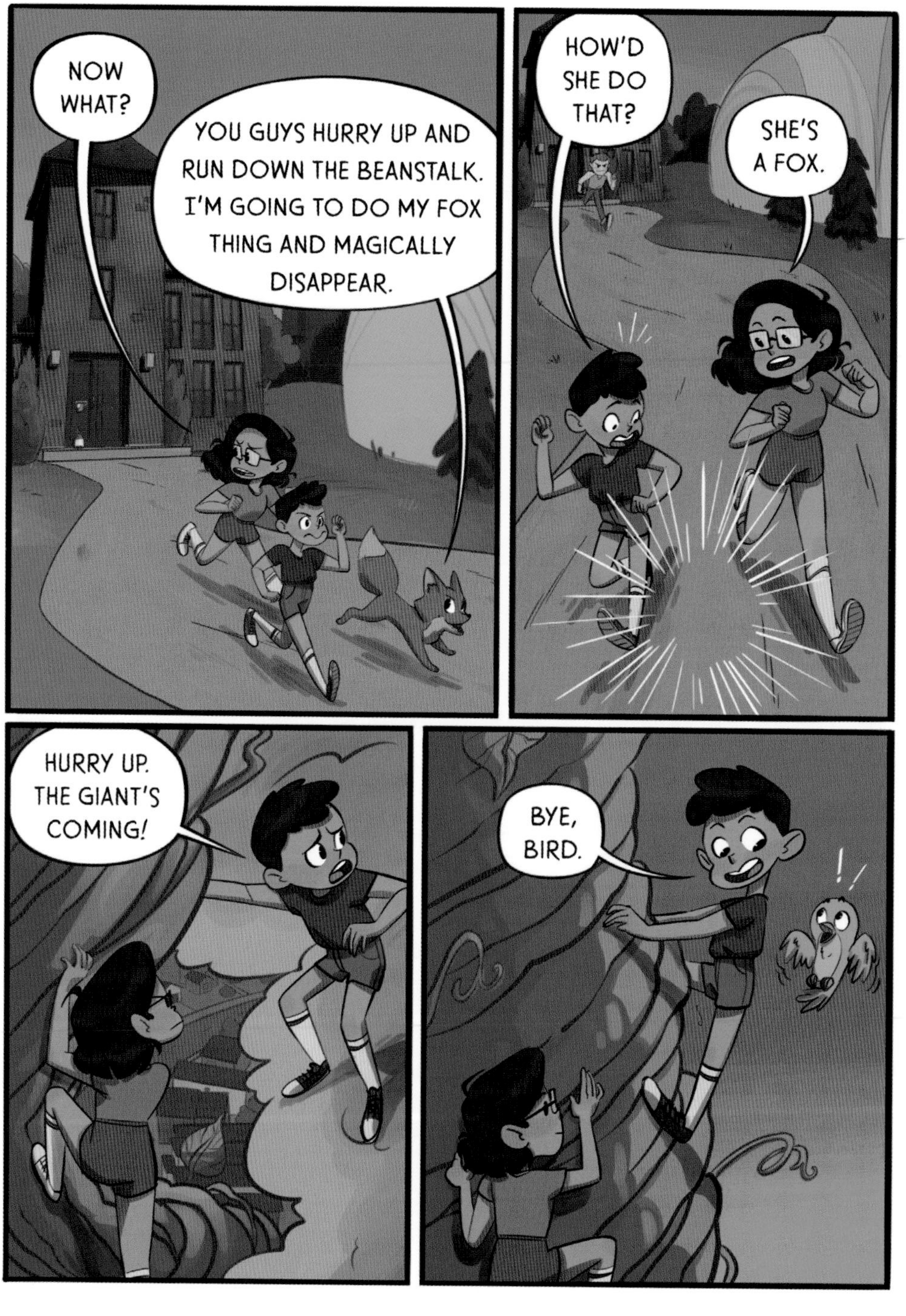
NOW WHAT?
YOU GUYS HURRY UP AND RUN DOWN THE BEANSTALK. I'M GOING TO DO MY FOX THING AND MAGICALLY DISAPPEAR.
HOW'D SHE DO THAT?
SHE'S A FOX.
HURRY UP. THE GIANT'S COMING!
BYE, BIRD.
!!

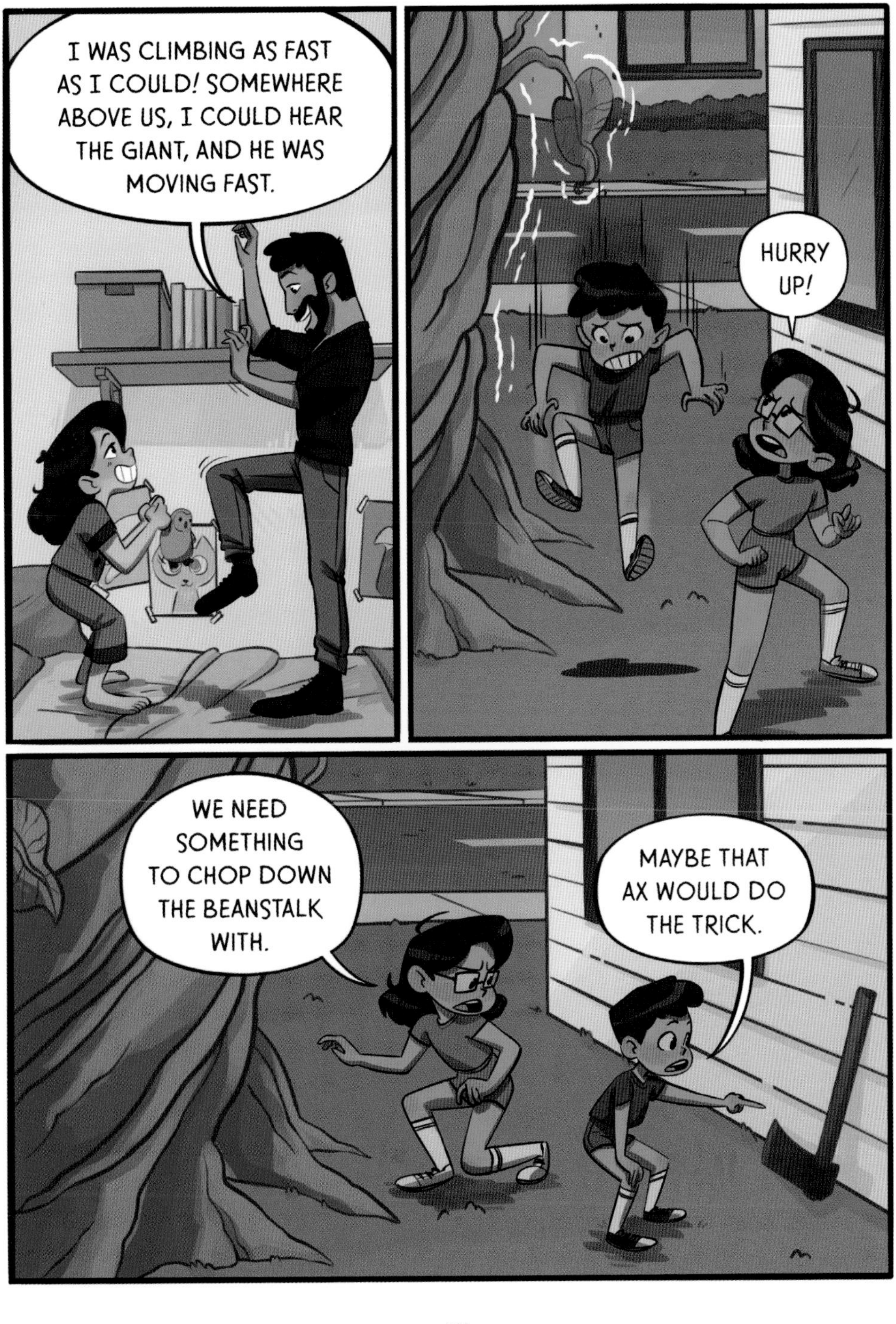
I WAS CLIMBING AS FAST AS I COULD! SOMEWHERE ABOVE US, I COULD HEAR THE GIANT, AND HE WAS MOVING FAST.
HURRY UP!
WE NEED SOMETHING TO CHOP DOWN THE BEANSTALK WITH.
MAYBE THAT AX WOULD DO THE TRICK.

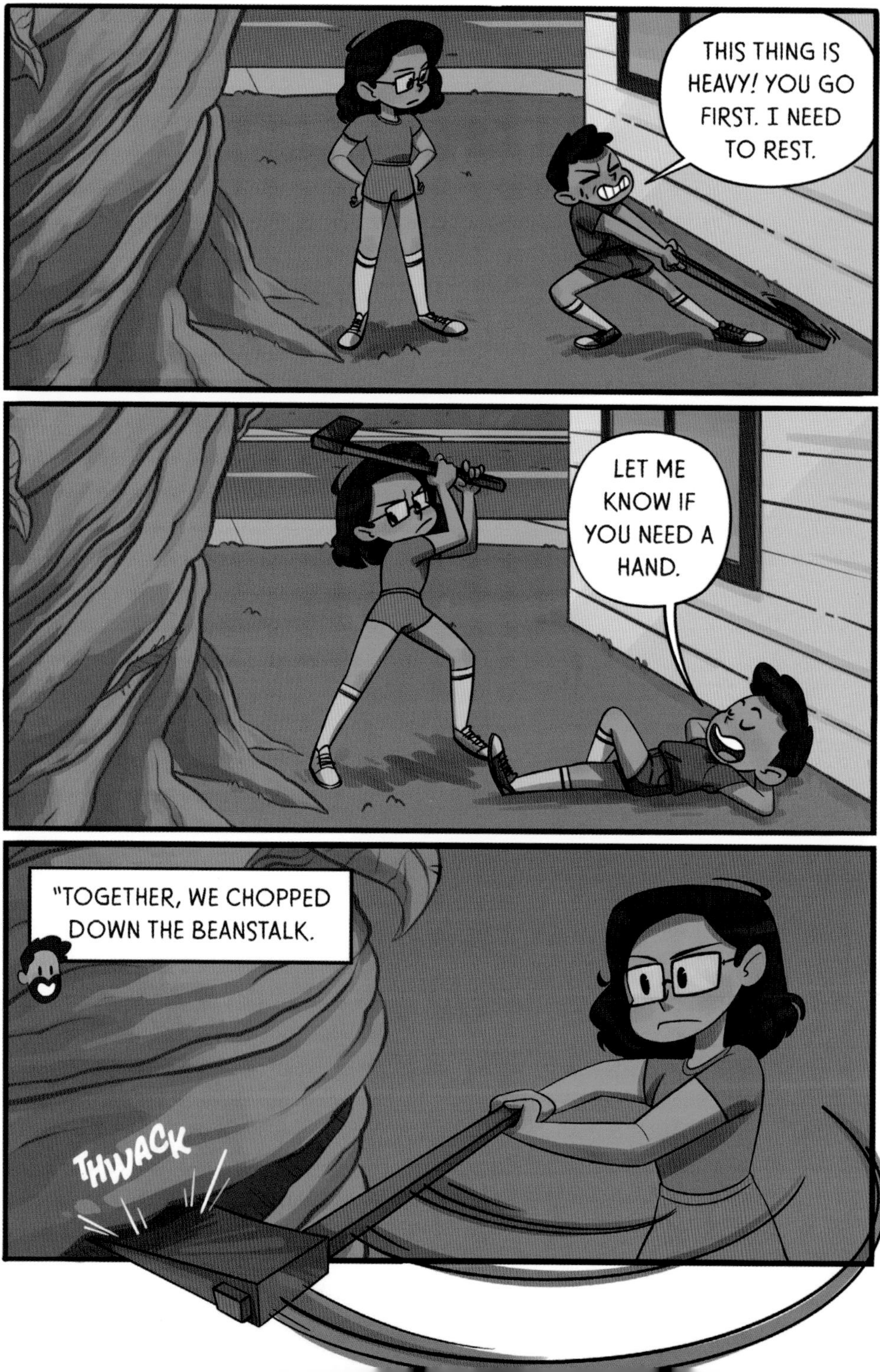
THIS THING IS HEAVY! YOU GO FIRST. I NEED TO REST.
LET ME KNOW IF YOU NEED A HAND.
"TOGETHER, WE CHOPPED DOWN THE BEANSTALK.
THWACK

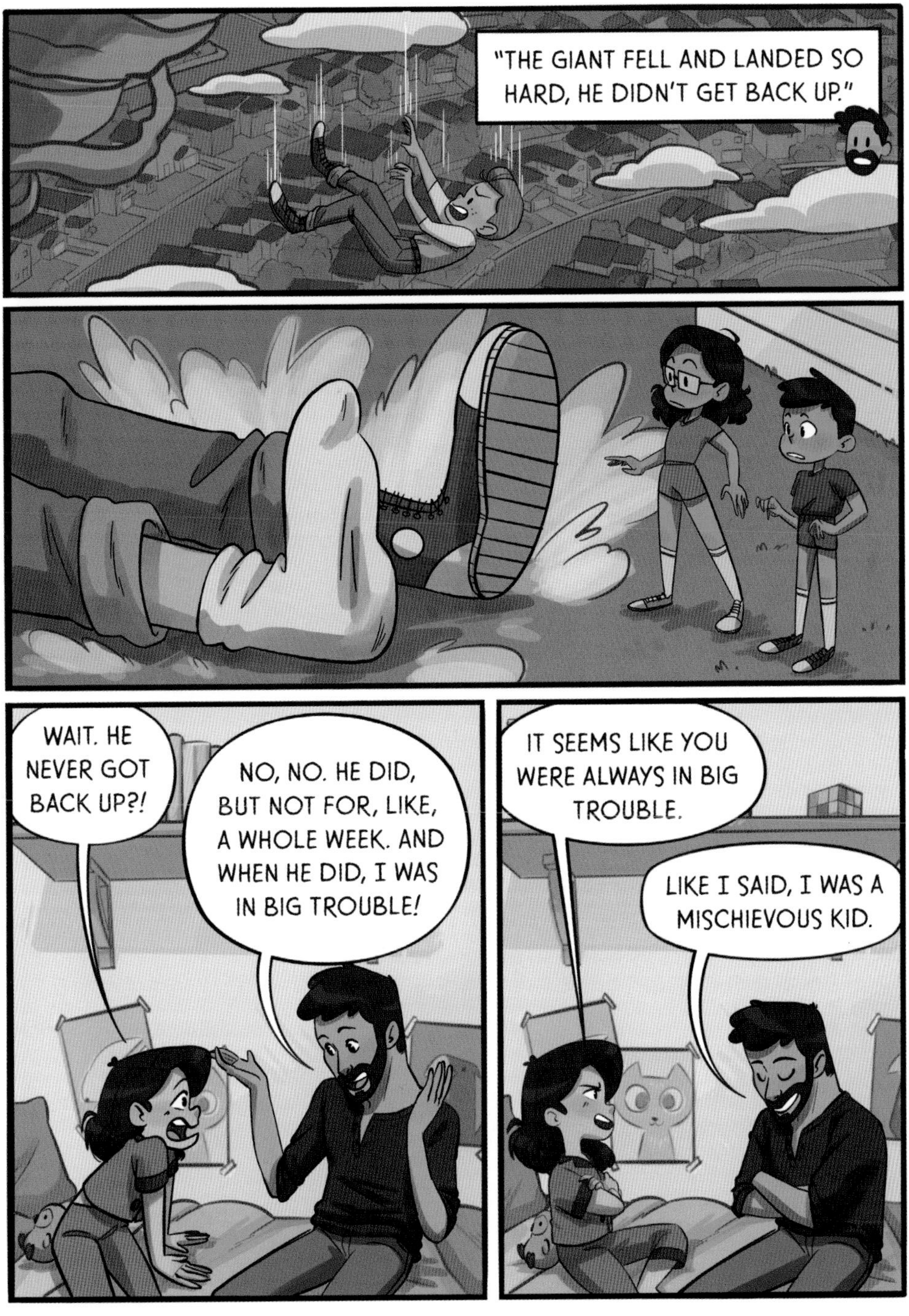
"THE GIANT FELL AND LANDED SO HARD, HE DIDN'T GET BACK UP."
WAIT. HE NEVER GOT BACK UP?!
NO, NO. HE DID, BUT NOT FOR, LIKE, A WHOLE WEEK. AND WHEN HE DID, I WAS IN BIG TROUBLE!
IT SEEMS LIKE YOU WERE ALWAYS IN BIG TROUBLE.
LIKE I SAID, I WAS A MISCHIEVOUS KID.

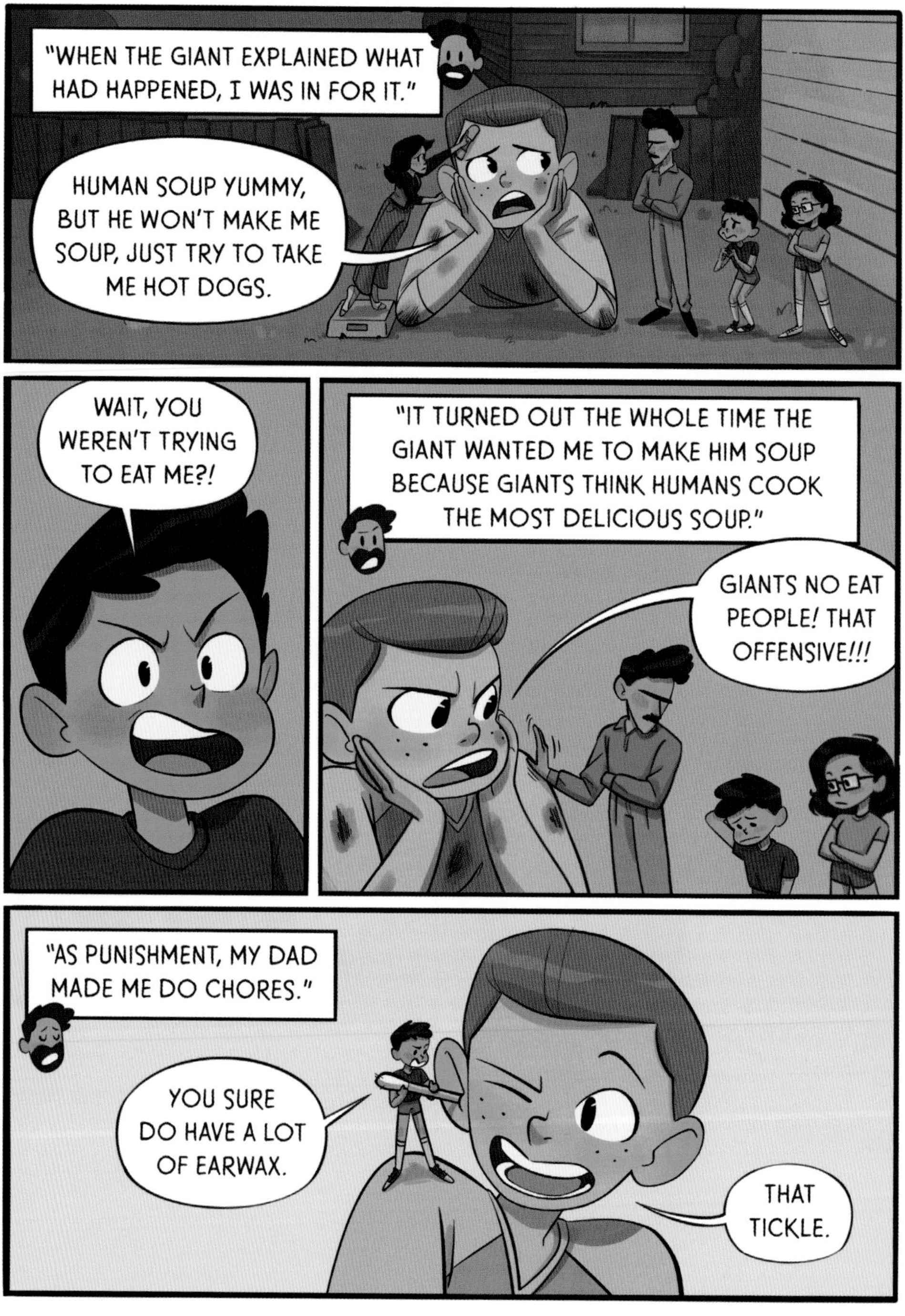
"WHEN THE GIANT EXPLAINED WHAT HAD HAPPENED, I WAS IN FOR IT."
HUMAN SOUP YUMMY, BUT HE WON'T MAKE ME SOUP, JUST TRY TO TAKE ME HOT DOGS.
WAIT, YOU WEREN'T TRYING TO EAT ME?!
"IT TURNED OUT THE WHOLE TIME THE GIANT WANTED ME TO MAKE HIM SOUP BECAUSE GIANTS THINK HUMANS COOK THE MOST DELICIOUS SOUP."
GIANTS NO EAT PEOPLE! THAT OFFENSIVE!!!
"AS PUNISHMENT, MY DAD MADE ME DO CHORES."
YOU SURE DO HAVE A LOT OF EARWAX.
THAT TICKLE.

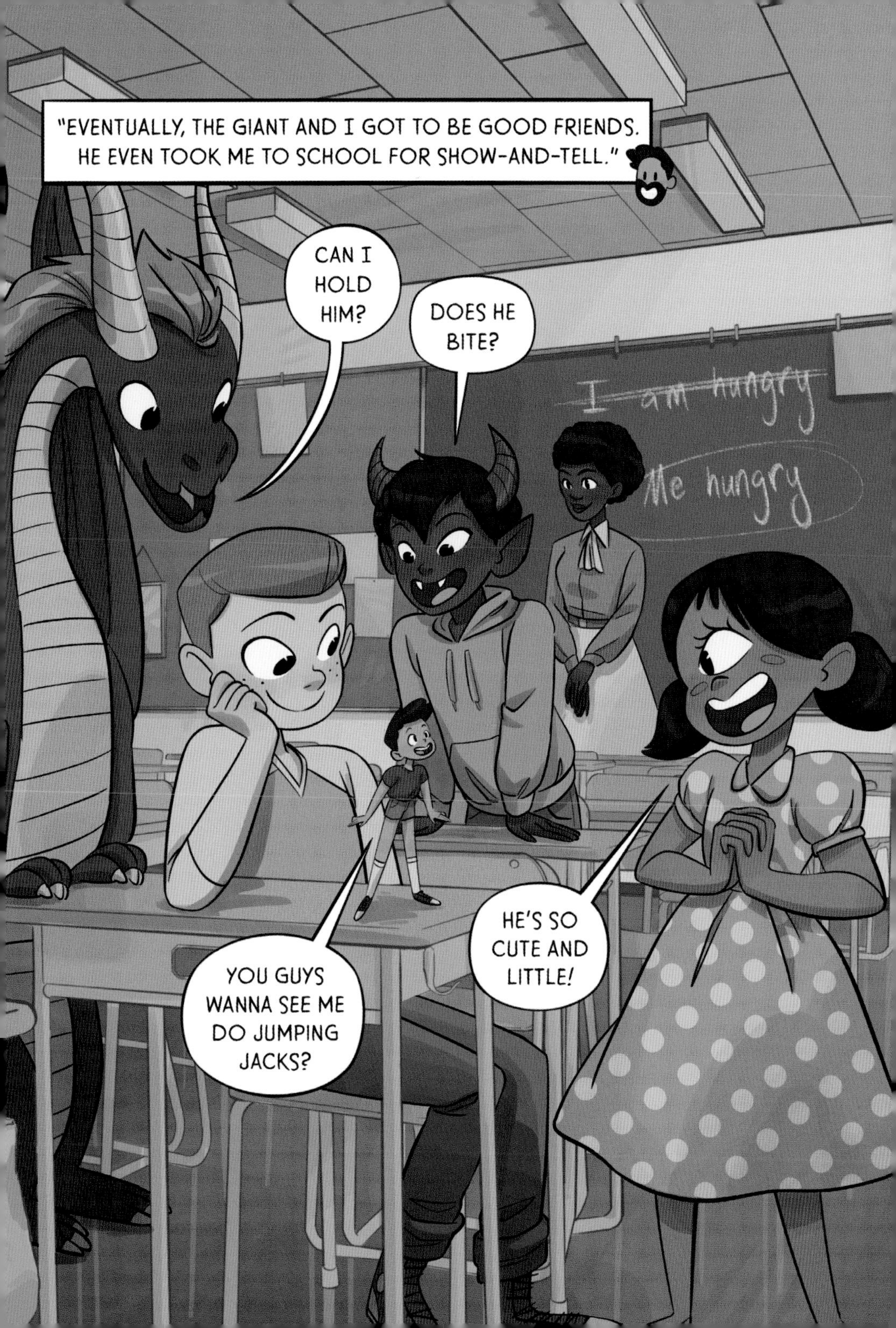
"EVENTUALLY, THE GIANT AND I GOT TO BE GOOD FRIENDS. HE EVEN TOOK ME TO SCHOOL FOR SHOW-AND-TELL."
CAN I HOLD HIM?
DOES HE BITE?
I am hungry
Me hungry
YOU GUYS WANNA SEE ME DO JUMPING JACKS?
HE'S SO CUTE AND LITTLE!

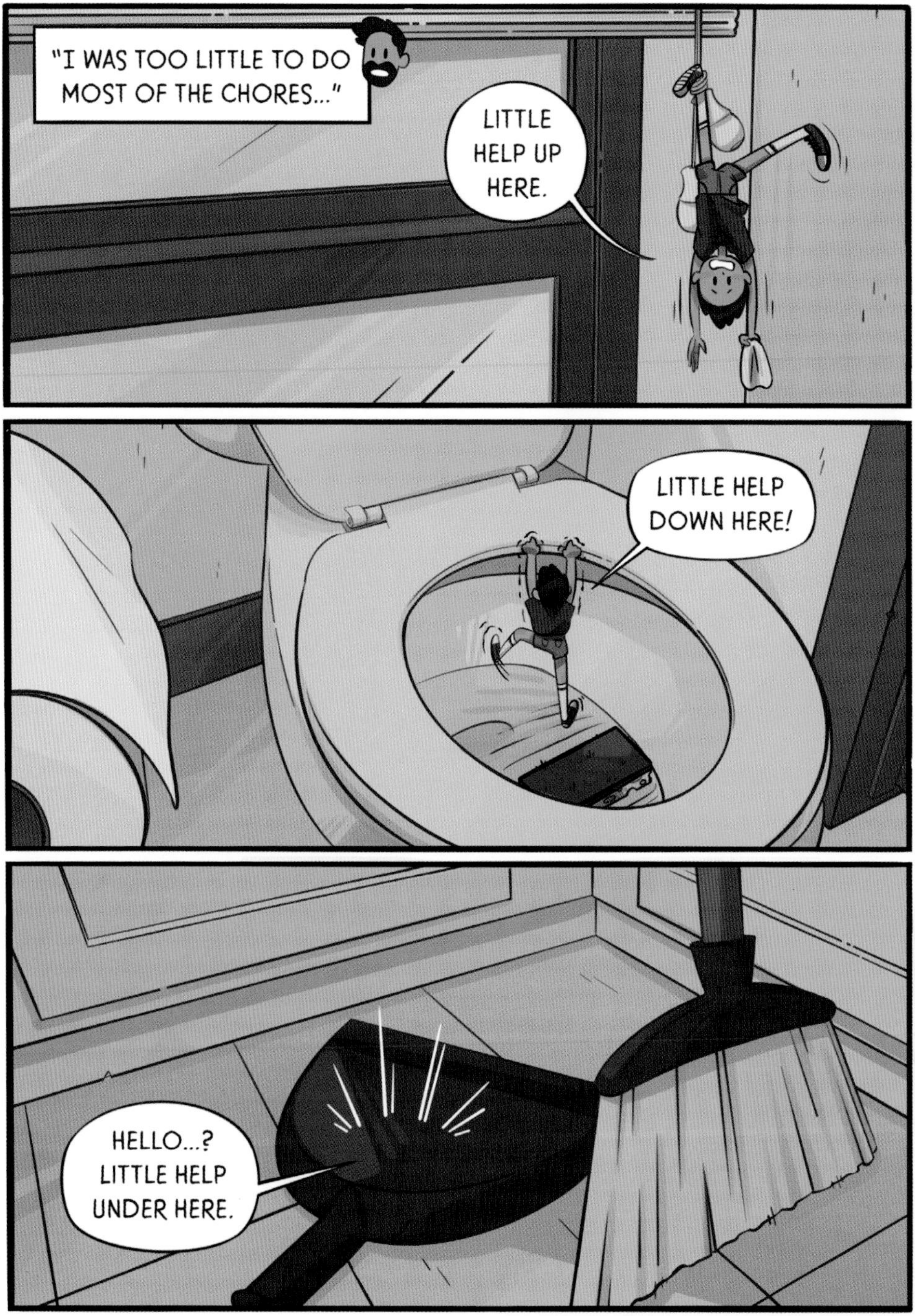
"I WAS TOO LITTLE TO DO MOST OF THE CHORES..."
LITTLE HELP UP HERE.
LITTLE HELP DOWN HERE!
HELLO...? LITTLE HELP UNDER HERE.

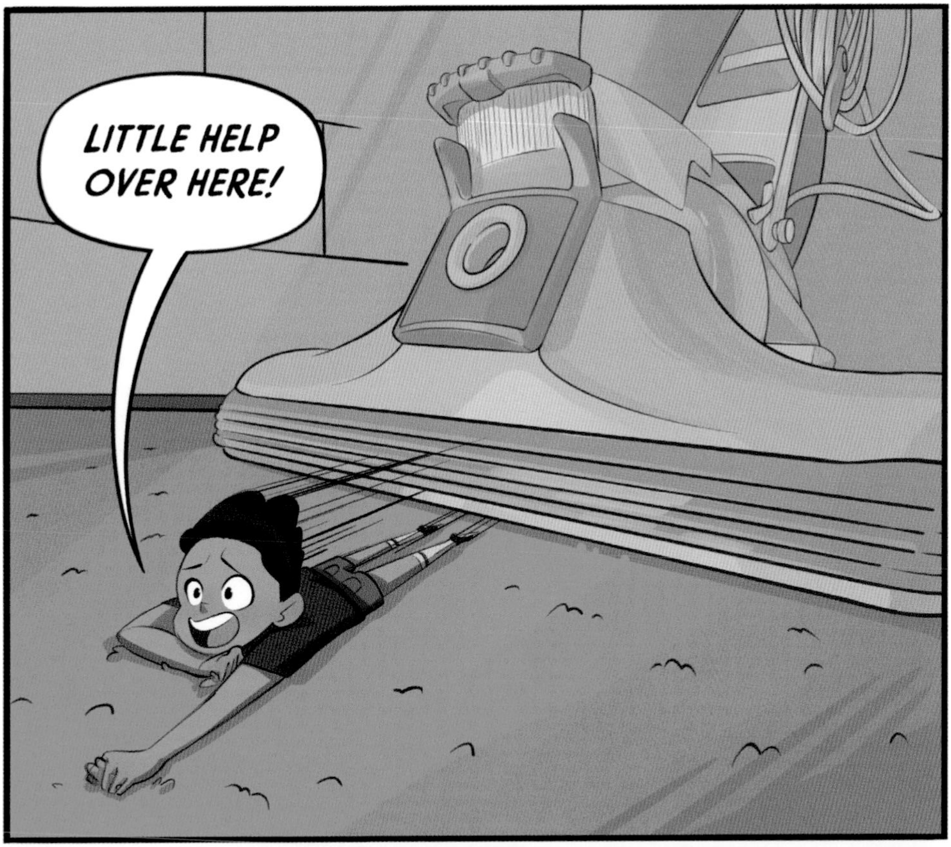
LITTLE HELP OVER HERE!

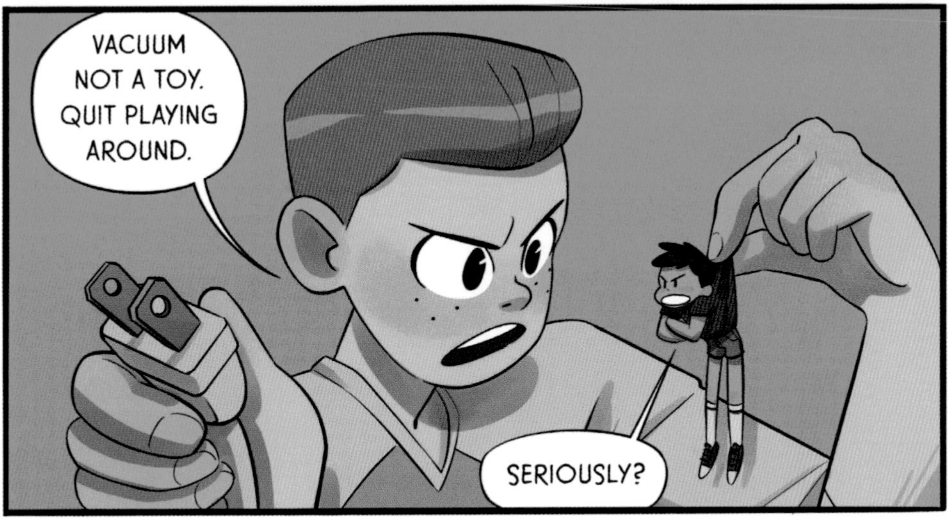
VACUUM NOT A TOY. QUIT PLAYING AROUND.
SERIOUSLY?

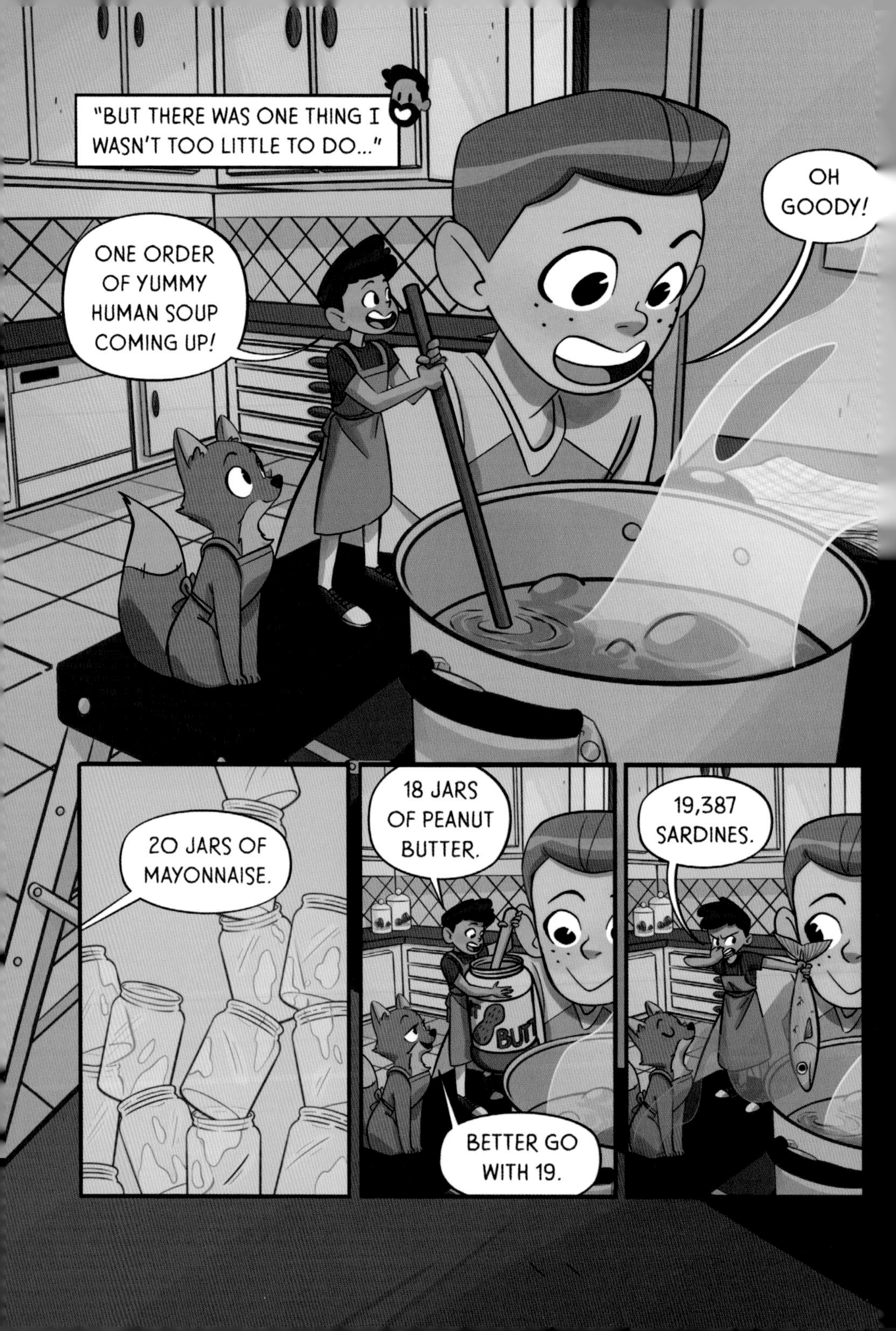
"BUT THERE WAS ONE THING I WASN'T TOO LITTLE TO DO..."
ONE ORDER OF YUMMY HUMAN SOUP COMING UP!
OH GOODY!
20 JARS OF MAYONNAISE.
18 JARS OF PEANUT BUTTER.
BETTER GO WITH 19.
19,387 SARDINES.

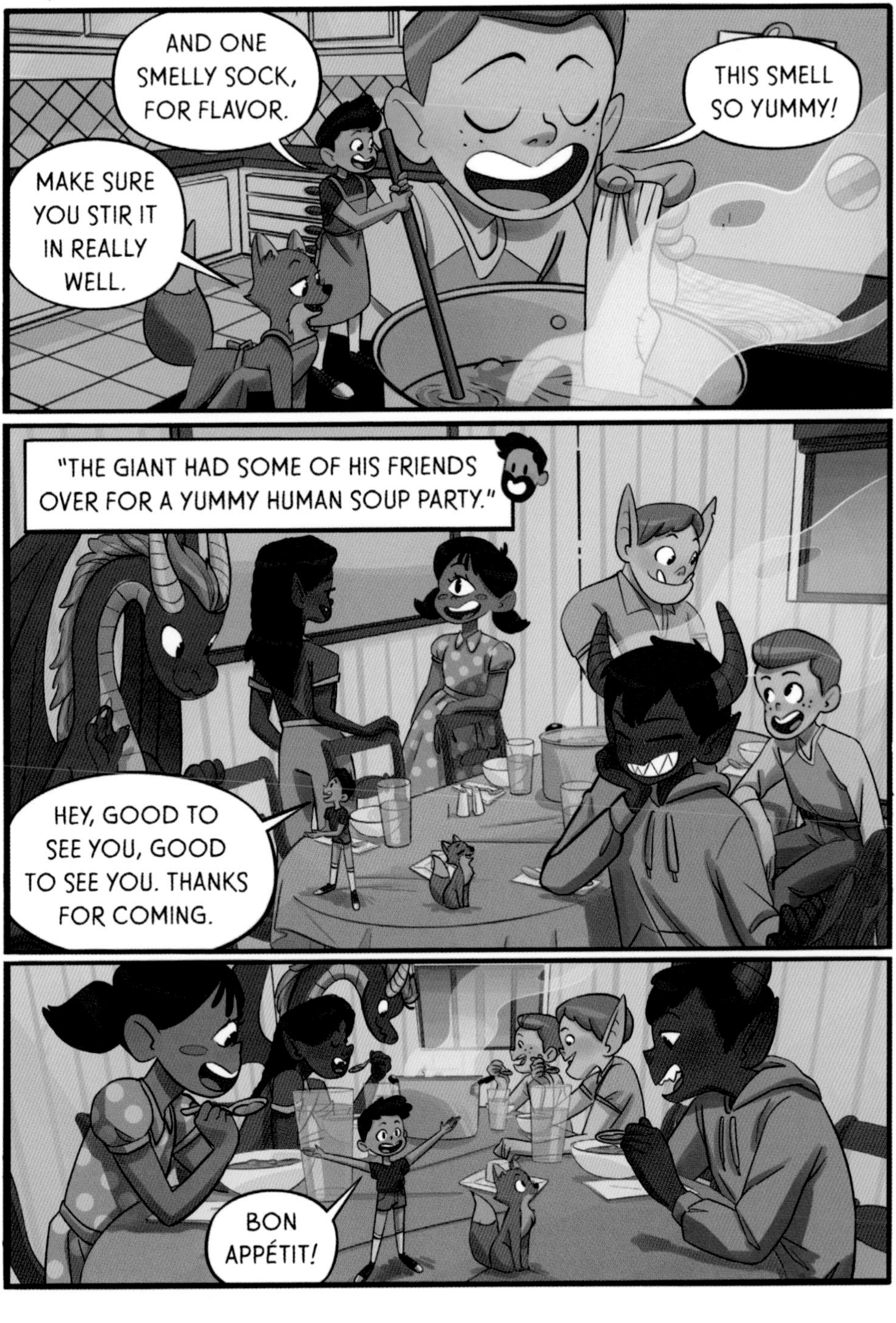
AND ONE SMELLY SOCK, FOR FLAVOR.
MAKE SURE YOU STIR IT IN REALLY WELL.
THIS SMELL SO YUMMY!
"THE GIANT HAD SOME OF HIS FRIENDS OVER FOR A YUMMY HUMAN SOUP PARTY."
HEY, GOOD TO SEE YOU, GOOD TO SEE YOU. THANKS FOR COMING.
BON APPÉTIT!

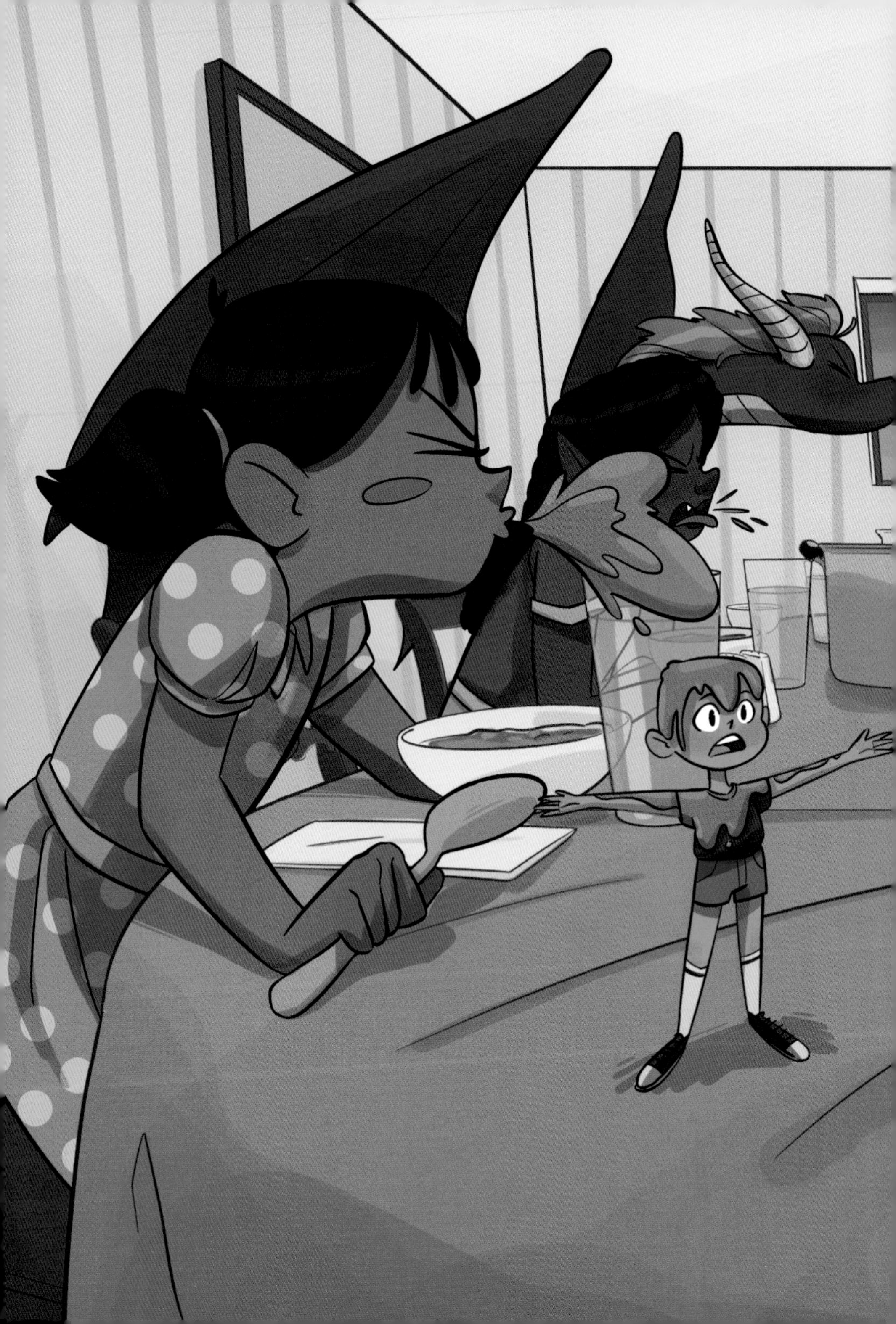

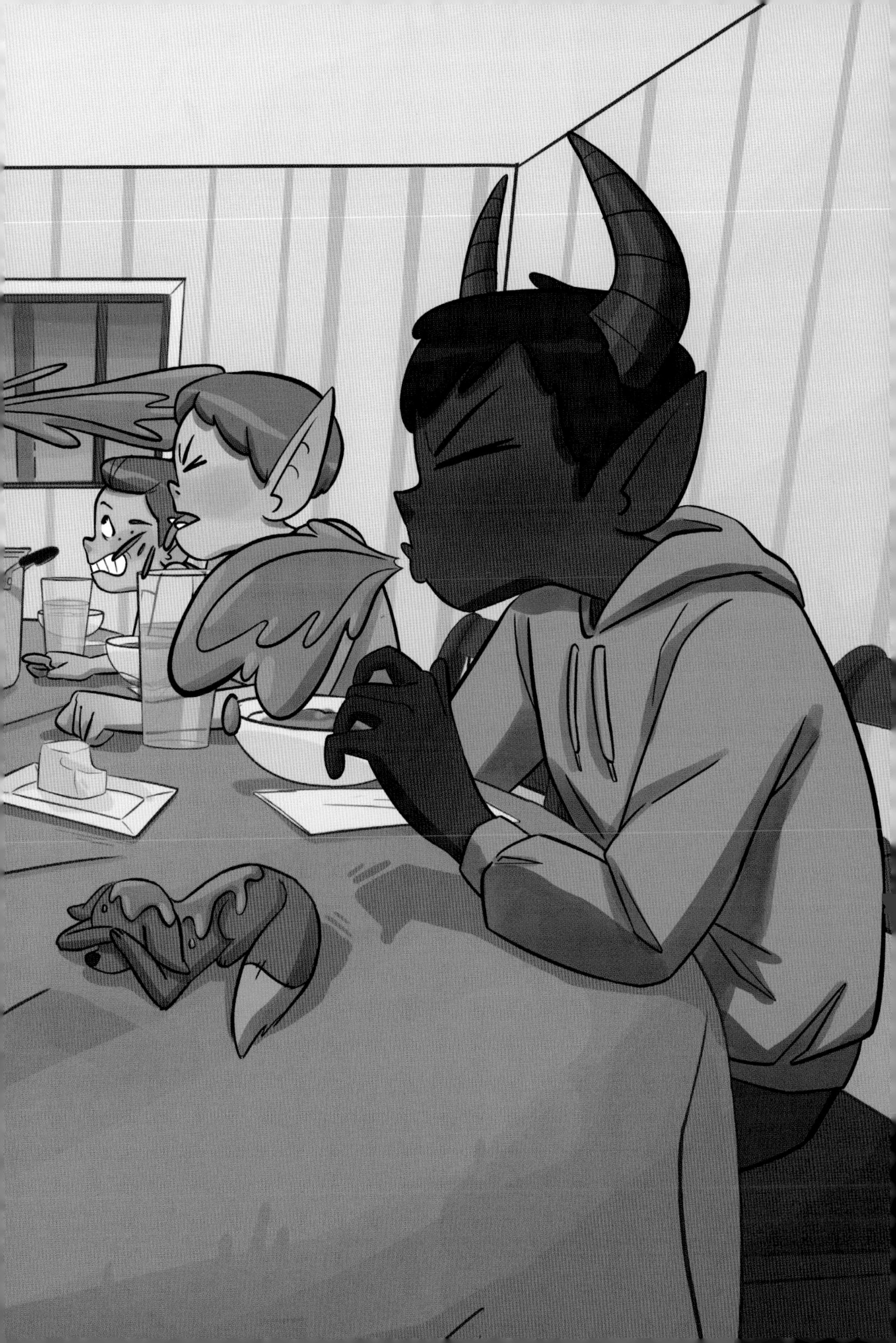

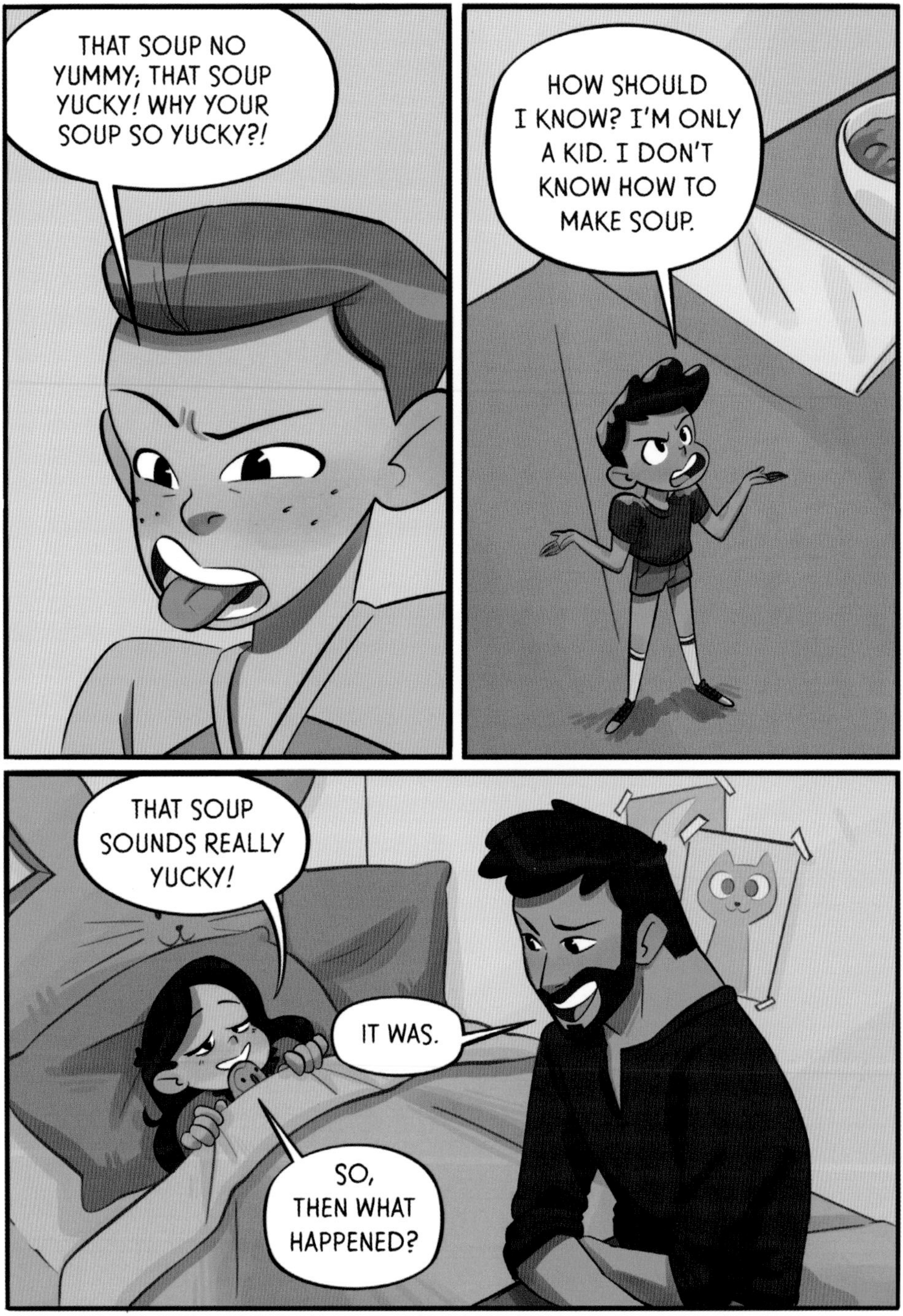
THAT SOUP NO YUMMY; THAT SOUP YUCKY! WHY YOUR SOUP SO YUCKY?!
HOW SHOULD I KNOW? I'M ONLY A KID. I DON'T KNOW HOW TO MAKE SOUP.
THAT SOUP SOUNDS REALLY YUCKY!
IT WAS.
SO, THEN WHAT HAPPENED?

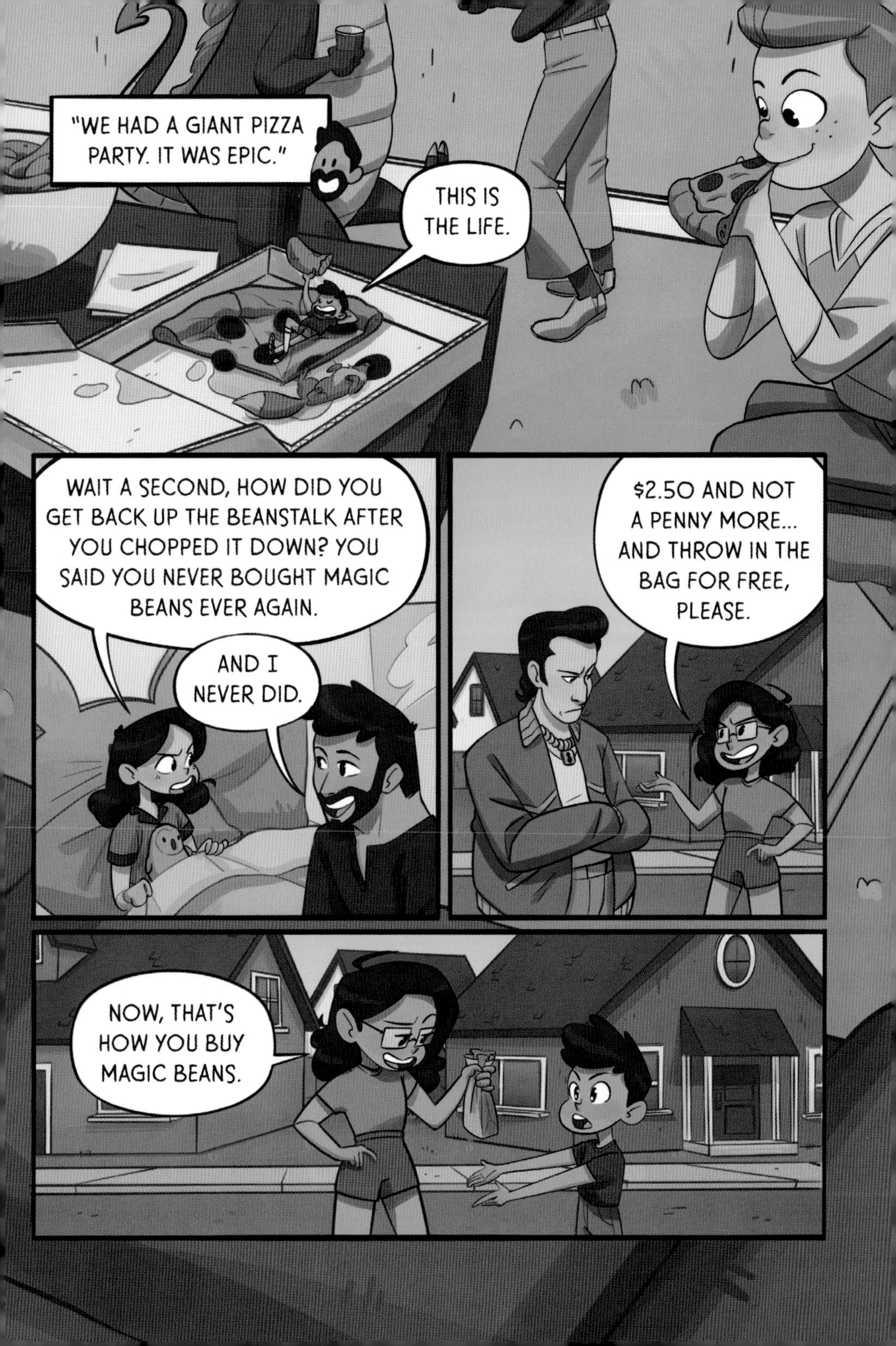
"WE HAD A GIANT PIZZA PARTY. IT WAS EPIC."
THIS IS THE LIFE.
WAIT A SECOND, HOW DID YOU GET BACK UP THE BEANSTALK AFTER YOU CHOPPED IT DOWN? YOU SAID YOU NEVER BOUGHT MAGIC BEANS EVER AGAIN.
AND I NEVER DID.
$2.50 AND NOT A PENNY MORE... AND THROW IN THE BAG FOR FREE, PLEASE.
NOW, THAT'S HOW YOU BUY MAGIC BEANS.

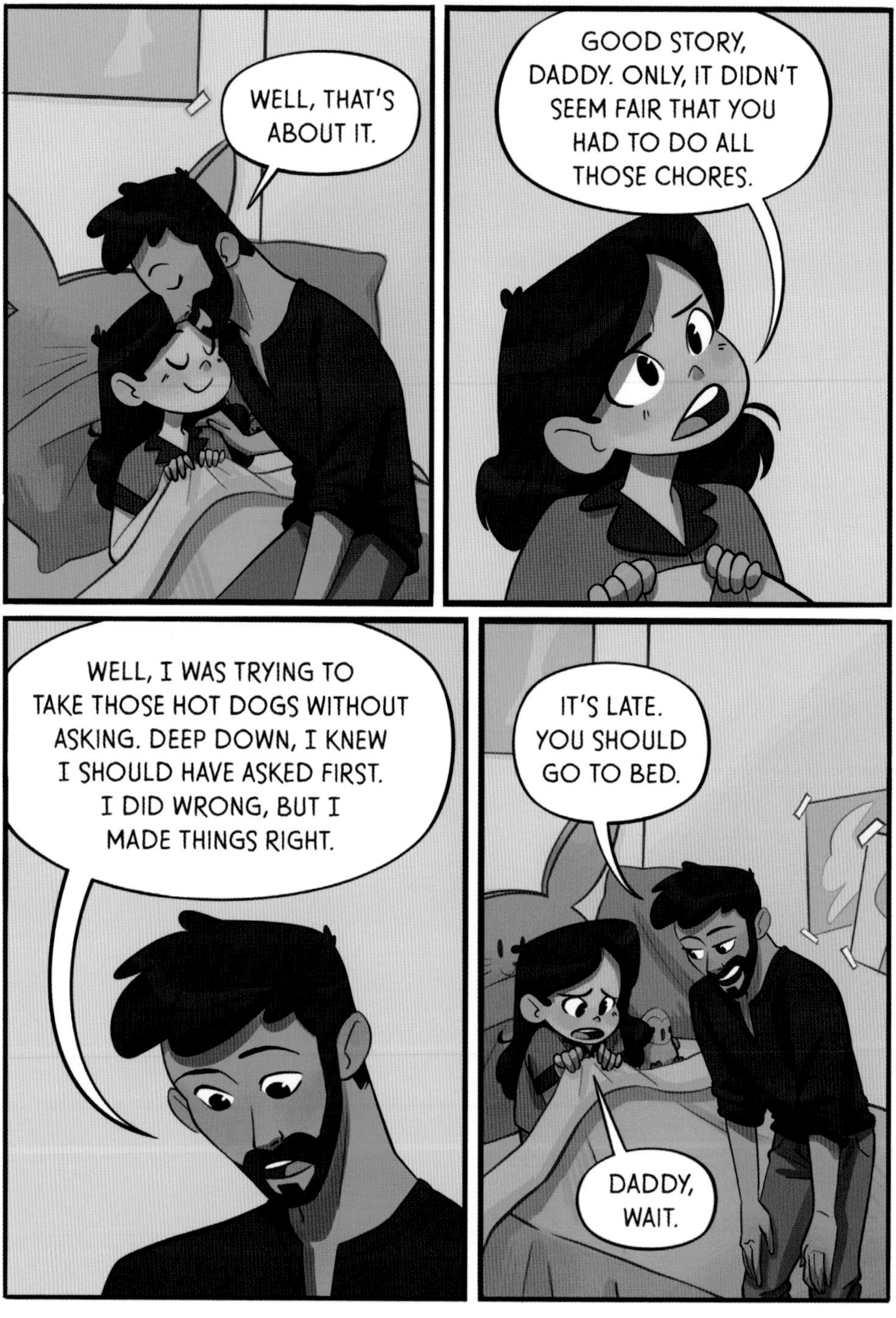
WELL, THAT'S ABOUT IT.
GOOD STORY, DADDY. ONLY, IT DIDN'T SEEM FAIR THAT YOU HAD TO DO ALL THOSE CHORES.
WELL, I WAS TRYING TO TAKE THOSE HOT DOGS WITHOUT ASKING. DEEP DOWN, I KNEW I SHOULD HAVE ASKED FIRST. I DID WRONG, BUT I MADE THINGS RIGHT.
IT'S LATE. YOU SHOULD GO TO BED.
DADDY, WAIT.

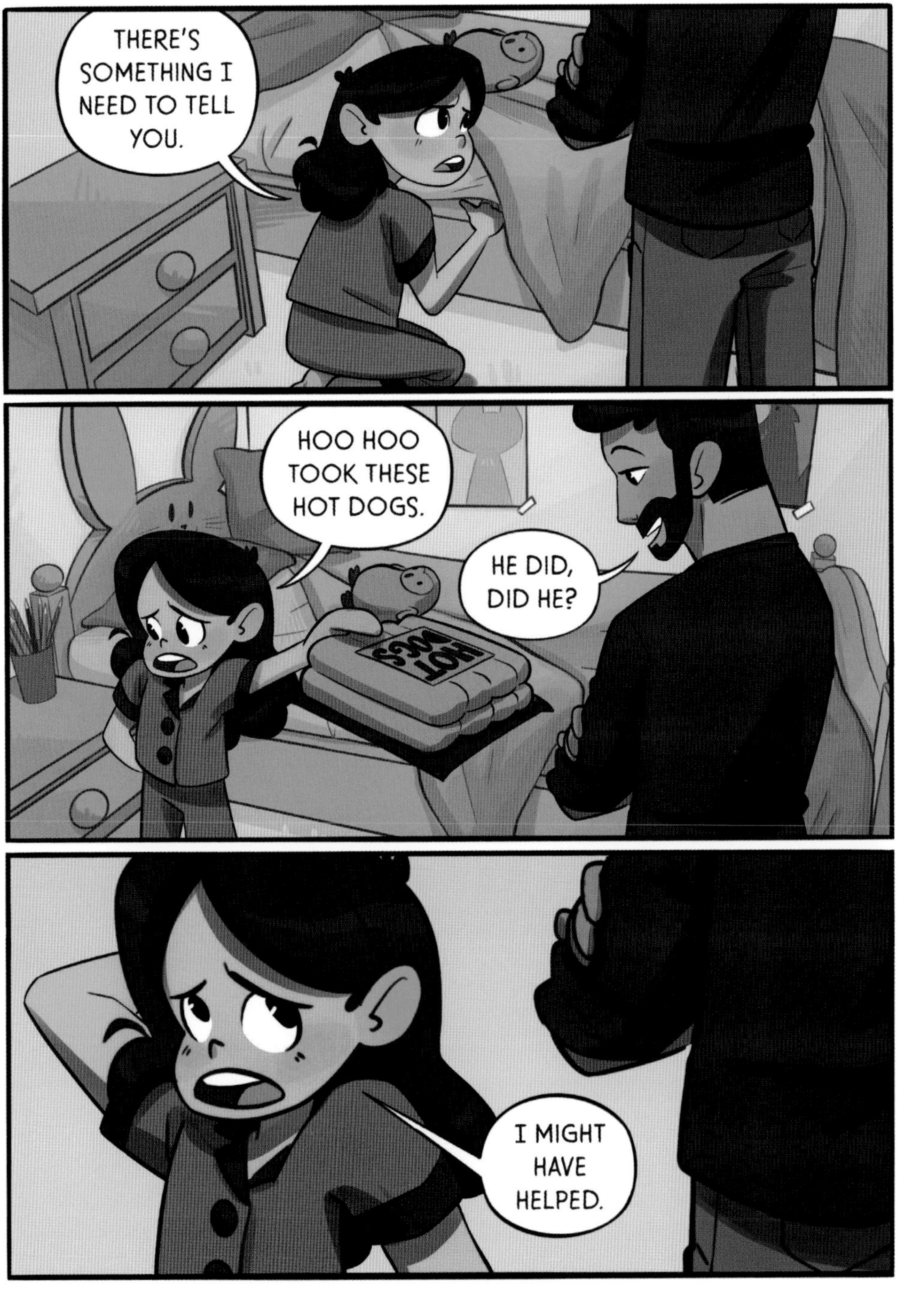
THERE'S SOMETHING I NEED TO TELL YOU.
HOO HOO TOOK THESE HOT DOGS.
HOT DOGS
HE DID, DID HE?
I MIGHT HAVE HELPED.

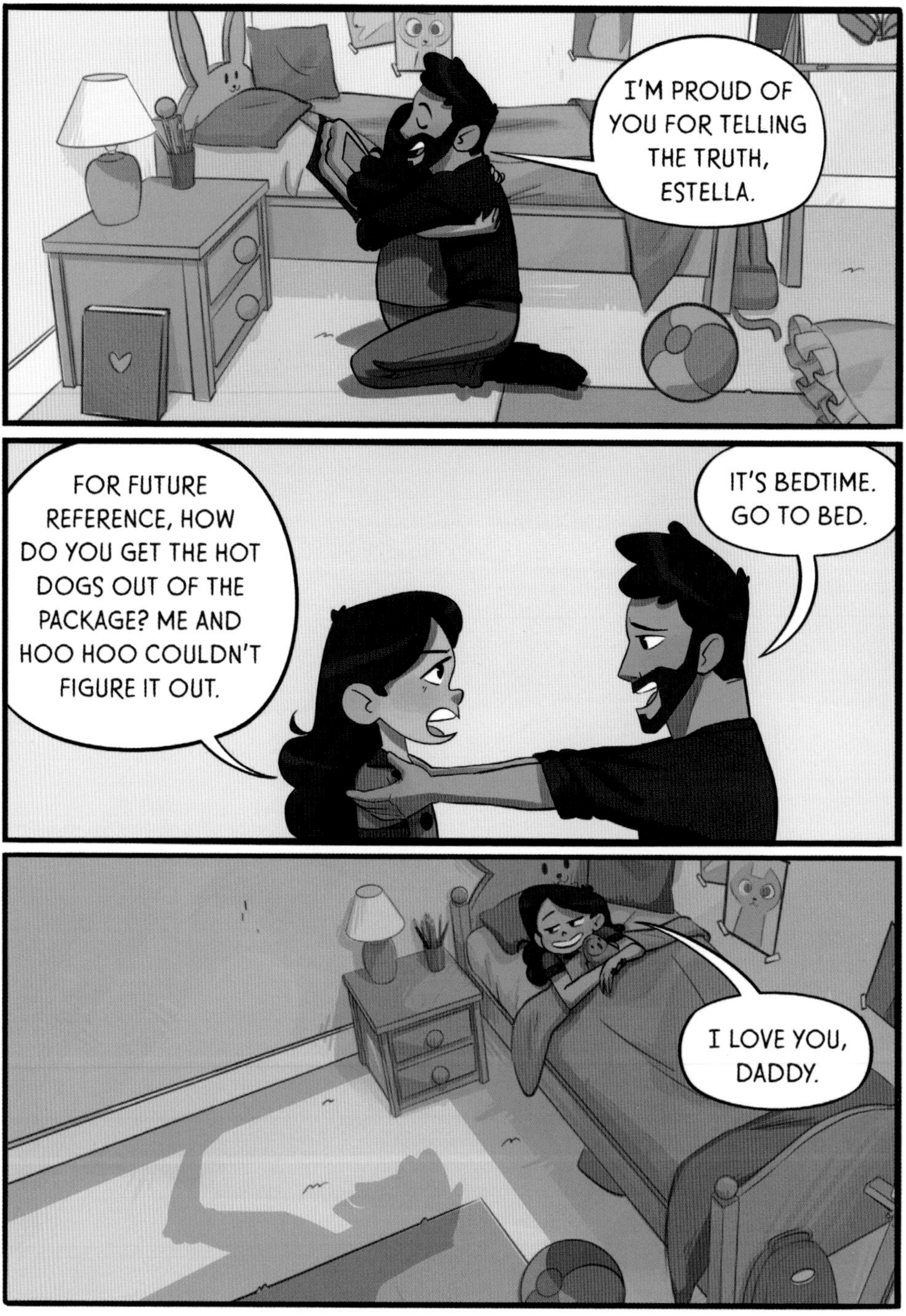
I'M PROUD OF YOU FOR TELLING THE TRUTH, ESTELLA.
FOR FUTURE REFERENCE, HOW DO YOU GET THE HOT DOGS OUT OF THE PACKAGE? ME AND HOO HOO COULDN'T FIGURE IT OUT.
IT'S BEDTIME. GO TO BED.
I LOVE YOU, DADDY.

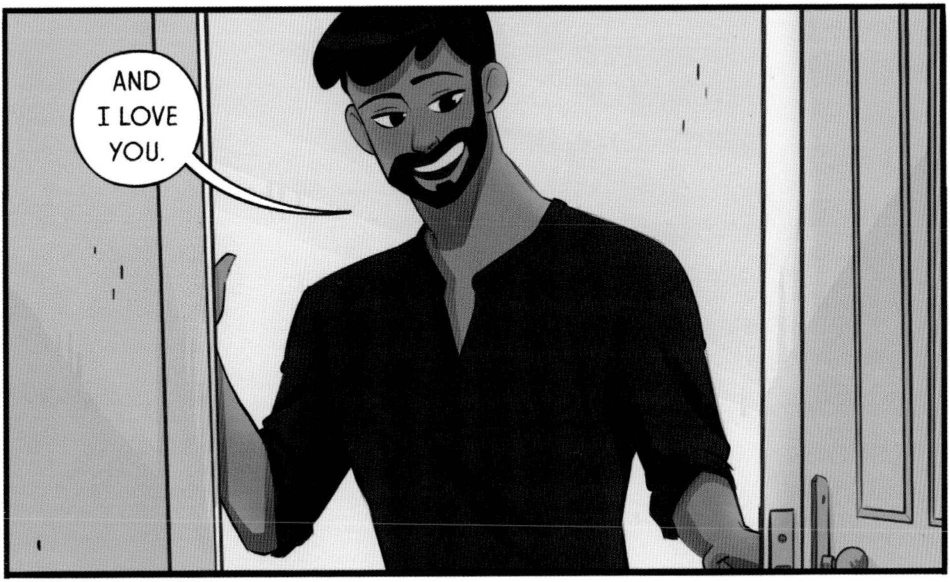
AND I LOVE YOU.

The End

And now for some knock-knock jokes!!!

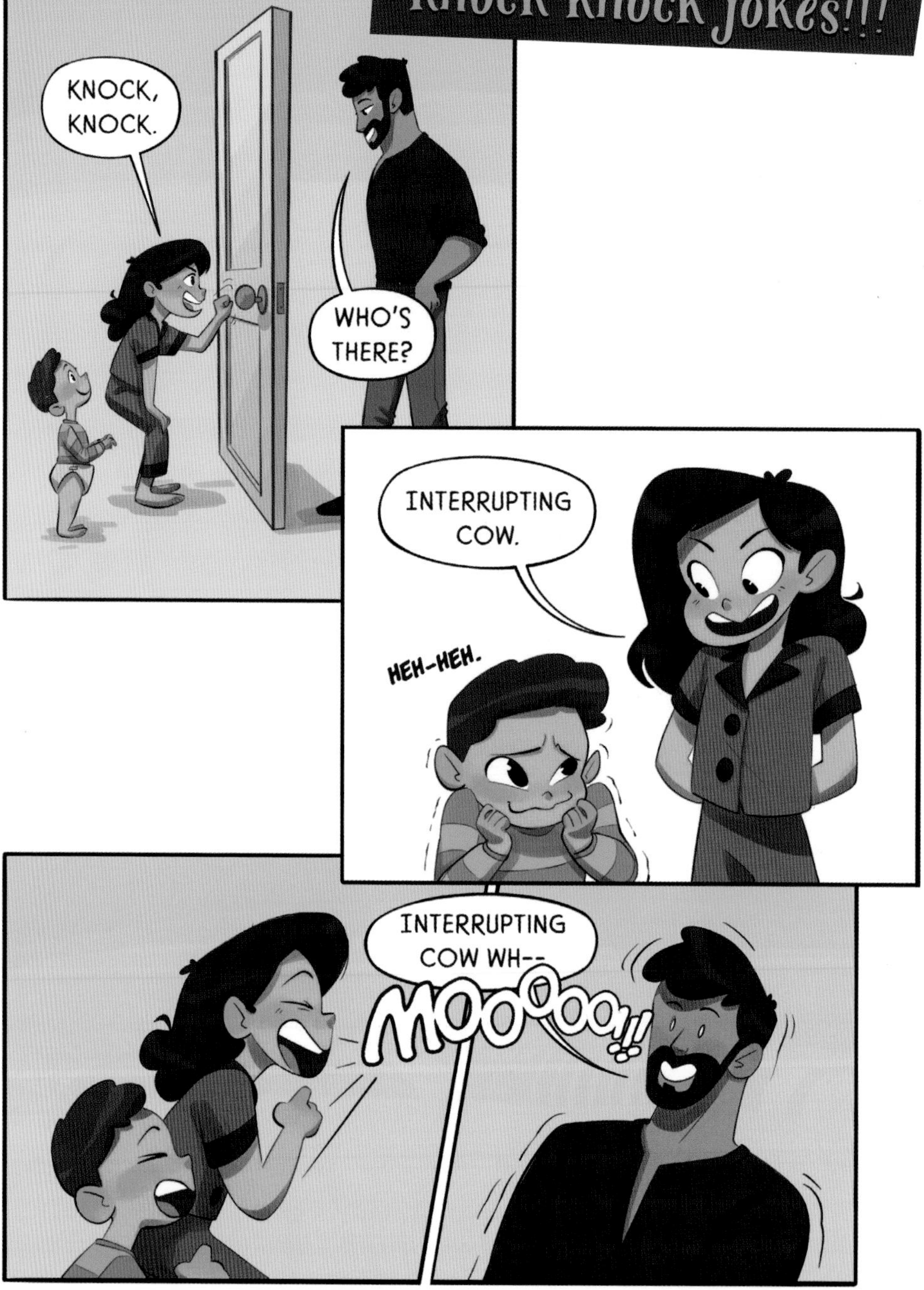
KNOCK, KNOCK.
WHO'S THERE?
INTERRUPTING COW.
HEH-HEH.
INTERRUPTING COW WH--
MOOOOO!!!

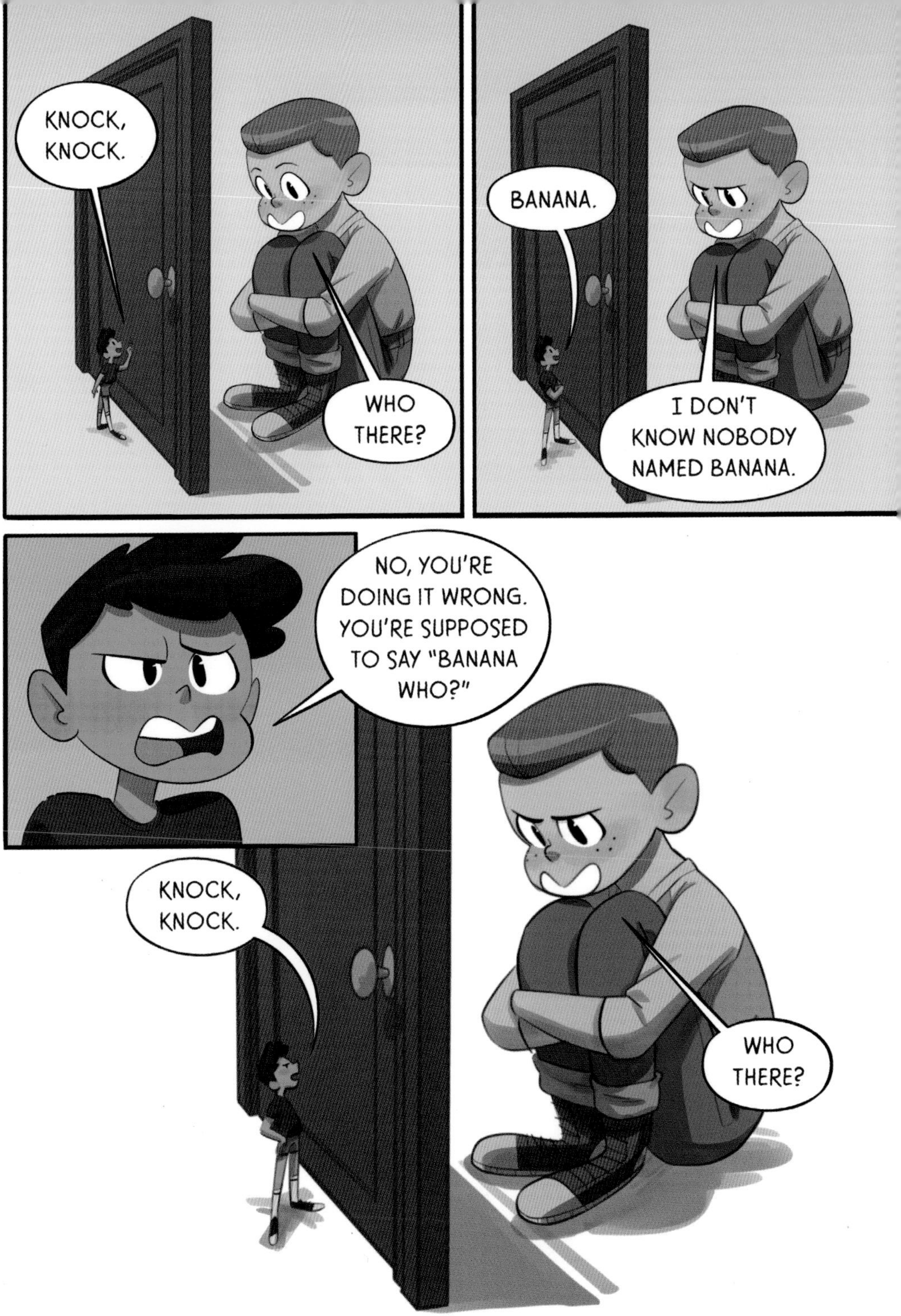
KNOCK, KNOCK.
WHO THERE?
BANANA.
I DON'T KNOW NOBODY NAMED BANANA.
NO, YOU'RE DOING IT WRONG. YOU'RE SUPPOSED TO SAY "BANANA WHO?"
KNOCK, KNOCK.
WHO THERE?

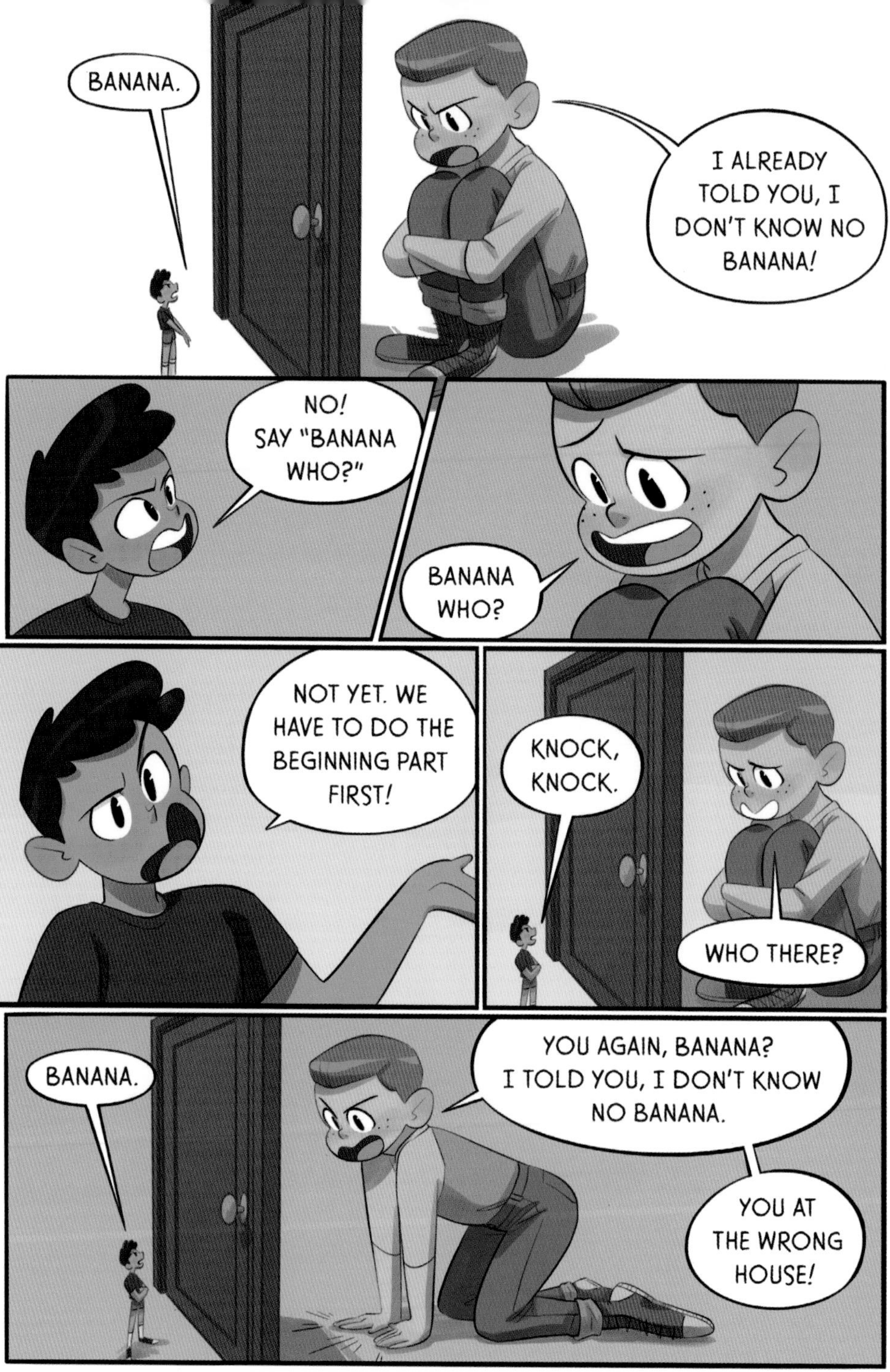
BANANA.
I ALREADY TOLD YOU, I DON'T KNOW NO BANANA!
NO! SAY "BANANA WHO?"
BANANA WHO?
NOT YET. WE HAVE TO DO THE BEGINNING PART FIRST!
KNOCK, KNOCK.
WHO THERE?
BANANA.
YOU AGAIN, BANANA? I TOLD YOU, I DON'T KNOW NO BANANA.
YOU AT THE WRONG HOUSE!

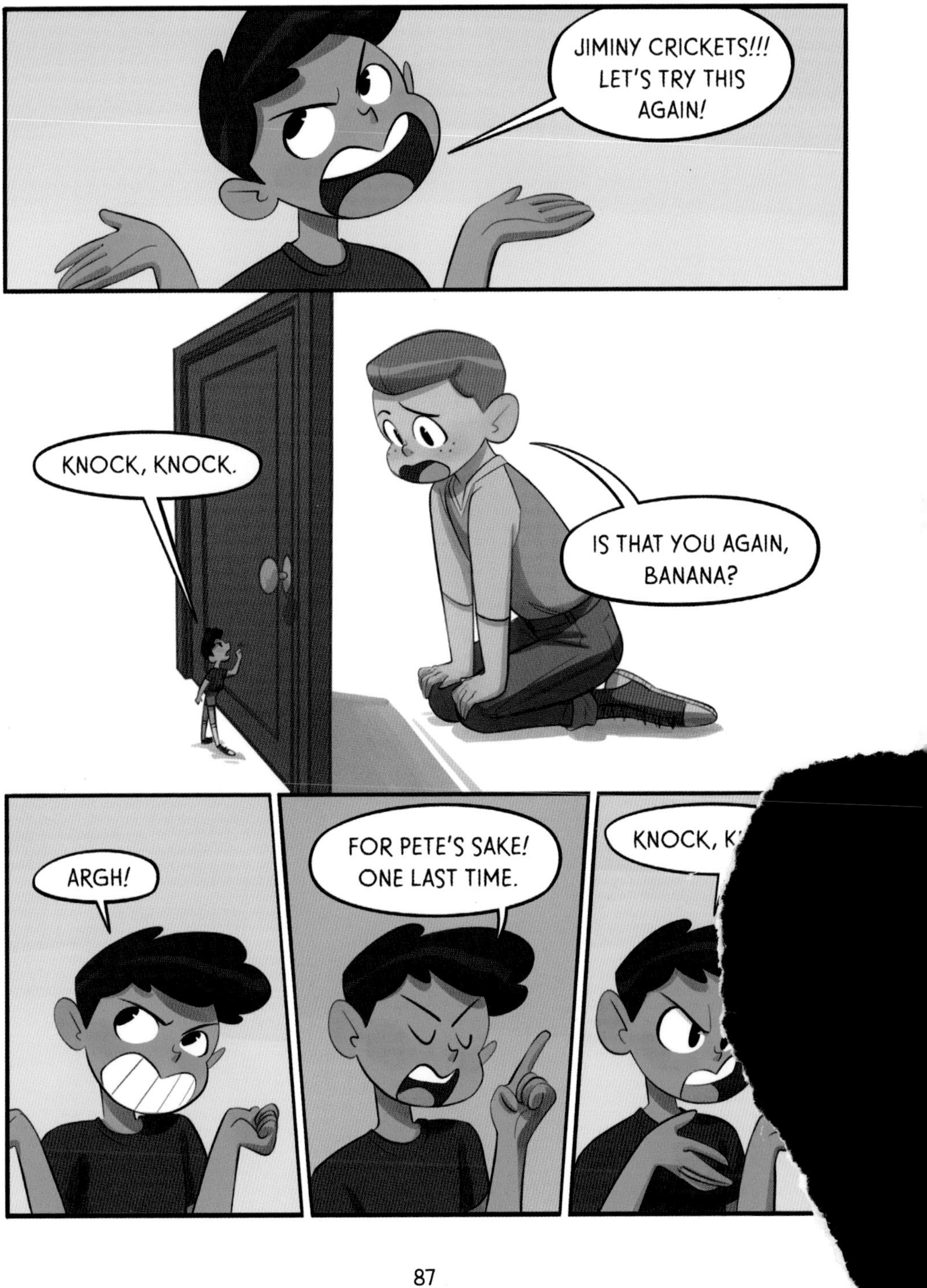
JIMINY CRICKETS!!! LET'S TRY THIS AGAIN!
KNOCK, KNOCK.
IS THAT YOU AGAIN, BANANA?
ARGH!
FOR PETE'S SAKE! ONE LAST TIME.
KNOCK, K

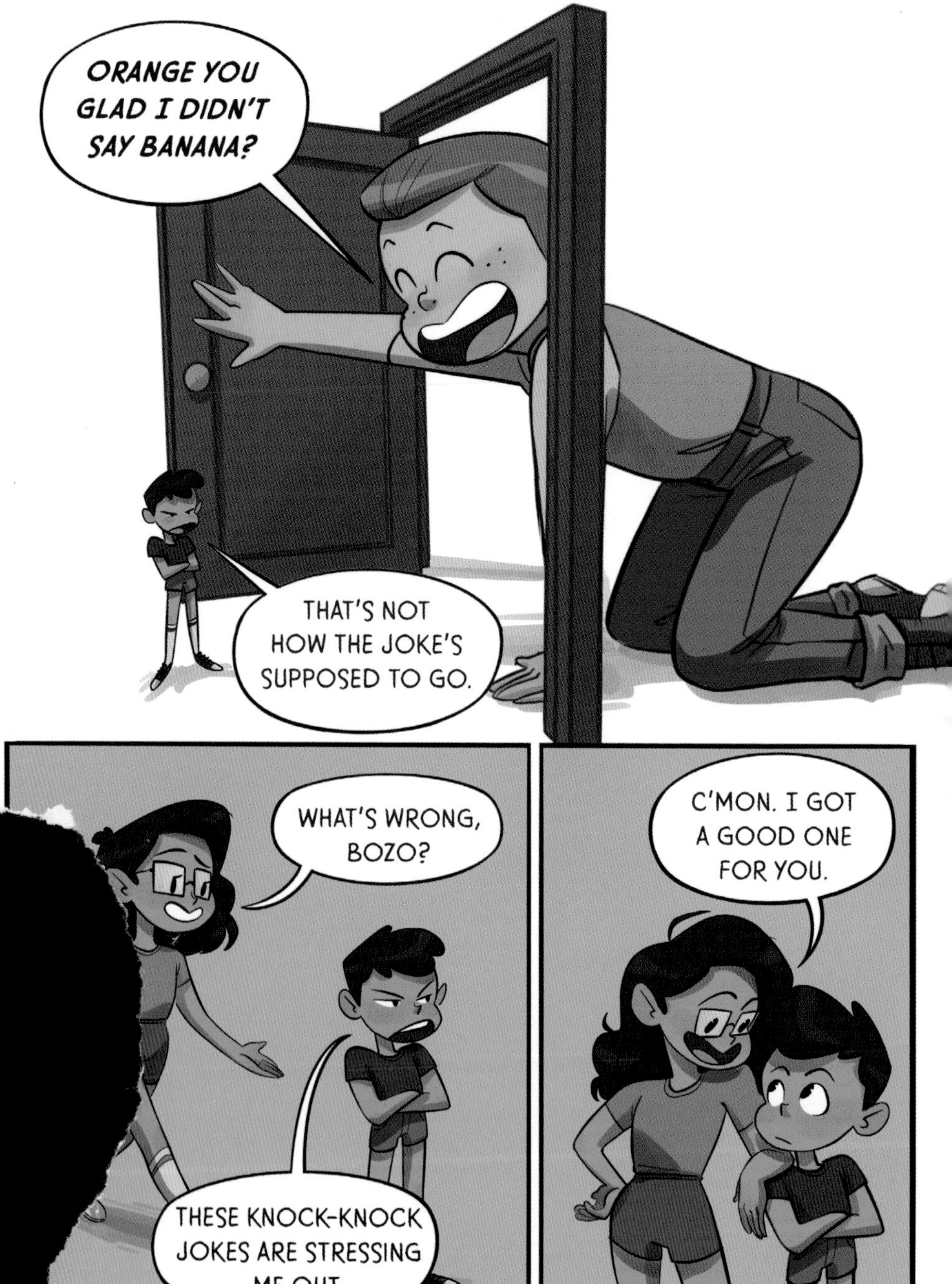
ORANGE YOU GLAD I DIDN'T SAY BANANA?
THAT'S NOT HOW THE JOKE'S SUPPOSED TO GO.
WHAT'S WRONG, BOZO?
THESE KNOCK-KNOCK JOKES ARE STRESSING ME OUT.
C'MON. I GOT A GOOD ONE FOR YOU.

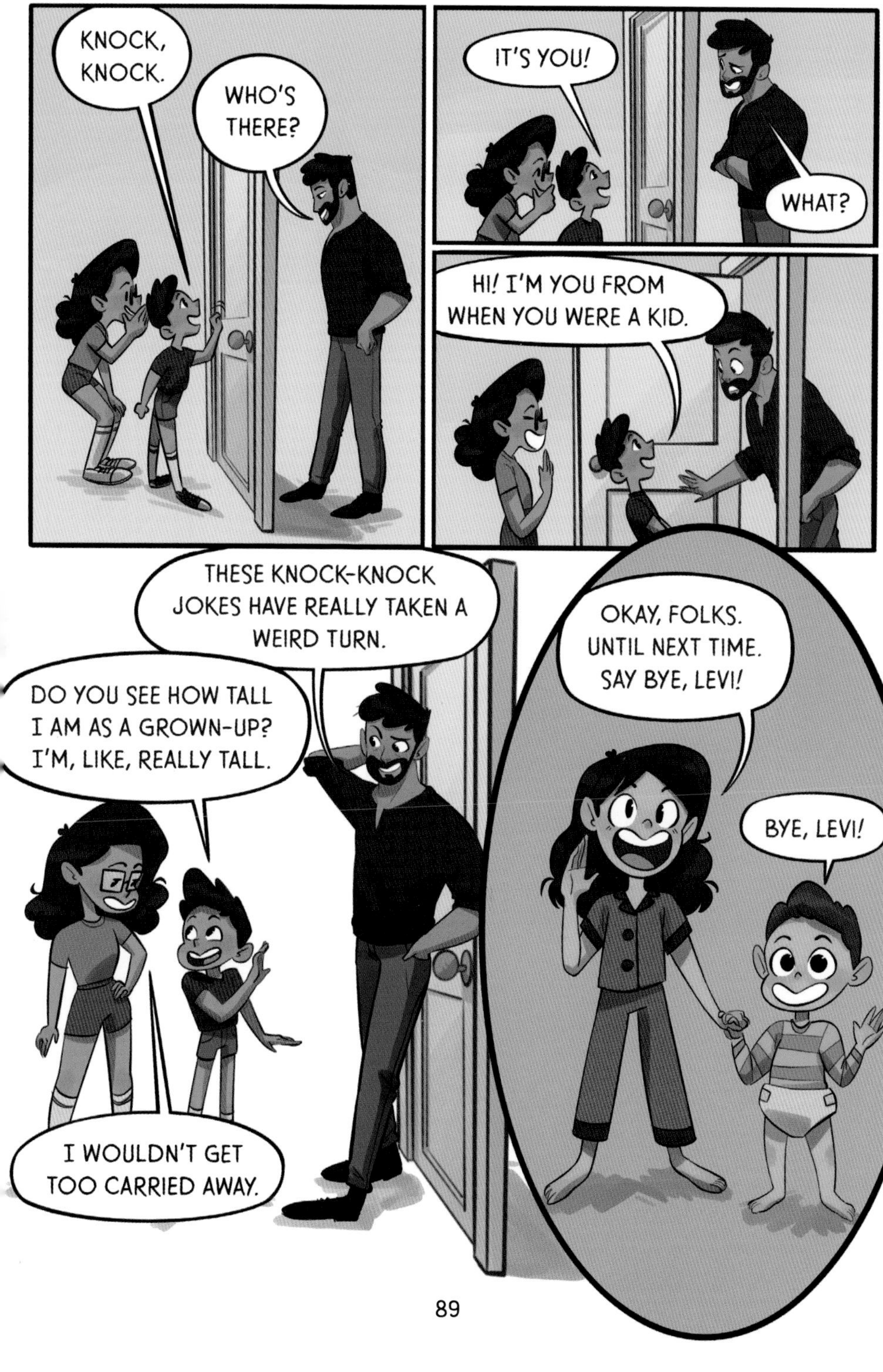
KNOCK, KNOCK.
WHO'S THERE?
IT'S YOU!
WHAT?
HI! I'M YOU FROM WHEN YOU WERE A KID.
THESE KNOCK-KNOCK JOKES HAVE REALLY TAKEN A WEIRD TURN.
DO YOU SEE HOW TALL I AM AS A GROWN-UP? I'M, LIKE, REALLY TALL.
I WOULDN'T GET TOO CARRIED AWAY.
OKAY, FOLKS. UNTIL NEXT TIME. SAY BYE, LEVI!
BYE, LEVI!

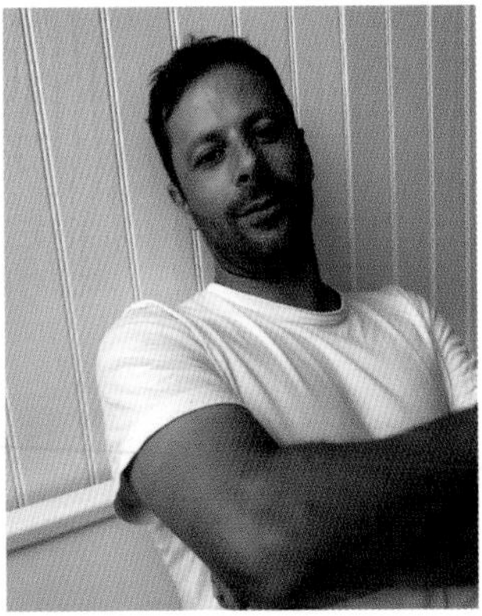

Andrew Weiner

Andrew Weiner is a graphic novelist, screenwriter and filmmaker, and the founder of the multimedia entertainment company Inner Station. Most recently, he cowrote and created the YA graphic novel *Girl on Fire* alongside Alicia Keys. To date, he has written, produced, and/or directed eight feature films. He lives in Brooklyn with his wife, his two small kids, and their giant cat, Waldo.

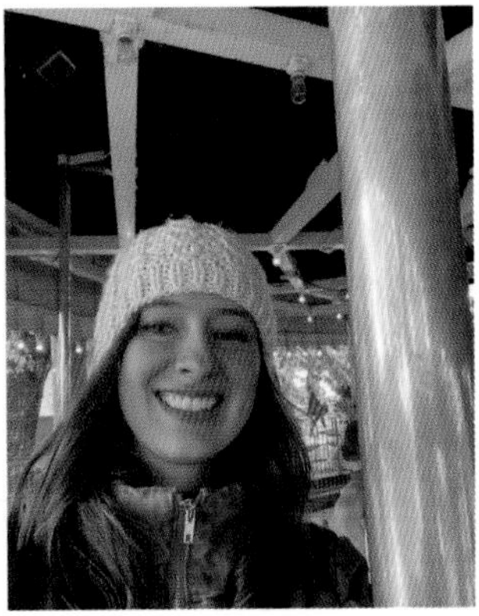

Chelsea Crandall

Bethany Crandall is an illustrator and designer based in Idaho. Bethany has illustrated children's books and for magazines. She has also worked doing designs for children's television. Bethany studied at Brigham Young University–Idaho and graduated with a bachelor of fine arts in illustration. She enjoys drawing and reading. She invites you to find her on Instagram @bethanycrandallart.